A. Lila Riley

**Ruby**

Or, a heart of gold

A. Lila Riley

**Ruby**
*Or, a heart of gold*

ISBN/EAN: 9783337224202

Printed in Europe, USA, Canada, Australia, Japan

Cover: Foto ©Andreas Hilbeck / pixelio.de

More available books at **www.hansebooks.com**

# RUBY; OR, A HEART OF GOLD.

## By A. LILA RILEY.

David C. Cook Publishing Company, Elgin, Ill., and 36 Washington St., Chicago.

## CHAPTER I.

### THE TEXT. *

DR. CARUTHERS did not know it, and I should not like to mention it to him, but the unusual interest of his congregation on this particular Sunday was due to one listener. And that which awakened the interest of the listener aforesaid was the text.

Ruby always waited patiently through the readings in the Prophets and Epistles for the text, and if it was not too long, and if the words were not too hard, he said it over and over till he had it all by heart to say to Aunt Sarah in the evening. He was very glad when the text was short, so that he could remember it, for it kept him from getting sleepy, and made him forget that he was hungry, to say the words over while the sermon was being preached.

His practice was to repeat the text twent; times, putting down a finger for each time, and going over the row of ten fingers twice. Then, if he felt his eyelids begin to droop, or if a strong desire to exercise his limbs came over him, he at once put himself under strict discipline and commenced to say it backwards, or to repeat each word twenty times in succession, and sometimes he became so interested in this occupation

RUBY.

that the closing of the book startled him, and, to his joy, there was an opportunity to stretch his legs.

Today he was ready with his fingers to count the words as Dr. Caruthers read them out, and was pleased when he stopped at four; easy words, too, and words that he knew, each one, only when he put them together in his mind he could not understand: "Christ liveth in me."

Ruby forgot to say the text over twenty times, for he was wondering about the meaning. He raised his little head and looked straight at the preacher and tried to take in every word.

Dr. Caruthers was a learned man. He preached long sermons about regeneration, condemnation, sanctification, justification, and other things like that, and Ruby always looked upon him with a reverence akin to worship. Almost every Sunday evening, when he and Aunt Sarah were talking over things, he would say: "I will be glad when I get to be a man, 'cause then I'll know what Dr. Caruthers says. I think Dr. Caruthers is a great man."

So Ruby sat so still that his father said, in his teasing way, at dinner, that he thought the boy must have been asleep. I am sorry to apply an old adage here: "It takes a thief to catch a thief." Ruby's father was always late home from the store on Saturday nights.

Copyright, 1899, by David C. Cook Publishing Company.

He sat so still that Mabel and Marian, whose devices for church entertainment were various, such as watching through the window the clouds, the trees, and chance passers, counting the pews and people within their line of vision, attempting to count the prisms on the chandelier, calculating how many doll cloaks and hoods could be cut out of the velvet on the reading desk,— Mabel and Marian looked to see what was on hand, and, seeing Ruby with eyes and ears fixed upon the preacher, turned their eyes and ears thitherward. For if Ruby was held, they must know what was holding him.

Then they all three sat so still that Aunt Sarah, who was in the rear, had not one opportunity to tap Mabel on the shoulder for swinging her feet, nor to shake her head at Marian for looking behind. Perhaps this was the first time Aunt Sarah had not met and seized these opportunities. In fact, so intent were the children that she followed their example; but then, Aunt Sarah always listened to the sermon.

Just behind Aunt Sarah was Dr. Matthews. Dr. Matthews always listened for the text, then he settled himself comfortably and thought over his cases, or some other doctor's cases that he was studying in the Medical Journal. Many a time he had reached some important conclusion, and, being a demonstrative person, had almost clapped his hands, but suddenly remembered his bearings. And the doctor had acquired the habit of partly shading his face with his hand, while resting his head upon it, because his wife told him that he sometimes smiled broadly and might attract undue attention. But nobody, not even his wife, knew how densely ignorant Dr. Matthews was of the homiletic discourse, for he could challenge the best of them for the text.

Away back when Dr. Tom Matthews was such a lad as Ruby yonder, there was a custom in his mother's house which was this: After the two-hours sermon the family assembled in the dining-room, the boys stood each at his place, and, beginning with the eldest and going to the youngest, Tom and his five brothers repeated that morning's text. It was a custom that by long usage had become law, a law which not a lad of them dared intentionally to break, for if one word was missing or misplaced, there was no loaf bread and butter, no delicious slice of cold meat, no glass of unskimmed milk, no dainty cake, no saucer of preserves—nothing for the unhappy one but banishment and hunger, gnawing hunger for two hours, when, if the letter of the law was fulfilled, he was received into the family circle and given one slice of bread and butter, but no meat. So these boys lodged in their heads many words of the sacred Book. I do not know how many they hid in their hearts.

It was the habit, though, the strong habit of childhood, that made Dr. Matthews, now a gray-haired man of fifty, listen for the text and remember it. And so among the masses he passed for a good listener. Not that he was a hypocrite and sought to make false impressions, but he was always ready with the text.

To-day, before getting deep into speculations, he caught sight of a little bright curly head just above the back of Mr. Vane's pew. It was not an unfamiliar head to Dr. Matthews, and had always been interesting to him from the time it had lain in the cradle. Many a time he had eased it as it tossed, feverish, upon the pillow, and many a time had he slapped Ruby on the back and called him a "great fellow" when he swallowed his medicine, almost without making a face. The intent, listening attitude of the head attracted him, and, like Mabel and Marian, he looked and listened to know what it was.

The doctor was a man of deep concentration, and, when he fixed his thoughts upon the sermon, was as completely lost to bacilli as formerly he had been to the sound of Dr. Caruthers' voice. He seemed to hear another voice, familiar yet unfamiliar, speaking away down within him, and it was as if a strong, strange light flashed all along his past and he saw himself, his true self, from the time that he stood at the Sunday dinner table, trembling, awaiting his trial, through the years of youth to frosted middle age. He seemed to see down within himself, deep down where the voice sounded, and he knew for the first time how tremendous, how fearful, was the gap between himself and this child. When Dr. Caruthers closed the book and raised his hand for the prayer, Dr. Matthews bowed his head and covered his face.

Just across the aisle from Dr. Matthews was Judge Lauder. The judge was a learned, a mighty man. There were many who thought the church highly honored by his presence there. Logic was his forte; logic and history. He always met some one down the aisle or at the door with comments: "Fine sermon. Good reasoner, Dr. Caruthers. Leads you on step by step from premise to premise, then the conclusion comes of itself: you can't get round it. He never lets go his thread, and he holds you by it, too; he holds you."

What made him notice that little curly head, and the half of the face which was visible to him? I don't know. But he did notice, and something in that intent childish face caused him, too, to wonder what it was, made him forget to count the premises and to grasp the strong thread of argument; made him, the great man, seek to descend to the child's level and see with his eyes and hear with his ears. And so it was that instead of the dry bones of argument, he found the rich marrow which is their life, and instead of the hard and empty husk he tasted the nutritious kernel for which the husk is but the cradle. That day when Judge Lander passed out of church he made no comments, but went by very quietly, much to the disappointment of certain who regularly lay in wait.

Across the church from the judge, and not far from the Vane pew, was Mrs. Wyman. Mrs. Wyman, the "healthy, wealthy, and wise," we might say. For a sight of her robust figure would naturally lead one to the conclusion that she was in health. A vulgar mind would have judged from much velvet, fur and feathers, that she was in wealth; and though outsides are often deceiving, we have authority to affirm the truth of that judgment. Lastly, she read many books and knew many things. One thing she knew was that Dr. Caruthers was getting old and prosy. He preached the same sermon every Sunday, using a different text. She felt that a change, an entire change, was necessary to her spiritual health. She had no children, and her husband, the small, wiry president of the bank, was not in many of her thoughts. A man twenty years your senior is not always agreeable company.

It is not to be wondered at, then, that Mrs. Wyman read many books, rode often in her luxurious carriage, "got up clubs," superintended church socials, fondled dogs and monkeys, and on stated occasions scattered cakes and small pence among the children of the poor.

She had taken up Ruby with enthusiasm. It was nothing uncommon for her to watch the bright little head in church. Dr. Caruthers looked drier than ever this morn-

ing; she was not comfortable, someway; she had not even heard the text. But when she saw the deep interest of her little favorite she smiled to herself at first, and then listened, too. Mrs. Wyman's mind was not well trained for listening, and often it wandered with her eye to Ruby, but as he sat so still, so intent, she could but feel the magnetism and was drawn each time to the preacher.

What Mrs. Wyman heard it is not the purpose of this paper to tell, but it seemed that she was listening to something which she had never heard before—some new doctrine, some latter-day revelation; and she wondered why Dr. Caruthers had never preached it until then.

I could go on and cover a great deal of space and tell you of others who saw with seeing eyes and heard with hearing ears, that day, but it is enough.

Attention, like many things, such as kindness and gentle speaking and acts of unselfishness, is contagious. It is like a current, too, that flows silently and swiftly from listener to speaker. When he feels it he takes on new life, the air is light and he breathes more freely, the blood goes tingling through his veins. So the good doctor, who was often despondent, and felt that his words had fallen to the ground; who many a Sabbath day sorely reproached himself, and with prayers, tears, and even fastings, sought deep down in his heart for the secret sin which was the cause of blessings withheld, felt that he had great liberty, and prayed and wept and fasted that day for gladness of heart.

———

## CHAPTER II.

### DESIRES.

AS that short winter afternoon was closing in, Ruby and Mabel and Marian gathered in the library round the glowing grate.

Marian was their cousin, a motherless child, and, Aunt Sarah said, as good as fatherless. Not that her father did not supply her with everything in a material way that a child could reasonably wish for; but Aunt Sarah had a supreme contempt for things that money can buy. "What will gewgaws profit her, if she loses her soul?

And that's what she will do if she follows his teachings." She never forgave, or thought she never forgave, her young and beautiful sister, Eleanor, for marrying a man who had no God but Science. And what was Science? If a man would spend all his time burrowing, no wonder he thought he was a worm; if he spent all his mind on apes and tadpoles, no wonder he came to think himself of the same kind. She was horrified at such a doctrine, yet always associated her brother-in-law with these strange companions. She was willing to do anything in her power for her sister's child, she said, but there were traces of bad blood — shaking her head.

As for Marian, she only knew that her father was a tall, stern, silent man, who left her almost entirely alone when she visited him, which she did once a year. Her uncle's house had been her home ever since her mother's death, and that was so long ago she could not remember it. Aunt Emily thought that Marian should visit her father once a year, as he could scarcely be persuaded to visit her. The month in midsummer was a dreary one indeed that she spent in the great, gloomy house, with its handsome, old-fashioned furniture, its straight, stiff, solemn, spotless housekeeper, and its dark, mysterious chambers upstairs, which Marian had always passed breathless by, and never dared to enter—her father's workshops.

Dinah, the colored maid who accompanied Marian on these yearly pilgrimages, enjoyed herself very well, for her time was spent in the kitchen with the cook and stable-boy, who were sociably inclined, and who, on the quiet evenings when Mrs. Green was "nowhere," told, in truly dramatic style, many a "sho' nuf" story of those dark upper rooms and their lonely occupant, until the whites of Dinah's eyes would gleam in the light of the pine torch on the hearth.

These stories, with helpful coloring, were duly repeated in the mornings as Marian's dark curls were arranged. It was well enough to be so entertained when the sun was shining through the east window, but at night, all alone, in that great white bed, black darkness around, or perhaps a faint streak of moonlight creeping through the blind only to show how large and shadowy the room was, then it was another matter. And many a night Marian lay shivering and sobbing under the sheet, and calling her dear Aunt Emily, and thinking there was no

place so good as the little room behind Aunt Sarah's, with its three small iron bedsteads in a row. It might be dark or light there, she was never afraid.

Marian and Mabel were eleven — their birthdays came very near together — and Ruby was seven. They were very good to the little fellow. The biggest, reddest apple must be saved for Ruby — "he's the youngest, you know."— and the prettiest picture must be his. They listened to whatever he said with a certain deference, and Ruby's word had much weight with them. Perhaps it was because he did not talk a great deal and had such a quiet, old-mannish way about him. If there was any disputing and loud talking between them, he never clamored to be heard, but waited very calmly for a lull, then in his sweet, childish treble he would give them some bit of information that quieted matters at once.

The two little girls were very fond of each other, and, though they quarreled sometimes, always made up with a kiss. They never quarreled with Ruby, though — Ruby wouldn't have quarreled with any living person, I think; and if any person had ever tried it upon him he would have been met by silence and two solemn brown eyes. And who could quarrel under such circumstances?

The three made a pretty group that evening, the two girls on one side of the fireplace, Mabel's head leaning on Marian's shoulder, the short dark curls above falling and mingling with the long tresses, soft and fine as yellow silk; Ruby on the other side in his low chair, both hands clasped about one knee which crossed the other, his eyes fixed upon the fire. The girls were talking about the book they had read that afternoon, but Ruby had sat for a long time and neither spoke nor seemed to hear.

"Now, girls," he said at length, "what did you think it meant?"

"Meant?" said Marian. "What?"

"Why, you know — the text. 'Christ liveth in me.' Is that true, and all the things Dr. Caruthers said? Somehow I could hear better to-day, but I couldn't tell what it meant all the way through."

"I don't know. But while Dr. Caruthers was preaching, I felt as if I just wanted to be good all the time," Marian sighed softly.

"Yes," said Mabel. "I thought I would ask mother about it, but I forgot. We will at bedtime, Marian."

"You see," Ruby continued, "it sounded

this way to me: Christ lives in us just as we live in this house. And you know what he said about the housekeeper; now, say that mother or Aunt Sarah is the housekeeper, she takes a broom and sweeps, and then she takes a bunch of feathers and brushes away the dust and cobwebs, and then she gets clean water and soap and washes everything and makes it nice and clean. He said Christ was the housekeeper of our hearts; he made them clean, he — what was the word?"

"Purified them," said Mabel.

"Yes, purified them. And then he said if Christ wasn't there keeping house for us, it was a bad, dark place, like — like what?"

"Oh, I remember!" cried Marian; "a cage of birds — of unclean birds. Oh, my! that is bad, isn't it?" And Marian shuddered. She was thinking, too, of those dark chambers in her father's house, into which she had dared to peep once or twice, but never to enter.

"I wish I knew if Christ was really keeping house for me," Mabel spoke very earnestly.

"It seems to me we ought to know. Why can't we know?" broke in Marian.

"Well, if we're good —"

But Marian broke in again. "If we're good! He said Christ came in and made us good, as the housekeeper makes the dirty, turned-up house clean and tidy."

"Well, then," said Ruby, as if a light had gleamed on him suddenly, "I reckon we're just to ask him in. Why, don't you know the verse mother taught us one Sunday? — 'Behold, I stand at the door and knock' — and something more. What was it, Marian?"

"'If any man — if any man' — oh, yes! I can't remember the words, but He said if any man would open him the door, He would come in and sup with him. Isn't it pretty? And the hymn:

"'Behold, a Stranger at the door!
    He gently knocks, has knocked before.'"

"It seems like anybody would be glad to open the door," said Mabel.

"You know, girls, I think it's this way: We keep the door shut when we want to do our own way. It is like not listening to the voice inside that mother tells us about."

"That's it, Ruby! I think that's just it!" said Marian; "and I mean to keep the door open all the time, for I want my house to be as clean as clean can be."

Mabel pressed her cousin's hand. "Mar-

ian, I think we could help one another; sometimes you might see how I was keeping the door shut when I wouldn't see, and sometimes I might see when you wouldn't."

"Yes," said Marian, "it will do us good to tell one another of our faults. You remember, when Aunt Emily came up to our room the first time after she had been sick two weeks, she told us the windows were dim. We hadn't noticed, because we saw them every day, and were used to it. I think it will be just the thing to tell one another of our faults."

Aunt Sarah came in then, and sat down next to Ruby.

"Aunt Sarah," he said, "we want to be good children, and want you to tell us of our faults, 'cause we can't always see them."

Mabel and Marian did not express, by their countenances, hearty approval, but they were in for it.

Aunt Sarah turned her keen black eyes upon Marian first and spoke without hesitancy.

"Well, one great trouble with Marian is, that she is always in a hurry. She doesn't take time to finish one thing before she begins another, and she doesn't take time to think before she speaks."

There was a dangerous sparkle in Marian's eyes, and she seemed quite ready to speak before she thought. But Aunt Sarah did not give her an opportunity. She turned to Mabel.

"And Mabel wants the best of what's going, and puts off her work till it's school time, and her mother has to do it for her."

Mabel took the sulks at once, bit her lip, and would have nothing more to say. But Marian, burning still, and unwilling to leave the field, asked:

"And what about Ruby?"

Ruby sat waiting his turn, his grave eyes fixed upon the fire. Aunt Sarah turned to him, and her face and voice softened as they always did when Ruby was in question.

"Well, Ruby hasn't got a real fault; or, if he has, I don't know what it is."

---

## CHAPTER III.

### THE SECRET.

AUNT SARAH spent the Sabbath, except that part which was given to public worship and works of strict necessity, in the privacy of her own apartment. Even

in the evenings she kept religiously apart.
Her brother's family was lax. "Philip was
not brought up that way; we studied the
catechism and read our ten chapters as sure
as Sunday came round, and there wasn't any
playing off. And there were no trashy Sunday-school books lying round, either."

Attendance upon meals was a necessity,
but one could easily see that though Aunt
Sarah might be unavoidably in the table
talk, yet was she not of it. The Sunday-
school books were profane literature; in fact,
much of the literature, a great part of the
songs, and almost all the conversation in-
dulged in by her brother's family upon the
Sabbath day, were profane, if we may use
this word in speaking Aunt Sarah's
thoughts.

Ruby spent the Sunday afternoons downstairs, listening to the pretty stories in the
books and the prettier ones in the Bible that
his mother read to them, and joining in the
singing, which he liked very much. There
was one hymn which he called his and that
he sang every Sabbath. You will know what
it is after awhile, for to know Ruby was to
know his hymn. But when supper was over
it was his custom to make his way up to
Aunt Sarah's room, and there he always
gained admittance.

This evening he found her, as usual, in her
high-backed, leather-covered chair, which
did not rock. "Taylor's Holy Living" in her
hands. Aunt Sarah fed during the day on
"Calvin's Institutes," "Apostolic Fathers,"
and "Edwards' Sermons;" at night she took
lighter diet.

Ruby sat down on his own little stool and
remained silent a long time. All at once he
broke out:

"Aunt Sarah, it was a lie!"

"A lie! What?"

"What you said."

Aunt Sarah's book dropped into her lap
and her black eyes were fixed upon the
child, but there was neither surprise nor
displeasure in them, only a silent interroga-
tion.

"What you said in the library. I know
you didn't know, 'cause I never told it; I hid
it, and I'm afraid that made it worse than
ever."

A pause, during which Aunt Sarah still sat
silently interrogatory.

"It's a bad feeling in here," laying his little hand upon his heart. "It's a feeling that
don't forgive."

Aunt Sarah's eyes came as near twinkling

as they ever did, but there was no other sign
of merriment upon her countenance.

"And what have you to forgive?"

"Well, Aunt Sarah," — very slowly — "I
don't know but one person that ever did me
any harm."

"Who was that?"

"I'd rather not call his name, but he goes
to our school, and he's big, and he hits the
little boys and throws their hats in the tree,
and sometimes he takes their lunch. Willie
Jones — he's just so high — he cried all one
recess 'cause he was hungry."

"And he takes yours, too, I reckon. He's
got to stop it!"

"He never did take mine but once, and I
don't seem to mind his teasin' me; it's the
way he does the little fellows."

Little fellows! Aunt Sarah's eyes were on
the verge of twinkling again.

"And why don't the little fellows tell the
teacher?"

"Well, you know, they cry and say they're
going to tell, and he says, 'Dare you,' and,
'I'll put you in the pond,' and 'Sic Teck
on you!' And they're just as 'fraid as they
can be of Teck, and he's one dog I don't
like. I'm sorry 'bout that, too. You reckon
it's a sin not to like a dog, Aunt Sarah?" —
very solemnly.

"Well, if it's a mean dog, how can you like
it?"

"But if anybody is mean, you ought to like
'em — you ought to love 'em, oughtn't you?
And isn't it the same with a dog? 'Love
your enemies.'" Ruby repeated, softly.

All Aunt Sarah's theological reading did
not seem to help her out. "Love your enemies," had always been to her as plain as
English could be, and she didn't know how
to make it any plainer. So she had no
answer for this child, so deeply in earnest,
sitting with his solemn eyes upon her.

"Oughtn't you?"

"Well, yes, I reckon you ought."

"And, you see, I don't, Aunt Sarah; and
I'm sorry all the time. Then," after a
pause, "he hits the dogs, too, and ties things
to their tails. There is one little dog that
goes by the school-house every day on three
legs, 'cause he broke one with a rock; and he
laughs when a dog howls or a little fellow
cries, just like it made him so glad!" Another pause. "And there is one other thing,
Aunt Sarah. It was S—I mean it was
this boy that"—here the voice broke—
"that gave something to Rover,"

"How do you know? Where is he?"

Aunt Sarah started up as if she would have pursued the "wretch," for by that name she knew the unknown who had given something to Rover.

"I thought so a long time, and I was afraid it was mean in me to think so, but one day, before Christmas — let's see; it's over a month now — he told me, and laughed right in my face, and said, 'Help it if you can.' Aunt Sarah, I can't tell you how terrible I was inside. I doubled up my fist, but something spoke to me and I didn't hit him. But I had to run hard to keep from it. I just hollered out once and ran in the house to my desk, and — and burst out crying."

But it was too much for the brave little heart. He broke down and burst out crying again, resting his head upon his knees.

There was something in the corner of Aunt Sarah's eye, something that made the eye brighter and blacker than ever, but she sat perfectly erect and said not a word.

After a time Ruby's sobs ceased; he raised himself, and in the depths of his glistening eyes was an untold tale.

There was a long silence, broken only here and there by a deep-drawn breath.

## CHAPTER IV.

### ROVER.

AND this was the tale: Among the first things that Ruby could remember was a shaggy creature with great, kindly eyes, that followed him everywhere. It was Rover that came to his bedside every morning and laid his great paw gently upon the little cheek to say the day had begun; it was with Rover that he shared breakfast, dinner and supper; and no apple or stick of candy was good unless Rover first had a bite; it was over Rover's great back that he had rolled, crowing and laughing, before he knew the use of his own tiny limbs or could call his playmate's name; it was with his curly head on Rover's black neck that he had slept many an hour, the patient creature never moving all the time, and allowing no one to touch

his little master till he woke. Ruby's mother might miss her boy for ever so long, but she was not troubled, for Rover was with him.

When Ruby's first school day came, the question of separating the two was a serious one.

"Why couldn't he go, mother?" he asked, stroking the shaggy head. Rover had stuck closer than ever to him all that morning, as if he knew of trouble near at hand. So plaintive was the look in his great eyes that Ruby was sure he understood and was begging to go.

"Why, dear, it would be as bad as Mary's little fleecy lamb."

"But Rover wouldn't make the children laugh and play; he would lie down right by me and mind every word I said. Wouldn't you, Rover?"

Rover wagged assent very diligently.

"How could the teacher mind? He's as good as anybody I know."

But these two must part company, there was no help for it. In the hall Ruby hugged Rover tight, called him a "dear old fellow," assured him he would be back before long, and dropped a tear on his great nose.

It was a more sorrowful day for Rover than for Ruby; for the faithful creature, who must needs be shut up in the washroom to keep him from following his little master, lay upon the door, howling dismally for a long while, and neither food nor drink would he touch; while the little master himself, in the new, strong excitement of "entering upon life," thought not once of the loving and lonely friend, till, the day's work over, he bounded up the front steps, to be greeted with a wild bark of joy, and found himself all in a pile with Rover upon the piazza floor.

Every morning there was the same trouble. Rover must be shut up or he would go to school, too. On a certain day, some one having forgotten to fasten the door, he slipped out quietly, lost no time in reaching the school-house, and, the door being open — it was a warm autumn day — rushed in without ceremony, and, with unerring instinct, found his master's desk. There was a series of glad barks, and Ruby, quite forgetting himself, cried out, "Oh, Rover!" as two great paws were laid upon his shoulders.

It was worse than Mary's lamb, I suspect. The children laughed out in school, and the teacher laughed, too; so she gave recess and let Ruby take Rover home.

But one morning Rover did not go up-stairs and lay his paw on Ruby's cheek, nor did he wake his master by scratching at the door, which he always did when he could not get in. Ruby was late coming down in consequence, and, not finding the faithful fellow on the stairs or in the hall, sorely puzzled, he opened the dining-room door, and, without waiting to say "good-morning" to anyone, asked, "Where's Rover?"

Everybody was blank.

"Rover!" said Mr. Vane. "Did Rover ever fail to call you up? And is that the reason you are late for breakfast?"

Nobody had seen him that morning, but nobody had thought about it till now.

Ruby felt a vague foreboding. "I must see about him, mother;" and he was gone.

He went to the kitchen and inquired of Janet and Dinah. "I ain't seen him sence you give him his supper," was all either could say.

He went into the yard and called and whistled and called again, but no response. Then he went to the stable, for Rover and Sukey were good friends. Sukey was chewing her fodder contentedly. Ruby stroked her face and asked, with choking voice, if she knew aught of Rover; but Sukey only chewed on and looked at him with her mild eyes.

Then—what was that? It sounded like a moan, a feeble moan. It was very faint. Perhaps he was mistaken. He waited. There it was again.

Then Ruby rushed out and, following the direction of the sound, ran behind the stable, and there, in mortal agony, lay Rover.

It took only one sharp cry to bring all the family out, for breakfast had gone a-begging all around since the first hint of trouble.

"It's all up with him, poor fellow!" Mr. Vane said, for he saw that Rover was in his death throes.

But Ruby cried pitifully, though his eyes were dry, "Oh, father! can't you help him? Oh, mother! Oh, Aunt Sarah!"—wringing his hands; and he would have fallen upon the great creature, writhing and foaming though he was, and clasped his neck, had not his father held him back by main force.

It was not long that they had to wait; death came mercifully soon and freed the faithful animal from his agony.

"If we only could have said good-by, Aunt Sarah!" Ruby said afterwards when

he could trust himself to speak of it; and that was not for many days.

He kept up until Rover was buried at noon in a corner of the garden; then, when the last shovelful of earth was pressed down over his loving and life-long companion, fled, without a word—indeed, he had scarcely spoken all day—upstairs to Aunt Sarah's room. There he gave way and there he wept, sometimes aloud, though not loudly, sometimes silently, all that day and all that night; for even when he slept, which was not many hours, Aunt Sarah, ever watchful, heard him moaning pitifully. And for many nights after she heard him moan and sometimes cry out. "Save him!" And sometimes he must have dreamed pleasant things, for it would be, "There, Rover, you're a dear old fellow!" or, "Come, come, try again!" as if he were teaching him "tricks." Then memory probably returned, for he would draw a long, deep sigh, and turn restlessly.

Neither food nor drink would he touch on the day of Rover's death, and on the next they could hardly persuade him to touch a little milk or tea. Aunt Sarah became apprehensive on the third day and wanted to send for Dr. Matthews, but the mother thought it was not necessary. Ruby stayed at home all that week, though, and when he went to school again, it was with a sad heart.

What evil spirit could have prompted a boy to such a deed? The first time that Ruby saw this boy, Sim Larkins, he was cruelly beating his own dog, the blear-eyed Teck. Ruby, whose sympathies were always with the oppressed, crossed the street, and, going up close, said, in his grave way:

"I wouldn't hurt him so if I was you; what did he do?"

"None o' yer bizness!" Harder blows and louder howls.

Unabashed, the young champion continued:

"Please don't; maybe if you'd be kind to him he wouldn't do bad. I never hurt my dog, and he's very good."

"You ten' ter you' dog. I'll ten' ter mine." The boy stopped and leaned against the tree to which the dog was chained.

"There, now, let's unfasten him," said Ruby, springing forward to lay hold upon the chain, for he thought, in spite of the boy's rough language, that his words were having effect.

But the tyrant had only stopped to gain

breath and strength. "Dare you to touch it!" he cried furiously, lifting the huge cudgel again, as if Ruby himself might be the victim. "I'm not to git all the beatin's for his aig-suckin'!" Then he came down upon the helpless creature again, and Ruby, seeing that his protests only increased the boy's rage, went away as fast as he could to get out of hearing of the poor animal's cries.

When Ruby entered school he was not particularly happy to renew the acquaintance of Simeon Larkins, nor did that young person take to him. Perhaps when in Sim's company, Ruby's face was never altogether free from a look of grave yet mild disapproval, for he never forgot their first meeting.

Sim sought from the first to prejudice the others against him by circulating rumors to the effect that he was a "stuck-up little chap," and lost no opportunity of guying and ridiculing the new scholar, calling him "toad" and "baby," and other names such as the occasion or his fancy suggested. But Ruby paid no attention — that is, he never answered back — so he lived down the slander and ridicule, for the scholars soon learned that he was the least "stuck-up" and the least babyish of them all.

It was not long before Ruby found out Sim's delight in making the little fellows cry; he has already told Aunt Sarah of that, so we will not repeat it, but he did not tell her how he brought trouble upon himself by seeking to comfort the little fellows, by getting their hats out of the tree, by sharing his lunch with them when theirs so mysteriously disappeared, by championing the persecuted dogs, by honestly and fearlessly

speaking his disapproval to the persecutor himself.

And so things went on. There was scarcely a day in which Ruby's spirit was not troubled by the boy's cruelty to himself or others, and there was not a day in which the spirit of hatred ceased to grow in Sim's bosom, because this little lad dared to

"PLEASE DON'T HURT HIM SO!"

withstand him without one sign of fear, and because he could not make him cry or "hit him" in helpless rage, as the other little chaps were ofttimes constrained to do. Some way to exasperate this self-controlled one, some way to "do him up," came to be his study night and day.

He did not have to wait a great while. That day when Rover bounded into the school-room and all but embraced his little master, when Sim saw the look of joy on that little master's face and heard his cry of glad surprise, his plan was made. It was just a week from that day that Rover failed for the first time to ascend the stairs in the morning and lay his great paw on Ruby's cheek.

From that time Sim's countenance changed toward the child whom he had so grossly injured. Instead of the former sullen scowl, there was a strange gleam of cunning in his eyes, and the surly growl had given place to loud and mocking laughter.

Ruby's silent grief was a luscious morsel that he rolled under his tongue and which to all appearances yielded abundant pleasure. It seemed bold to tell it, but that was half the triumph, and his calculations were shrewdly made.

" Ef the ole man er any on 'em gits after me, I'm jes' to say, 'Sumthin' was suckin' my ma's aigs continual, an' she 'lowed I'd best put some "rough on rats" in a biscuit and lay it in the barn.'"

## CHAPTER V.

### THE HOUSEKEEPER.

 WAS some days, perhaps a fortnight, after the consultation in the library, that Mabel and Marian sat in their bed-room with troubled faces. They had come upstairs arm in arm, and each knew well why the other was sad and silent.

Marian spoke first. " I might as well give up; it isn't in me to be good, I reckon. People in books are not like us, Mabel, do you think?"

Mabel sighed. " They have tempers and faults like ours, but somehow they seem different, too. I'd like to see some of them."

" I don't believe there ever was one of them better than Aunt Emily."

Aunt Emily came in then. " Why, you two children! I thought I'd find you ready for bed, and here you haven't commenced to undress." And she sat down between them and saw that they were troubled.

" Aunt Emily, we want to tell you all about it. We thought we were going to be so good, and here we are worse than ever."

" Are you?"

" It was the day Dr. Caruthers preached about the housekeeper that we said we wanted Christ to keep our hearts. Right away we got angry because Aunt Sarah told us our faults. She said I was always in a hurry, and spoke without thinking. I knew it just as well as anybody, but I didn't like to hear it. And then, since, I've been worse than ever, I'm sure. I've talked too much to the girls at school, and I almost believe I've been pert to Miss Long, and you know what I've done at home — you know I've wanted to have my say before anybody, and how I answered Aunt Sarah to-day about my music."

" And I know," began Mabel, " I know that what Aunt Sarah said of me is true. I neglect my work, and — and I'm very selfish."

" You're not a grain more selfish than I am," broke in her cousin. " I believe I have all the bad things in me, Aunt Emily, and I'm afraid I won't ever be good at all." Marian was very sorrowful and very much in earnest.

" Well," said Aunt Emily, " we won't talk about it any more now, for I have a story to tell you."

They were all attention.

" Now, there was a woman, a small, feeble woman, who lived all alone. She was very rich — that is, she had a great house, handsomely furnished and richly adorned; but the woman had never allowed any one to sweep or dust or clean her house for her, or put it in order. She had just sat still and the dust and dirt had accumulated, as they will, until her house, which would have been so beautiful if cared for, was dark and unpleasant to live in. But this state of things had come on so gradually that the woman did not notice and never thought her house unpleasant. Besides, she never let the sunlight in at the window, so she really could not see how bad it was, and was well content.

" But one day a child came on an errand, and opened the window and saw the woman sitting there in her dirty house. And the woman, as the light streamed in through the window, saw the great spots upon the floor, the layers of dust upon the tables and chairs and ornaments, and the cobwebs hanging in long festoons from the smoky ceiling. She was horrified, and rose up and said, 'I will clean my house this day.'

"But she did not know how small she was; she could not reach higher than the middle of the window. Neither did she know how feeble she was; her limbs trembled so that she could scarcely stand, and her hands were too weak for the task. So she sat down again and cried.

"While she was crying some one knocked at the door. The woman tried to dry her eyes and opened it. A stranger stood there; she asked the woman what her trouble was.

"'I have lived in this house all these years, and I thought it was beautiful; I did not even know it was dark, I thought I was a strong, happy woman. But to-day the light shone in; I saw the dirt and disorder, but when I arose and tried to set my house in order I was as weak as a little child.' And the woman wept again.

"'Take heart,' said the stranger.

"'But what shall I do? I cannot live on so another day, and I cannot make my lot any better. Who will help me?'

"Then the stranger said, 'Let me in, and I will cleanse your house and set it in order.'

"The woman was afraid. 'I do not know you,' she said, and half shut the door. Then her eyes met the eyes of the stranger, and she saw how honest and kind her face was. She looked strong and fit for the task, too.

"So the woman opened the door again and bade her visitor come in. The stranger did so and lost no time. She began with the cobwebs, brushing them down carefully. But the woman soon grew impatient; she had never cleaned house and did not know that the dust and cobwebs must be all taken away before the washing begins.

"'You take too long for that!' she cried. 'Here you've been working an hour and everything is so dirty yet. I want to see the floors clean and the windows bright.'

"The stranger tried to make her understand that this must come first; that she must not expect to see great improvement right away; that she must have time. But the woman only grew more impatient and irritable, and at last bade the stranger leave; she must have some one who would work faster than that.

"Sadly the stranger went away, and for many days the woman sought help. There were many who offered, and some assured her they could do the work in a short time.

She tried them, one by one. Some began with the windows, some with the floors, some with the furniture. Some pleased her greatly for a time, but the window was open, the light was shining in now, and she soon saw that what she had thought to be improvement was only aimless daubing; that there was no dirt removed, washed away—only pushed aside from one spot to make another more filthy.

"Someone passed one day and told her that her house looked worse than before. He was a plain man and plain-spoken. 'It's just a daub here and a daub there, and just water enough to make slush.'

"So she sat down helpless and hopeless, and while she was weeping came a knock at the door, a gentle knock. She thought she knew whose it was. She went timidly and opened. There stood the stranger, and her face was kind as ever. 'I have come again,' she said.

"The woman was glad and humbly asked the stranger in. Again the work was begun, slowly and carefully as before.

"At first the woman sat patient, and waited, but the time seemed long. After awhile she commenced to complain again, but the stranger worked on quietly. When she came to the windows the woman broke out anew. 'Nobody else washed them that way! You must use more soap. Oh, you will break my windows, my handsome windows, and I shall never be able to get others like them!' Then she sprang forward and interfered so that the work could not go on. 'You must do it my way,' she cried, 'or not at all.' So the stranger went away, sad again.

"The woman then took the window cloth herself. 'I am much stronger now and will mount the ladder,' she thought. But the effort was too great; her weak limbs gave way, her trembling hands could find nothing to lay hold of, and she fell unconscious to the floor. She knew not how long she lay, and when she came to herself there was a knocking on the door. She was too weak to rise, too weak to call out at first. After awhile she gained strength to answer feebly. It was only a faint whisper, but the stranger heard and came in.

"The woman wept and said not a word; the stranger went to work again. After a while she said, 'Suppose you sing while I work.'

"The woman sang all she knew, then the stranger taught her other songs. Very beautiful they were, and the woman's voice grew stronger and sweeter as she sang.

"A little boy was passing and stopped to listen; he was a ragged little fellow, with dirty face and hands and uncombed hair. The stranger looked at the woman, and she read a message in the look. She called the little boy to her and gave him food, and water to wash his face. She combed his hair. Then she found cloth and made whole, new garments for him. With a glad heart the little fellow went on his way. And with what surprised joy the woman saw her house growing clean and beautiful under the stranger's strong hands!

"'Do you not think I could help some?' she pleaded.

"But the stranger shook her head. 'You can never do this, but your hands are strong enough to feed the hungry and clothe the naked, and you need never cease from singing. You will forget that the time is long; many a one will go away with a blessing, and I will rejoice in the sweetness of your song.'"

"I see, mother," said Mabel, when the story was done. "We cannot make ourselves good, but we become good as we take Jesus to live with us. Yes, and that was what we said in the library, but we forgot."

"Yes," said Aunt Emily. "And now I don't mean that your hearts are dark and altogether bad, but there is evil in us all, and you know how the dust and dirt and cobwebs will accumulate every day in a house which is not cared for.

"There was one thing I didn't tell you in the story; the stranger's work was never done. Suppose Aunt Sarah and I should give this house a thorough cleaning and say, 'Now, that's the last of it,' and not touch it again for a month or even for a week. It is a constant work."

"And how can we hinder him, mother?"

"By forgetting him and thus shutting him out of your heart, and by opening the door of your heart, your thoughts, to evil passions."

"But how can we help their coming in, Aunt Emily? How can we help the bad thoughts and feelings? They just come."

"Yes, but it is when you invite them in that Jesus turns away. As you love him, he becomes ruler, and then he will conquer and turn them out. But it must be long past your bed-time, so you must be off. I want to say just one more word, my little ones. Think of the best, the kindest person you

have ever seen or heard of, and remember that the dear Jesus is so much better and kinder that you cannot compare them. He is never far away, and is much more eager to come in than you are to ask him."

Over in the corner of the room under the warm covering, was a third listener, for Ruby, though very still, was not asleep. His mother went over and kissed his forehead, and he opened his eyes.

"There, dear, did I wake you?" She tucked the blanket snugly round him and went out.

"Mother says Jesus will turn out the bad feelings. Then I will not worry any more. I will ask him to turn this out, and just wait." And so Ruby went to sleep.

---

## CHAPTER VI.

### THE WRECK.

ONE cold day in February Mr. Vane came home to dinner with a shade of anxiety upon his usually cheery face.

"Emily," he said, but glanced furtively at his sister, "Dr. Matthews told me to-day that a—a cousin of ours was in the hospital."

"What cousin?" asked Aunt Sarah.

Her brother Philip fumbled with his fork, stooped to get his napkin, which had dropped below the level of the table, and, while his head was below the level of the table, answered:

"Alex—Alex Harmon."

When he regained his proper attitude he glanced again at his sister. She was eating her dinner with no change of countenance.

"Is he very ill, Philip?" asked Mrs. Vane.

"Yes. And Emily,"—this time he avoided Aunt Sarah altogether—"do you think we could take him here? The hospital is overcrowded; he cannot receive proper attention nor be made comfortable, and I would be glad to care for him. He is not a near cousin, but was like a brother in our house years ago."

"Humph!"—from Aunt Sarah.

"I never loved any one as I did Alex,"

Mr. Vane continued. "I had no brother; and he was more than one to me, though some years older. I tried to keep up with him, but he did not answer my letters, and for years I have not known where he was. Dr. Matthews was telling me this morning of a stranger who was found very ill in his room at the hotel. He had but little money and was taken to the hospital, though it was already full. I inquired his name, and found it was Cousin Alex. I will go over this afternoon, and, if you are willing, Emily, will bring him back with me, if he can be moved. I will engage a nurse."

"By all means, Philip. We will do what we can for him."

But Aunt Sarah's eyes flashed. "Bring him here indeed! An outcast!"

Mrs. Vane looked inquiringly at her husband, and seemed troubled. Mr. Vane looked not at any one, and seemed relieved that the matter was settled.

Pretty soon Aunt Sarah left the table without ceremony, and, with elevated chin, passed out of the door and up to her own room. She heard footsteps going up and down the stairs, and passing her door; she heard sounds of preparation in the east room, the airiest and prettiest room in the house. It was at the back and had two great windows, one looking toward the rising sun, the other toward the south.

Aunt Sarah did not offer her services to fit the east room for the sick man, neither did she show herself at all. She shut close the blinds of her front window, seated herself in the high-backed chair, and sewed vehemently on the garment she was making for the washerwoman's child.

The afternoon wore on. There was a sound of wheels without, a vehicle stopped at the gate, some one alighted. It seemed a long time before the door was reached, then

AUNT SARAH.

there were footsteps, slow and careful, as of several feet — a burden was being borne up the stairs.

The footsteps passed her door, passed down the hall into the east room; they passed back down the stairs, not noisily, but less carefully, more quickly, and out at the front door. The vehicle moved away.

Aunt Sarah sat and sewed on until the garment was finished. She hunted for some place that might have been overlooked, put in unnecessary stitches, made unnecessary buttonholes, sewed on unnecessary buttons; it was done and overdone. Then she laid it in her drawer, and went downstairs.

In the dining room she found her sister-in-law laying the table for tea. That was a work she always claimed for herself, but she did not offer to do it now. She sat down, before the fire and began to talk.

"So, I reckon, if it comes to it, Philip Vane will turn his own family out of doors to make room for men who have thrown away their religion and their own souls. The best of the house must be given him. No man had better chances, but he deliberately threw them away and turned his back upon his God. And now that his God has forsaken him, is it our place to take him up? He made his choice; now let him have his reward. There's no patience in me for honeying up deliberate sinners; let them receive the wages of their sins. He made his life; let him live it."

"But he has come to death now, perhaps," interposed Mrs. Vane gently.

"Death! What have we to do with that? If an injured God calls him to the bar, is it not justice? And a brother to Philip! 'Brother,' indeed! It was nobody else's influence that turned Philip Vane from the ministry, which father was bringing him up for, and made him the milk-and-water

Christian he is now — if he is a Christian! A trained nurse, too! — giving herself airs, and ordering what's to be done and what's not to be done, from cellar to garret!"

Her sister-in-law turned away, for her cheeks were hot. If she had not known the deep, true heart beating beneath this hard and pricking outside, she would have answered. As it was, she went on with her task, saying nothing.

All through supper Aunt Sarah's face was like a flint. She never once spoke except to answer questions, and her flashing eyes would not meet any one's. She left the table before the others, went to the library for a History of the Reformation, and with it sought her own apartment.

The shadow of Aunt Sarah's displeasure gone, conversation passed more freely round the tea-table. The children could not resist asking many questions about the invalid whom they had seen borne upstairs.

"Poor Cousin Alex!" said Philip Vane sadly. "He was a noble fellow, Emily, brainy and a very eloquent speaker; one of the handsomest men, too, I have ever seen, and of splendid physique. But now — a wreck!"

Ruby made friends at once with the nurse, when she came down to her supper. She was a short, plump little woman, with round, white arms, blonde hair and a smiling face. She wore a blue dress and white apron, but no cap. She was a home-raised nurse and not altogether conventional. Ruby stood near while his mother poured the tea.

"I think you will like mother's tea, Mrs. Cole," he said. "She makes very nice tea, and toast, too; but the tea is nicer. Mother gives me toast every night when she has it, but only a little taste of tea now and then. She says milk is best for me."

He watched a moment as Mrs. Cole dipped sugar for her tea.

"I'm glad you've come, Mrs. Cole."

"Why?" asked that lady, smiling, and dipping more sugar.

"Because you look pleasant, and I like to have pleasant people in the house. I think you are a good nurse, too."

"Do you?" said Mrs. Cole, laughing. "When you get sick I will come and nurse you."

"Thank you; but Aunt Sarah and mother and Dr. Matthews nurse me. And I'm not sick often."

"You're an odd little fellow!" said Mrs. Cole.

"What's that?" asked Ruby.

"Well, it's right hard to tell just what it is;" and Mrs. Cole took her third piece of toast.

"You like toast better than tea, don't you, Mrs. Cole? Mother never lets me have but two pieces. And you like sugar in your tea, don't you?"

Mrs. Cole's fair, smiling face was turning a little red.

"And you like to ask questions, don't you?" said his mother. "Suppose you run up and ask Aunt Sarah for the sideboard key."

The next evening Mr. Vane was late from the store. As soon as Ruby had finished his supper, he went upstairs and knocked softly on the door of the east room. Mrs. Cole opened it and smiled a welcome.

"Father hasn't come from town yet, so I've come to take your place while you go down to supper."

"Did your mother say so?"

"Mother wasn't in the dining-room when I left, but she won't mind, I know. I will take good care of the sick gentleman, Mrs. Cole."

Mrs. Cole stood in doubt a moment, but the little face was so grave and earnest she concluded she might trust him.

"He is asleep now, Ruby. Just sit quietly here, and if he wakes and wishes anything before I get back, call or come for me. But I will not be long."

Then she left, and Ruby sat down noiselessly on the stool and looked up at his charge. He was almost frightened at first, for he had never seen any one look like that.

The sick man was not in bed, but in an invalid's chair, packed around with pillows. Almost as white as the pillows was the face resting upon them; there were deep hollows in the cheeks, and the thin and straggling locks, falling over the temples, were streaked white and dark.

Ruby sat for some moments in his favorite attitude — his knees crossed and his hands clasped about them. He could not hear the invalid breathe; he sat very still and wondered if it would not be better to call Mrs. Cole; and, while he was thinking, there was a slight sigh and the invalid opened his eyes. They were great eyes, without much color or light in them, and underneath were dark rings.

Ruby waited until he thought his patient

was wide awake, then went to him with outstretched hand.

"How do you do, Uncle Alex? Father calls you Cousin Alex, but I will call you uncle."

Uncle Alex did not offer his hand, nor did he speak; he only looked at Ruby with his dim eyes that did not seem to see.

But Ruby went on unabashed. "I'm glad to see you, for I haven't any other uncle except Uncle Rede, and I don't see him often. But I'm sorry you're sick. I think Mrs. Cole will soon make you well, though; she is so nice."

Ruby had taken the long, thin hand lying upon one of the pillows, and held it caressingly in his own. All the time he looked into the white face that never relaxed, and into the dim eyes that gave no sign of seeing.

"Uncle Alex,"—he spoke very slowly—"what is a wreck? Father said you were one, and he loved you very much. You like to be a wreck, don't you?"

Suddenly a wave passed over the pallid face, as if consciousness had but just returned, and with it all the gall of bitterness. The sick man dropped his head forward and moved his hands, as if he would have raised them to his face, but they were too weak for that. Great tears rolled down his hollow cheeks.

Ruby saw the look of pain, saw the tears, and began to weep outright himself. "Oh, Uncle Alex, what is the matter? Did I do anything wrong?"

The knob turned, and Ruby was both relieved and conscience-stricken at sight of Mrs. Cole.

"Oh! Mrs. Cole, I must have done it, but I didn't mean to! I tried to do just right!" And he wept afresh.

Mrs. Cole drew him towards the door. "It's just weakness. There, now, don't mind. It's just weakness—he can't help it. I've seen 'em do that often."

"I thought it was something I did," said Ruby, under his breath, drying his eyes. "Let me tell him good-night, please, Mrs. Cole."

"Just good-night," returned the nurse; and Ruby, somewhat comforted, went back, took the thin hand, and laid his little ruddy cheek against it.

"Good-night, dear Uncle Alex. I hope you will be better to-morrow."

# CHAPTER VII.

## AUNT SARAH.

AUNT SARAH'S eyes had always been black and bright, and fiery, too, on occasion, but there was a time when a glance from them was not like a two-edged sword, and when they did not seem to penetrate to your inmost motive and turn it wrong-side out before the world. There was a time when she did not wear her hair, black then as now, blue-black as a raven's wing, in a small, hard knot at the back of her head. There was a time when her figure, tall and straight as now, was neither spare nor prim, and when her tread was not that of a sentinel on duty. A time when her mouth was like a thread of scarlet, with no deep-cut lines about it; when her lower jaw was not rigidly set; when sternness did not sit, as a vigilant watchman, upon her countenance. In short, little as you might think it, there was a time when Miss Sarah Vane was young, a time when Aunt Sarah could laugh.

From early youth Miss Sarah Vane had been exceptional. Besides being the handsomest, the most graceful, the most daring as horsewoman or mountain-climber, and the wittiest, she was in every way the wisest young lady of her neighborhood. She could do all manner of housework; her cook-book was eagerly sought after by ambitious neighbors, and her style of dress, of house-furnishing and flower-bedding, was the undisputed standard for a radius of five miles. Besides, she was a deep student, especially of sacred literature. Novels she contemned, as did her father before her. She read some poetry, mostly "Paradise Lost" and "The Course of Time," and kept up with the news of the day, social, political, religious. Withal, she was a leader in good works. In fact, Miss Sarah Vane was just the person to have about, whatever your needs. If you were hungry, she could place before you the wholesomest and daintiest of meals; if footsore, she could produce the softest of slippers, her own embroidery; were you weary with mental exertion, she could waken sweetest of harmonies from the piano; were subjects of church or state under discussion, she could give the Rev. Dr. A's or the Hon. Mr. B's opinions, and her own, too; were you a beggar, she would send you on your way rejoicing, warmed, clothed and fed — also, if an able-bodied beggar, you would receive some solid advice as to how to better your condition. And Miss Sarah was not vain of her many accomplishments. Too proud to be vain, as I have heard said of another, she had not that light head which flattery can turn.

When Aunt Sarah was about twenty Alex Harmon came first to her father's house. His father was a remote cousin, who had sought frontier life. Alex, the only child, his mother's pride, was sent back home at eighteen to be educated. Two years he had been at school in the city before Mr. Vane found him out; then, charmed with the young man's appearance and manners, and pleased with the report of his talents, he took him into his own family as a son. Alex had two more years at college, and all his vacations and days off were spent at " Uncle Reuben's."

Uncle Reuben's was six miles from town and just such a comfortable, old-style, country place as one loves best to be in. And Cousin Sarah was no small part of the attraction. These two cousins were contrasting enough, if that draws people together. She with her dignity, her worldly wisdom, her strong and careful judgment; he, unconventional, warmly affectionate, impulsive.

It was during this time that his parents died, within a week of each other and suddenly, so that Alex could not reach them. He would not go afterwards, for the thought of the empty house was too much for him. He wept many days, and Mr. Vane himself went to settle up his affairs. He found that Alex was wealthy, though the young man himself had not suspected it.

It was in those days of grief that, catching sight of sympathetic tears in his cousin's black eyes, he had ventured to speak all his heart and his mind. It is of no use to tell what was in his heart; we can all guess that. One thing upon his mind was the thought of his mother's prayer, which was that he should enter the ministry. This thought was with him all the time, the influence of his mother's prayers he felt from day to day, but — was he worthy? The responsibilities, the vows! Was it for him to undertake so sacred a task? He had always hoped that some day his mother might see her desire fulfilled, but it was a dream, a

something dim and distant. Now his college days were drawing to a close; he was twenty-one, it was time for decision. More than ever now since his mother had passed from earth, did he desire that her prayer might be answered.

Aunt Sarah's countenance never betrayed her, but secretly she rejoiced. The ministry was her highest ambition for a man, and Alex, with his gifts, was fitted for great things. She never hinted so much as this to him, though, but went on with her sewing with a steady hand, and spoke such cool wisdom that he was almost disappointed. He was right; it was a great work, an awful responsibility, and no man should venture to undertake it who did not feel undoubtedly called. Much self-examination was necessary; motives must be tested; if this work were undertaken for anything but the glory of God it were better to leave it alone.

Self-examination only showed his own unworthiness to himself, yet if he knew his own heart it was for nothing save that — the glory of God — that he would undertake this work. But how could he know if he were called?

There were many tests; she dared not judge for him. Desire was one, and a constant burden upon him—the burden of souls.

At length Alex came to a decision, and then, when satisfied it was the result of prayer, Aunt Sarah let her joy shine forth.

With decision all doubts vanished away, and no man was ever happier, more enthused, more wholly given to his calling, than Alex Harmon. But three theological seminary years! How could he wait? The cry of souls was coming up from all over the land; was it not wasting time, precious time?

Aunt Sarah's steady hand was needed to clip his wings. The cry was great, but not for raw material. The greater the work the more preparation was necessary. Did a man attempt to cure bodies until he had learned something about the bodies and what they needed? Was a body better than a soul?

He reminded her that Christ's disciples never saw a seminary.

But they had a Teacher sent from God. They learned of Him three years and then tarried at Jerusalem till the Spirit was sent upon them. There was a louder cry of souls then than now.

Alex's sober second thought showed him the justice of these arguments.

There was one more college session to be gone through, and he set himself to diligent study. He did not care for honors now, but for Sarah's sake he must not lose them. The sudden shock of unexpected wealth did not turn his head. " A gift that God has placed in my hands that I may the better carry on his work," he said.

It is a great pleasure to have plenty, though. He gave lavishly to good causes; indeed, some proved to be doubtful ones. " But," he said, " it is better to throw away food to a full man than to let a hungry man pass your door unfed."

Then he commenced having small parties in his rooms, for he had a tasteful suite now; first to college men exclusively, then young men from the city were invited, for they sought the acquaintance of this charming, this eloquent, this generous young heir. Among the civilians was a lawyer, a gentleman some ten years Alex's senior, whose attractive personality and calm power as an orator had before now drawn out the young student's admiration. It was not long before these two became chosen friends. When Alex went to Mr. Vane's, which was now unreservedly called home, he could not speak in high enough terms of the young lawyer. He had made a wonderful speech in the court house, and gained what everybody said was an impossible case. It was town talk. But the family did not seem to relish the new friendship, and his Cousin Sarah searched him with her keen eyes. " Milton Crie is no Christian," she said.

After that Alex did not mention Milton Crie in his letters to his cousin. He wrote less and less of his plans, too; of his mission school, of his Bible study. There was no show of eagerness to begin his life-work.

Aunt Sarah's eagle eye was not fully developed at that period, but it was not dull. She took her lover-cousin's spiritual temperature with each epistle; she counted his pulse with the first five lines.

There was no abatement in his ardor as a lover; that seemed to increase without measure. But she laid a firm check upon his enthusiasm; forbade all " my darlings " and " my preciouses;" said " my dear Sarah " was most pleasing to her, but stretched the line to " dearest " on special occasions. Who knows but it was jealousy that caused this strictness? Who knows but she felt, avowedly or secretly, " He must bottle this, or it, too, may be spent "? Aunt Sarah was a wise woman, but a woman still.

Alex did not visit the homestead often during the last term; when he came, his visits were flying ones. Yes, he admitted he was working for honors — " But you know for whose sake, dearest cousin."

The honors were his; the highest all round that a student had ever received in the institution. It was a proud moment for Aunt Sarah when she heard that, and saw him there in his manly beauty, the admired of all that large assembly.

He went home with them the next day, and then Aunt Sarah found, too soon, a confirmation of her fears. He was reticent on the subject of his life-work, avoided all mention of religious topics, and at length — he knew his cousin's eyes were reading him well — made his confession. He could not see his way clearly — not yet. She must remember what her own words had been; he could not dare attempt this great work except he were undoubtedly called; and he hoped, he prayed, that her confidence in him would not be shaken, that she would not call it weakness. He was impulsive, he had been hasty; the thought of his mother's prayers — his voice choked — had moved him when grief warped judgment. Though there is always a sense of shame in turning back, how much better to halt and turn, rather than take a false step which could bring only shame now and forever!

Aunt Sarah's eyes were burning with a strange fire and her face was pale, but she was very calm and said it was better. Then, her eyes never leaving his face, " You have chosen the law."

He flushed up to the roots of his hair and would not look at her when he said it was true.

She turned and went away.

But Aunt Sarah did not throw him over. She knew at a glance the difference between a shallow nature and an impulsive and undisciplined one. That Alex's failings sprung from impulsiveness she did not doubt, and when the burden of life came upon him, as it came upon every man, he would learn judgment, patience and quietness of spirit. She reasoned with herself about him and bore with his weaknesses more like a kind elder sister than a sweetheart. In fact, she always felt as if she were the elder, the more experienced, although he had the advantage of her in time by a few weeks.

There was no coolness between them except it might be on that one subject; rather, those two subjects — the profession he had given up, and the one he had chosen. And there was one name he never mentioned in her presence; it was Milton Crie.

The law Miss Sarah had always looked upon as an unlawful business. She inherited that distrust from her father. There were some noble men in the profession, he was accustomed to say; there were his classmates — Judge Neal and Judge Lawrence — they were, and always had been, men of honor; the latter a man of eminent piety; but they were exceptions. A young man who went into the law ran a great risk of losing his soul. He had had a friend who practised law five years and gave it up, "because," he said, "I cannot do this and be a Christian." If a man could battle through the flood, he was no doubt a stronger man, but — if he were drowned in the rush of waters!

The summer, so sweet and all too short, was ended and Alex returned to the city to study, this time with Milton Crie.

His visits to the homestead were frequent, and Sarah, though secretly sorrowing still, secretly rejoiced also, for she thought she could see each time that he was leaving the fickleness of youth and developing into a robust and tempered manhood.

Yet there was a shadow which sat upon Aunt Sarah's heart, sometimes lighter, sometimes darker; still it sat, and never lifted. There were times when she would reproach herself for distrust; there were times when she would weep and wish that her eyesight were not so keen. Once her boast, this magnified vision was now an affliction.

No, the shadow never lifted; Alex was gaining in judgment, in stability, in self-control, but was he not losing in spirituality? He was laying aside childish things, and, among them, the trusting and open heart which is a part of the Kingdom. Where was the desire to learn of the Master and follow in his footsteps, which had characterized the young man? Where was the zeal to take up that Master's work?

Two years passed. Alex's maiden speech was received with great éclat. That was the town talk now, and the country talk, too, for that matter. Mr. Vane, though disappointed in Alex's course, went to hear it, and with him Philip, a mere lad.

Sarah waited in secret excitement for their return. Mr. Vane was not talkative, but looked pleased. "After all, some good

men should be lawyers," he said at dinner, "to uplift the profession."

Philip was wild with delight. "Some people said Mr. Crie would be nowhere to Cousin Alex in a few years."

It was not long before Alex began to talk of marriage. He was settled in life now; he had abundant means. He had long ago picked out the spot for their home; he would have her to go there and see if it were not a beautiful place. She assented that it was, but would not hear of preparations for building. He almost grew impatient, but she gave in not an inch.

In fact, the shadow sat upon her heart, darker than ever. Sometimes this strong-minded young woman tried to argue with herself that she was over-strict. If Alex were losing in spirituality, was it not so much the more reason she should become his wife, that she might influence him more perfectly? Was there anything that a wife could not do? But she brought herself sternly to task each time. There could be no union for her with a man who left his God. Such an one were worse than a heathen; for it were better never to have known Christ, than, having professed him, to trample him, the Crucified One, under foot.

There were certain rumors afloat, too, and they came to Sarah's ears soon enough. It was her mother who first opened the subject; she had had a visitor from the city. "Sarah," she began, "did you know — had you heard, that — that Alex is becoming indifferent about religion? Mrs. Crayton says he never comes to prayer-meeting or Sunday-school now, and but seldom to church. He has never been known to say a word against Christianity, but his actions show he is leaving it out. And everybody knows what Milton Crie's belief is."

Aunt Sarah made up her mind. Alex was to be there that day.

Probably he saw, all through dinner, by her silence, by the light in her eyes, by the bright spot in either pale cheek, that something was coming.

And it came. When the cool of the evening drew on, she went to Alex in the library and asked him to walk with her. They passed through the side yard, under the grape arbor, and down to the fern-grown spring. She looked him in the face and asked him the plain question, "had he given up his religion?"

He could not look her in the face nor answer plainly. He played in the pool with a froud of fern. He had not given up his religion, but there were many things which he thought of now that he had never thought of before; there were doubts that troubled him now. She could not understand; she had never been where he had been. He could not help these doubts; he had struggled with them, but they grew with him until now he could not know anything, he could not see—

If Aunt Sarah had seen any sign of a troubled spirit she might have acted otherwise, but to her it seemed that he was well enough content; that if he had struggled, he had ceased; that there was one consuming passion now in his breast, one god that he sought after, and it was the fame of his profession.

If she had laid her hand upon his and asked him to confide to her his doubts, that they might meet them together; if she had pleaded with him to open his heart to her and keep nothing back, it might have been different. But Aunt Sarah's proper course was very plain to her eyes. She rose up and told him, without a quaver, that their engagement was at an end; that henceforth she was his cousin — she would never forget his claim as a kinsman upon her—but as to anything else, that was blotted out forever.

It was a terrible blow to Alex. He could not take in her words until her retreating figure was half-way up the path. Then he rose and stretched out his arms and cried: "Sarah! Sarah! Sarah!"

She passed on as a deaf woman might have done.

He knew her too well; he did not seek her that night, but went to the city.

In the silence of his room he wrote a long, humble, pitiful letter. If he had waited a week! If he had put it in another envelope! But he could not even wait till morning; he went out in the dead of night to post it, and Aunt Sarah got it the next morning at breakfast. Her heart was still hot within her, and when she saw on the corner of the envelope, "Milton Crie, Attorney at Law," she went immediately to the desk, inclosed the unopened letter in another envelope, and directed it to the writer. Perhaps that was the only very hasty act of which Aunt Sarah was ever guilty.

If she ever regretted it no one knew; she was firm as a rock, and from that day commenced her unrelenting warfare with unrighteousness and the unrighteous.

She never saw Alex's face after that.

Stung to desperation by the unopened letter, he left the city in a week, went to Europe, and was there five years.

Philip, who did not understand things so well then, lamented and wondered at this hasty departure without farewells. He found out from Mr. Crie where his cousin might be addressed, wrote many letters, and received in return a few short ones, from London, Paris, Rome, Switzerland.

When Alex returned, Philip had settled in business at Greenville, Mrs. Vane was dead, and Sarah was living alone with her father.

Mr. Vane was very feeble; he never went to town. But gossip was not slow to reach the country homestead. Alex Harmon was an avowed skeptic; Milton Crie never went to anything like his lengths. He did not pretend to practise law, either, and was fast spending his substance in riotous living. He was given to an excess of wine. "What a pity! What a pity!" said many a one who partook of his reviving cup.

He did not stay in the city six months, but drifted westward. Within another year news came, through Milton Crie and others, that his property was all gone, that he was living a wild and godless life; and there were some dark sayings, for Crie had charge of his young partner's affairs and had become suddenly affluent. A new house on the spot Alex had selected for his own home, elegant furniture, handsome grounds, servants in attendance — such things will make talk.

Ten years are gone by. Old Mr. Vane has quietly passed away, but Aunt Sarah still lives at the homestead. She is the autocrat, not only of the plantation, but of the neighborhood. She rules with a mighty hand. Philip has his own home now, and pleads with her to come to it. She is doing very well, she says. She does not see how she could live in town, and she does not approve of the worldliness of her brother's house. Not but that Emily is a good Christian woman, she believes, but Philip is lax and his wife is more or less influenced by it.

But a little boy comes to her brother's home. Aunt Sarah's heart is not withered, and it thrills all through; she names him Reuben Vane at once. She makes up her mind to go to see him. In the next letter Philip says Emily is very ill; will she not come? She goes, and that is her home henceforth. Her brother is her brother, her sister-in-law is a good woman. Mabel is a promising child, though too much of a house plant; but none of these could have kept Aunt Sarah away from her own kingdom. Nothing but that little dawning life which, from the first, took possession of her own. If he had been like some boys he would have ruled this ruler of others with a rod of iron; as it was, he ruled her, but with a different kind of a rod.

Everybody called him Ruby right away; it was so natural. Aunt Sarah was indignant and tried her best to make it Reuben, but without success. She dropped into Ruby, too.

"It is a shame!" she often said: "there is Mabel named for my mother, and Ruby for my father, and who would know it?" Marian, too, was a pretended namesake of her grandmother, Mary Ann Vane. The genuine article was the thing for use, she thought; but times had changed.

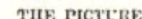

## CHAPTER VIII.

### THE PICTURE.

UBY told his mother that Uncle Alex had cried. "I was afraid it was me, but Mrs. Cole said people would cry when they were sick and weak. Maybe I talked too much, mother."

His mother said it might be better not to go back till Uncle Alex was stronger. So Ruby only knocked gently at the door of the sick-room every morning before going downstairs, and, when Mrs. Cole showed her kind face, asked how Uncle Alex was.

After three weeks' nursing the invalid grew stronger; he ate a little and could talk some, though he seldom wished to. Mrs. Vane sat with him awhile every day, and he seemed glad to have her. One day he asked why Ruby did not come.

That evening Ruby ascended the stairs and took Mrs. Cole's place.

"Now, if I talk too much this time, Uncle Alex," he said, placing himself on the low seat, "and you begin to get tired, just say, 'Ask Mrs. Cole to come up,' and I will understand, and not mind at all. I think you don't look so white," he went on. He

thought his uncle's eyes seemed to see better, too, but he didn't like to say that. They were large and sorrowful eyes still, and rested constantly on the child's face except when the sick man closed them, now and then, as if he were very weary.

"You don't know my Aunt Sarah, do you? She said she had not been in here. But don't mind that; she thinks you are too sick to have company now. She will come when you are better. My Aunt Sarah is a very good woman. She has black hair, and black eyes that just shine sometimes. There is nobody as good to me as Aunt Sarah, except mother and father and Janet and Marian and Mabel and — why, everybody is good to me! I don't know who is best.

"Aunt Sarah reads great big books. She says they are very good books, but they don't have stories in them, like the ones mother reads to us. When I get to be a man I will read them, too. Aunt Sarah is kind to the poor people; she makes clothes for Mrs. Watson's baby — Mrs. Watson is our washerwoman. She used to make clothes for Tom Watson — he's a big boy, higher than I am — and taught him out of the catechism on Sunday after dinner. She always gave him a nice plate of dinner, too. But Tom got so he wouldn't study the catechism when it got over to the long answers; sometimes he'd eat his dinner and slip out of the kitchen before Aunt Sarah knew it. Then Janet said Tom used bad words in the back yard, and went to chicken fights when his lesson was over. So Aunt Sarah would not let him come any more. Father said Tom came for the loaves and fishes, but I don't know what he meant, for we don't have fish for dinner on Sunday. Aunt Sarah said she would not cast pearls before swine. I don't know what that meant, either, about Tom, for Aunt Sarah doesn't like to tell the meanings of things always, and I didn't ask her. But I remembered the words, for I have read them in the Bible and heard people read them. Don't you like to read the Bible, Uncle Alex? I think the story about little Samuel is a nice one. Sometimes when I wake in the night and it is all dark and still, I say to myself, 'Suppose God should call me three times, "Ruby, Ruby, Ruby."' Marian says she would be afraid, but I would be glad; for God is so good, I know his voice would be kind.

"I used to think mother and father and Aunt Sarah and Janet gave me everything, but now I know it's God; for he gives me them, and they could not give clothes and shoes and bread and butter and apples and milk, if God did not make things grow in the ground. I learned some of that at school. Miss Long says nearly everything we have comes out of the ground, someway. I said we got milk from Sukey, and she told me that Sukey couldn't give milk if there were no clover and grass and things for her

it, for I feel better; and if I keep it back and she finds it out some other way, she comes and tells me about it, and sometimes punishes me; but she is never angry with me, only sorry, and I am sorry, too. It's the same way with God, I reckon.

"I love the stories about Jesus best," the child went on, after a short pause; "don't you, Uncle Alex? They always make me

THEN RUBY SANG IN HIS SWEET LITTLE TREBLE.

to eat. God is good, isn't he, Uncle Alex? Once my Sunday-school teacher asked me if I wasn't afraid of God when I did wrong. I said, 'No, ma'am,' and one of the little girls said, 'Why, Ruby!' 'Well,' I said, 'God loves me, and I'm not afraid of anybody that loves me.' 'But God doesn't love you when you do wrong, does he, Miss King?' the little girl said. Then I told them, 'Mother loves me when I do wrong. I always like to go straight and tell her about

think of my hymn; would you like to hear it?" (Mrs. Cole opened the door just then.) "Maybe I'd better go, though, now."

"Sing your hymn," said the sick man, faintly.

Then Ruby stood on the hearth rug and, lifting his bright, curly head, sang, in his sweet little treble:

"I think, when I read that sweet story of old,
When Jesus was here among men,

How he took little children as lambs to his fold,
　I wish I had been with them then,
I wish that his hands had been placed on my
　head,
　That his arms had been thrown around me,
And that I had seen his kind look when he said,
　'Let the little ones come unto me.' "

"Isn't there another verse?" asked Mrs.
Cole, her eyes glistening.
"Yes'm.

" Yet still to his footstool in prayer I may go
　And ask for a share in his love,
And if I thus earnestly seek him below,
　I shall see him and hear him above.

"There is some more, but I don't know it.
I will get mother to teach it to me next
Sunday. Good by, Uncle Alex. May I come
again sometime?"
But Uncle Alex did not answer. One thin
hand covered his closed eyes. Ruby took
the other, which rested on the pillow.
"I am sorry, Uncle Alex; I hope I didn't
talk too much this time."
He was so earnest and so anxious that the
sick man shook his head — he did not open
his eyes — and whispered feebly:
"No, no."
Ruby went down the hall and knocked at
Aunt Sarah's door. Aunt Sarah was sitting
erect in her high-backed chair, reading.
"May I come in, Aunt Sarah?"
"Oh, yes."
He took his stool and watched the fire
awhile.
"Uncle Alex is a nice old gentleman," he
said at length. "He sits right still and don't
say anything. I told him you would go in
to see him when he was able to see com-
pany."
"Who said I would?"
"Nobody; but I knew you would, because
you always go to see sick people. You never
saw Uncle Alex, did you?"
Aunt Sarah did not answer, but Ruby was
accustomed to her being silent when she
wanted to be.
Then suddenly — "Why, Aunt Sarah, if he
was like father's brother, wasn't he like
yours, too? You used to see him at grandfather's house, didn't you?"
"Yes."
"Did you like him, Aunt Sarah?"
No answer.
"Ma'am?"
"What?"
"Did you like Uncle Alex when he used
to be at your house?"

"Oh, I suppose so."
"Father said he loved him very much;
why didn't you?"
"I told you I liked him well enough."
"That doesn't sound like it was very
much. I think you would like him now,
he's so quiet and looks so sad. Aunt Sarah,
his eyes are as big as this," — making a
circle with thumb and finger — "and they
look straight at you, but I thought he could
not see out of them at first. They have a
fady color, too. Were they always that
way?"
"Of course not."
"How did they look?"
"Like anybody else's."
"I mean what color. They were not
black like yours, were they?"
"No."
"Were they brown, or blue?"
"Neither."
"What then?"
No answer.
"Ma'am?"
"What do you want to know?"
"What was the color of Uncle Alex's
eyes?"
"Oh, well, hazel, I suppose you'd call it."
"Like Mabel's?"
"No."
"Like whose then?"
"Nobody's that I know of."
A pause. Then:
"Was his face white and creasy, with
great big dents in his cheeks?"
"Of course not; he's sick."
"Yes'm. Did he ever have any red in his
face like father?"
"Why, yes."
"And his hair, Aunt Sarah, it's nearly all
white now, only in some places it's got dark-
ish stripes in it. Was it always that way?"
"Why, Ruby, you know hair turns gray
when people get old."
"Uncle Alex is very old, isn't he?"
"Oh, not so very; as old as I am."
"Why, you are not old, Aunt Sarah."
"I'm not young, am I?"
"But your hair isn't gray a bit. What
made Uncle Alex's get so white?"
"How do I know, child?"
"What color was his hair when you used
to see him?"
Silence again.
"Ma'am? Was it like yours?"
"No."
"Was it like father's?"
"No," — positively.

"Like mine?" running his hand through his short, bright curls.

"Darker than yours."

"Whose then, Aunt Sarah?"

Silence.

"Ma'am?"

"You know Miss Caroline Mauly, don't you?"

"Oh, yes, the young lady that gave me a lily once. Was his hair like hers?"

"Something; not exactly."

"That's kind of red; what do you call it?"

"Auburn."

"Yes, auburn hair. What a pity!"

"A pity?"

"I mean what a pity Uncle Alex's hair has turned white; Miss Caroline's is so pretty. Did his curl?"

"Not exactly."

"Not exactly? How was it then?"

"Oh, well, Ruby, aren't you tired asking questions?"

"Yes'm—I mean no'm. But I'll stop. Only if it didn't curl like mine, and wasn't straight like yours, how was it?"

"Well, then, it waved. Now, that's enough, isn't it?"

"Yes'm. But it doesn't wave now, Aunt Sarah; it just hangs thin round his forehead."

Ruby paused for a time.

"Could he talk out loud and laugh, Aunt Sarah, and walk fast, like father?"

"Yes, yes, child."

"Do you think he'll ever get well?"

"How do I know? God only knows if people will live or—die."

The next day when Ruby came from school, he ran directly to Aunt Sarah's room. He had turned down six, and got head.

The door was partly open and he rushed in, but Aunt Sarah was not there. He was about to run out, when he saw something on the bed. It was a velvet case, open, and a picture was inside.

It was the face of a young man, very good to look at. He took it in his hand, for Aunt Sarah never said "hands off" to him.

The young man had round, rosy cheeks, full, red lips, large, soft, hazel eyes, and rich auburn hair, waving like a girl's round a white forehead.

Ruby looked at it awhile. The eyes and mouth seemed to smile at him; the young man looked very happy, and he wondered who it was. Then he remembered the conversation of last night, and went with the picture in his hand to the east room. Mrs. Cole let him in with a welcome.

"Uncle Alex," he said, going up to the invalid, "is that a picture of you?"

Though Uncle Alex was stronger now, he could not hold the picture long, his hand was so unsteady, but he looked at it a moment and said, "I think it is."

"I thought so," said Ruby. "I found it on Aunt Sarah's bed."

## CHAPTER IX.

### FATHER PAUL.

 WAS one bright April morning—the white lilacs under the east room window had bloomed out in the night—that Aunt Sarah, answering a knock at the door, met a stranger. There was that in his face and mien which awakened at once respect and trust. She thought at first sight he was an old man, for his shoulders, though broad and strong, were slightly stooped, and his hair, when hung in soft ringlets almost to his shoulders, was white as snow. But the face showed no sign of age except slight wrinkles about the mouth and deeper ones across the forehead, which was broad and high. Aunt Sarah thought she had never seen a mouth at once so firm and gentle, nor eyes so penetrating and kind. When he spoke there was that sweetness and purity of utterance which we associate with purity of thought and speech. There was something about him to make you think of a Quaker, though he did not "thee" and "thou," nor did he wear the gray.

The stranger stood with his broad straw hat in his hand as Aunt Sarah approached. He wanted to know if Alex Harmon was there, and if he might see him.

Aunt Sarah was gracious to the stranger, and led the way upstairs. Then she pointed to the door of the east room and went down to the library where Emily was.

"How was he dressed?" asked Mrs. Vane, when Aunt Sarah had told of the visitor.

"I don't know; I didn't see anything but his face."

It was an uncommon thing for Aunt Sarah

to express admiration, or even unusual interest in any one. She did not express herself now in words.

"I mean, do you remember if he were
dressed very plainly? If so, he must be Mr.
Nesbit, of Factory Hill. I have seen him a
few times."

"Well, I didn't see any sign of finery that
I remember. I think his clothes were plain
and darkish, not black, not much show of
collar or shirt front."

"I don't doubt but it is Mr. Nesbit—
Father Nesbit, the people call him."

"I hope he's no Catholic priest!" Aunt
Sarah bristled.

"No; just a very good man whom everybody loves for his uprightness and kindness.
He regularly visits the hospitals, I have heard
Dr. Matthews say how the patients love to
see him. He brings flowers at all seasons;
sometimes he has been known to walk miles
for trailing arbutus or rhododendron to place
beside some bed. He brings choice flowers
in winter, some from his own hot-house,
which, I have heard, is always blooming.
Dr. Matthews says Father Nesbit cures as
many sick as he does. He is known wher-
ever there is poverty and suffering."

"Where does he live?"

"On Factory Hill."

"He's no factory hand."

"Yes. One would take him for a man of
exceptional culture, but he has been working in this position for years and seems content. He does not attend our church often
—they have a church on the hill—but he
was at prayer-meeting once when I was
there, and made one of the most, if not the
most, near-to-God prayers I ever heard. I
have never forgotten his petition; even some
of the words are with me yet. God's goodness to sinners, the worst sinners, and his
reclaiming power, was the burden of it. I
wondered how he could so feel it, for I think
of him as a man who has always lived apart
from sin."

"I should say so!" interposed Aunt Sarah.

"Mrs. Wyman was charmed with his
'beautiful dignity,' and tried to take him
up ("Humph!" from Aunt Sarah), but he
was not the kind to be made much of. He
would not go to her house, so she contented
herself with an occasional visit to his cottage, and with scattering buns and small
pence among his Sunday-school."

Father Nesbit stayed upstairs an hour, perhaps. Aunt Sarah was in the library when
he went out.

At dinner they were talking about the
visitor.

"A remarkable man," said Mr. Vane. "He
is known not only for his kindness to the
sick and poor, but for his integrity. Without making a parade, he is so scrupulous
about the smallest matters that he is called
'The Honest.' Mr. Newel, the superinten-
dent of the factory, says his influence
among the operatives is wonderful; not a
man among them, old or young, will use bad
language in his presence. And the women
and children go to him with their troubles
and ills, as if he were a woman and a
physician besides. He is allowed the priv-
ilege of working when he chooses, and sometimes he spends whole days in his ministra-
tions."

"Has he no one—no family?" asked Mrs.
Vane.

"No; he lives alone, and nothing is known
of his past."

When Ruby went up to have his evening
talk with Uncle Alex—he was a regular
visitor now, coming in and going out when
he pleased, for the invalid was much
stronger; too strong, in fact, to need a
trained nurse and Mrs. Cole had gone—he
asked about the visitor.

"I think Aunt Sarah liked him," he said
in the course of his remarks. "She didn't
say so, but when she talked about him her
voice sounded different, and her mouth didn't
look like this."

Whereupon Ruby attempted to make his
lower jaw rigid, and draw his rosy mouth
into a thin, straight line, without intending
the least reflection upon his beloved aunt.
Then he wanted to know if he might see the
stranger the next time he came, if he were
not at school, and Uncle Alex said he might.

Father Nesbit came again, after a few
days. It was one evening while the invalid
was taking his tea. As soon as Ruby finished his, he went upstairs. Uncle Alex told
the stranger who he was, and Ruby, ad-
vancing, held out his hand. He stood
awhile, his hand in the stranger's, looking
into the gentle blue eyes.

"Why, I know you, he said; "you are
Father Paul."

"How do you know me?"

"You see, I was in Mrs. Wyman's carriage—she was taking me to ride because
I had been sick and it was such a nice warm
day. We went by the factory; it was such a
pretty road down by the river, and some
children were all around you, under a big

tree. It was a heap of children, and you were talking to them and some of them sat in your lap. I thought you were telling them pretty stories, like the ones mother tells me on Sunday — that was Sunday; and Mrs. Wyman stopped the carriage and spoke to you and the children. Some of them came running up and asked her if she didn't have any cakes and pennies, but she told them they oughtn't to be beggars, and that she didn't have something for them every time. I expect Mrs. Wyman is a very good lady, don't you, Father Paul? She told me that was what the children called you. Do you know what it made me think about, when I saw you there with the children all round you? It made me think of my hymn. It is such a pretty hymn. I will sing it for you."

Then, standing erect and putting his hands in his pockets, as he always did when singing, Ruby sang in his sweet, childish treble:

"I think when I read that sweet story of old,
When Jesus was here among men,"

and all the rest of it.

Uncle Alex's thin hand was laid across his eyes, as it always was while Ruby sang, but Father Paul sat with his quiet eyes fixed upon the little singer.

"Don't you like it, Father Paul?" Ruby asked, after a short waiting.

"Yes, my child."

"And which part do you like best? I like the second verse that says:

"'I wish that his hand had been placed on my head.'

"And I like the part that says, 'Still I may go to his footstool,' and 'all who are washed and forgiven.' Will you sing that again, Ruby?"

"Yes, sir.

"Yet still to his footstool in prayer I may go,
And ask for a share in his love;
And if I thus earnestly seek him below,
I shall see him and hear him above,
In that beautiful place he has gone to prepare
For all who are washed and forgiven;
And many dear children are gathering there,
For of such is the kingdom of heaven."

They were quiet awhile, then Ruby suddenly remembered something.

"Father Paul, why do people call you 'The Honest'?"

"Do they?" the visitor asked quickly, as if much surprised: and a swift look of pain passed over his calm face.

"Father says so. Why do they? What does it mean? Sir?"

There was no getting away from Ruby's questions.

"Well, my child," — taking the little hand and looking straight into the earnest eyes — "it means not to lie, not to make believe, not to — not to —" He stopped.

"Why, I know now!" cried Ruby. "Not to take things. We had a boy once — Joe was his name — he used to take things. He took a pair of shoes and father's brand-new buggy whip, and father said he couldn't keep him because he wasn't honest. But I forgot about that; I didn't know what father meant when he said people called you 'The Honest.' Aunt Sarah taught me the commandments, and the eighth is, 'Thou shalt not steal.' But I don't know why anybody would want to steal, do you? It seems like I would feel so bad that I wouldn't want it if I took it from anybody."

Mr. Vane came in then, and there was a break in the conversation.

---

## CHAPTER X.

### WHOSOEVER.

SPRING wore on. Father Paul still came to visit the invalid. Sometimes they sat, on the bright mornings, by the east window, and breathed "the breath of God" from the lilacs, then the roses. Sometimes in the cool evenings, when the sun was set, they drew near the crackling blaze upon the hearth.

Ruby was often with them. His mother was afraid he might be in the way, but they both begged that the child might come whenever he wished. Sometimes he talked, and his quaint simplicity was very refreshing to these two men upon whose heads the world and time had laid ungentle hands. More often he sat still, now watching and listening, now seeming not to hear, looking into the fire.

One night he had sat so a long time, and

the two were talking more earnestly than usual.

"For any other sin there might be pardon, but was not mine the 'unpardonable'? Deliberately to sin against light and knowledge. No, no!"

That was Uncle Alex, and Father Paul remonstrated gently. "It is not for us to set limits to infinite love, nor to make our near-sighted interpretation of Scripture. 'Whosoever' is the best word I can find. Whosoever! Can you bound that?"

But no light came to Uncle Alex's pallid face; he laid it back against the pillows and closed his weary eyes. Weary eyes they were; weary of the light of day, weary of the long night-watches, weary most of all of the visions that rose up before them, moment by moment, and passed not by.

"Alex," said the low voice, "do you need to go any farther than me? and do I need to repeat the story of my own shame and sin-sickness? If God's love can blot out that, why should you fear?"

Something like a flush passed over the sick man's face; he raised himself and spoke almost vehemently in his weakness.

"Paul Nesbit, what are you saying to me? You did not sin! It was a lie they told!"

"Alex! Alex! You did not know? You! I—" Father Nesbit's strong frame quivered, and pain, deep and intense, was in his face. "Can it be? I never thought! And all along you have believed in me!"—his voice choked. "Look here!"

One hand snatched nervously at his collar and laid bare his breast. There, across it, were dark, ragged lines. The dim eyes of the sick man could see nothing else at first. Then Father Paul's straight forefinger traced them, and he knew they were letters—five; slowly he made them out—T—H—I—E—F—burnt into the flesh.

"It was in those first days of desperation, when there was for me no friend on earth, no God in heaven, that I did it; when I loathed myself, and called on death, and would have taken my own life if I could; and when I found death would not come at my bidding, but that this despised frame was growing stronger instead of weaker, and might drag out an existence for years to come, I branded it thus. But God caused the madness to abate, and without help of man, only by the voice within me, was I brought to behold his love, to know his yearning over me. And now, Alex! Alex! what is left for me to say? Whosoever! Whosoever!"

When Father Paul left the room a little figure slipped out with him; a little figure that was not noticed.

Father Paul went downstairs and out upon the street, but Ruby knocked at Aunt Sarah's door and opened it softly. He stood gravely by the high-backed chair for a little while.

"Aunt Sarah, what does it spell, in big letters—T—H—I—E—F?"

"'Thief'; don't you go to school?"

"Thief! Aunt Sarah, are you sure? every time?"

"Yes, child."

"And a thief is a—a—"

"A man that steals."

A pause.

"Then, Aunt Sarah, what—why was it written on Father Paul's breast?"

"Father Paul's breast! Ruby, you've been asleep in yonder, and dreaming some outrageous dream. Wake up, child!"—shaking him a little.

"No, Aunt Sarah, I wasn't dreaming; it was the very truth; and Father Paul looked all strange and talked fast, and Uncle Alex is sorry 'cause he says God doesn't love him. What makes him think that, Aunt Sarah? Why, God loves everybody. Mother says we're his little children. And Uncle Alex sits so nice and quiet all the time he's sick, and don't fret any. I know God must love him a heap."

Aunt Sarah's theological reading didn't seem to help her out this time, either. She put the over-sensitive child to bed.

---

## CHAPTER XI.

### A NEW NURSE.

AY passed, and June was at its height. Uncle Alex had grown gradually stronger, but had never left his room. When Mrs. Cole went away he had a long talk with Mr. Vane.

"There is doubtless room for me now at the hospital, Philip, and I must go there. I may be chained to my chair for months yet, and it is too much for you. I can never thank you and Emily for taking me in and caring for me so tenderly when nothing but death was before me. But no one knows — Dr. Matthews himself cannot tell me anything; he says candidly that I may recover in time, or may linger for weeks or months, only to meet the end at last. In either case there is no hope of speedy recovery, and as I am helpless and must be a burden, it must be upon public charity and not upon you, Philip."

"A burden, Cousin Alex."

"No, Philip, I know your generous heart. I know what it was when you were a boy, and you have not outgrown it. But do not argue with me."

"We will not talk of it at all now, Cousin Alex. We will see what Dr. Matthews says, and you must rest content for the present. If you must go, there is no haste. Why, what would Ruby do? And Marian and Mabel are so proud of being your nurses now, it would be a pity to disappoint them by taking away the important trust. I will see Dr. Matthews, though, and in the meantime just wait patiently."

So spoke Philip, because he knew the sensitive nature with which he had to deal; more sensitive than ever because of the bowed head and broken spirit.

"Dr. Matthews shall have his orders before he sees him."

And so he had. "No, no, my fine fellow, no moving yet!" was his answer to the invalid's petition. "Philip can put up with you a little while longer; time enough to talk of changing quarters. Now, you just walk around this room when you begin to feel stiff, and read a little now and then, and talk to Ruby and Mrs. Vane and the bonnies and — Miss Sarah. Miss Sarah is a host within herself, you know."

So the sick man tried to content himself to wait the doctor's will.

The days went on, and the weeks; whenever he broached the subject of removal, there was some plausible excuse. It was too cold, or too hot, or too damp, or too threatening; or if the weather was perfect, the doctor's twinkling eyes would become suddenly anxious; there would be a feeling of pulse and taking of temperature, a shaking of the head, and "Not to-day, not to-day," until Uncle Alex began to suspect the plot. He was making up his mind to face them both with his suspicions when he found himself, one June morning, unable to rise from his bed. Philip and Emily and the children ministered to him, and in a week

he was able to be in his chair again, but helpless, almost, as when they bore him from the hospital.

Then one morning Mrs. Vane found herself unable to rise and sent for Aunt Sarah. Aunt Sarah was used to carrying the keys, so needed few directions. But later her sister-in-law sent again.

"Philip went for Mrs. Cole, but she is not in town, so he did not go for a strange nurse before consulting you. If you prefer, he will engage a neat serving-woman, who can do everything under your directions."

"I'll have none of them," cried Aunt Sarah, and one who knew her less would have thought her wrathful. "No trained nurses for me, whipping by you on the stairs and taking their ease all day; and none of your serving-women, either, just as full of themselves in their way and just as lazy. Emily Vane, do you think I never managed a house and sick people? Was there ever a trained nurse in my father's house in the forty years I lived there?"

Janet and Dinah knew they must move when Miss Sarah was on guard. Janet said she wanted to go every way at once, and her feet "jes' got tangle' up" in her haste to have the meal up on the stroke of the clock, and Dinah spilled the gravy on the table-cloth while watching Miss Sarah pour the coffee. The children must be off to school right away, so Philip carried the invalid his breakfast.

But at eleven, when the house was set to rights, and the servants set to weeping because there "wa'n't nuthin' they could do to please Miss Sarah," — that is true of the tender Janet; Dinah, however, had been rendered callous by a thick epidermis — the new housekeeper knew that there was one duty which must be performed. She had never forgotten it all morning, and, if there was such a thing as repentance in her heart, repented at leisure that she had taken so much on herself in hastily refusing a nurse. She was not one to put off the inevitable, but she made no haste in her preparations. There was the soup, which must be so thick and no thicker; the crackers, which must be so brown and no browner; the tea, which must be of a certain sparkling amber.

When the dainty waiter, just such as she had carried to her father's room for years, was ready, Aunt Sarah ascended the stairs with her measured tread, and knocked at the east-room door. Uncle Alex knew that

Emily was sick, but he probably had never suspected who was to be his nurse. The knock was unfamiliar. In another moment the door swung open and Aunt Sarah entered, the waiter in her hand. Whether two decades and more had passed so lightly over her, or whether it was only because he was aware of her presence in the house, he knew her at once, but said nothing.

Aunt Sarah was prepared for much, but not for the sight of that shrunken figure packed in pillows, that bony hand, those sunken eyes and hollow cheeks, that sad and inexpressibly weary countenance. She was not one to be lightly shaken, but the dishes rattled in her hand. Then she walked up to him, and said:

"Do you know me? I am Sarah Vane. I have brought your soup."

He did not say anything, but took the spoon when she had made everything ready upon the little table beside him. But his poor hand could scarcely hold it, and the soup was spilled on his dressing-gown. There was no other way; she took the spoon and fed him like a baby.

There was no word spoken except, on her side, to know if the soup was salt or cool enough, or if he wanted the cracker in it, and if the tea was sweet or bitter. On his side was no word at all; only slight motions of the head in assent or otherwise.

Aunt Sarah went through her task without a break; no observer, however observant, could have discovered one sign of anything working below that even surface.

And no one knew how, when the invalid had taken all he could and she had wiped his lips with the damp towel and removed the spots from his dressing-gown, when she had carried the dishes away to the kitchen and given directions for dinner — no one knew, when she had ascended the stairs again and shut her door behind her, how she fell upon her knees beside the straight, high-backed, leather-covered chair, and poured out her soul before the Lord.

## CHAPTER XII.

### UNCLE REDE.

AUGUST came and with it the time for Marian's pilgrimage to her father's house. Ever since the holidays began Marian had looked forward with a certain uneasiness to this event. She would gladly have found some excuse for not going, and as the day drew near awoke every morning wondering if she had not a headache or other premonition of illness. If she were sick Aunt Emily would not let her go. But she could not get up a headache or any kind of ache, and kept a remarkably good appetite.

She and Mabel and Ruby had been having such a nice time this vacation. Uncle Alex had gone back to the hospital a month ago. They missed him very much, but found they could still help to nurse him. For every morning there was a waiter or basket made ready, and the three carried it by turns over to the hospital and up to Uncle Alex. Sometimes mother got the waiter ready, sometimes Aunt Sarah; and there was always the choicest flower that the garden afforded to go along with it.

One morning as they were starting off, Aunt Sarah called Ruby to the corner of the piazza and gave him three roses from her own pet climber which no one else ever touched. They were cream roses with the delicious odor of tea. She often pulled the flowers for the table or sideboard, but it was seldom that she honored a visitor with a bud.

Aunt Sarah did not tell Ruby what to do with the three sweet roses, but he knew very well. He went straight up to Uncle Alex with them.

"These were the prettiest ones on the bush," he said. "Aunt Sarah's bush; she sent them to you."

Uncle Alex was learning to put his own construction upon Ruby's statements. Ruby was honest as the day, but in perfect good faith often allowed himself wide latitude. Nevertheless, the sick man took the roses and laid his cheek upon them an instant.

Mabel and Marian were well pleased when they were permitted to uncover the tempting viands, and if Uncle Alex could eat, their joy was great. He always tried to eat to please them, but sometimes it was too much for him, and they would let him off with the promise to take some after awhile.

Marian said it was the happiest vacation she had ever had, and Mabel said so, too; as for Ruby, he said little about it, but every day seemed a quietly happy one to him.

"I think it's because we are doing something for somebody," Marian confided to Mabel, "that the time passes so fast, and we like every day so well. But, Mabel, it's passing too fast for me."—a deep breath here. "Next week I'll have to go—" She thought she ought to say "home," but it didn't sound right. Then a bright thought struck her. "Why, Mabel, why can't you go with me? I'll ask Aunt Emily right away. You will, if she lets you, won't you? It will be so different if I have you. I won't mind Mrs. Green and—everything."

Mabel was not so enthusiastic; she was sorry that Marian must go, but some of Dinah's stories had reached her ears and she felt a strong dread of the gloomy mansion; and of Marian's father, too—the tall, stern, silent man whom she had seen once when he came to visit his little daughter. But Mabel tried to forget herself for Marian's sake.

"Why, yes, Marian, if mother says so."

But mother did not say so. Mabel had had two chills, her complexion was waxy, and she ate next to nothing. She could not be spared from her mother's sight now.

Mabel kissed Marian and said she would have gone if her mother had been willing; but she could not say she was sorry, and she could not help the short sigh of relief. Marian felt it a little, but did not blame her cousin. She was feeling very sad just two days before her departure, when Ruby found her sitting in the library in the twilight, her head resting on the window sill.

"How would you like me to go home with you, Marian?" he asked.

"Why, Ruby, I would just love to have you go! Now will you?"

Ruby had not consulted headquarters, but he did at the tea table, and there was some discussion that night. Father and mother thought it might be possible, he was so

"HERE WE ARE, UNCLE REDE!"—SEE PAGE 30.

much in earnest, and they were sorry for Marian. But Aunt Sarah would hear none of it. She gave out all sorts of reasons, but the truth was she had never been separated from the child but one night since she had first laid eyes on him, and that night was one too many for her.

Somehow, she gave in at last; perhaps it was the sight of Marian's tearful face and the thought of the child's homesickness. It was the more remarkable as Aunt Sarah was not often accused of giving in.

So Mabel was left alone to minister to the invalid, and the two set off on their journey. There was a long ride on the cars, then they got off in the midst of so much stir and bustle and noise of vehicles and talking and laughing and men calling out something at the top of their voices about "this way," and "Mansion House omnibus," and such things, that Ruby was really bewildered, and held tight to Marian's hand. And Marian was glad that Dinah was with them, though she had been very sure they could get on without her.

Dinah was no veteran in the service, but she had strong arms that gathered up the outlying luggage and pushed through the jostling crowd. They made their way to the waiting-room, where the neat waitress looked after them till Prof. Rede's carriage rolled up, and Pete's dusky countenance, upon which always sat a chronic grin, showed itself from the driver's seat.

Dinah, upon whose impassiveness the joy of meeting or the sorrow of parting made not the slightest impression, returned a careless nod to the delighted salute from the driver's seat, and busied herself packing children and bundles.

Ruby shook hands with the colored waitress when he said good-by, and said he was much obliged to her. Then Pete cracked his whip over the black horses, and away they went, out of the city and over four miles of beautiful country road, gently rolling, to Glenwood.

"Uncle Rede has a pretty place, Marian," Ruby said, as they drove up the avenue of water-oaks.

He did not like the house so well when the carriage stopped in front of the door. It was such a dark red and looked like the jail where they put people who did bad things; but he thought he'd better not tell Marian that.

Mrs. Green opened the door as they came up the steps, and Marian thought she was taller and straighter and cleaner than ever. She held out a stiff right hand, which Marian touched with hers, but Ruby caught and shook it heartily.

"I am glad to see you, Mrs. Green. Where is Uncle Rede?"

Mrs. Green was not accustomed to children or to anyone else who asked questions or expressed pleasure in her acquaintance. Marian had come in and out many times, but had never asked "Where's father?" and it had seemed natural enough.

The housekeeper looked with some curiosity at this new specimen, and answered, with great precision, that Prof. Rede was in his study.

"Does he know we have come?"

Mrs. Green answered in the negative, and Ruby said, "Oh, well, you needn't trouble; we'll just go up. Come, Marian; you know the way."

But Marian shrank back and glanced up at Mrs. Green. That lady said nothing, but turned her eyes toward this strange young creature making for the stairs.

"Come, Marian, make haste before he hears. We'll just run up and s'prise him."

Marian did not know what to do but follow. Ruby kept in the lead. When they reached the landing he whispered behind his hand:

"Won't he be glad!"

They did not hear any response to the knock, but to Ruby a father was a father, and he was not afraid to enter without a bidding.

Anyone but Ruby would have been taken aback at sight of this long room, lighted by two windows, yet strangely gloomy; with its rows of glass cases round the walls, in which were all manner of flying, walking and creeping things, and its skeleton, not in the closet, but in full view. And not the most attractive object was the gaunt figure bending over a table before one of the windows, looking at something through a glass.

"Here we are, Uncle Rede, Marian and me! We did s'prise you, didn't we?" and Ruby advanced, quite joyful that his plan had succeeded. He not only held out his small hand, but put up his rosy lips to be kissed.

The tall man looked at him as if he did not understand, then stooped and touched the lips with his own. When Marian drew near, trembling and almost pale, he kissed her forehead, or touched it with his lips, and asked how she was.

Marian caught Ruby's hand and said hurriedly that they had better go and get off their things. But Ruby was of another mind.

"What were you looking at when we came in, Uncle Rede? May I see it?" he asked.

The silent man lifted him up to the level

of the table with one hand, and with the other put the glass to his eye.

"Oh, where did it come from? It wasn't on the table just now! Oh, Marian, come and see! It's all shiny!"

Marian, curious to see, but afraid to get too near her father, came up timidly to the other side of the table and looked over. She didn't see anything but a very small object, a tiny bug in fact, but Ruby continued his exclamations.

"Don't you see, Marian? There, just look! Why," taking his eye from the glass, "it's gone again! Is it in the glass, Uncle Rede?"

The gloomy face of the scientist seemed almost interested in the child's wonder. He showed him the tiny object upon the table, then placed the glass over it and told him how the strange creature he saw was not in the glass, but only the little bug seen through the glass.

"And how does the glass change it so?"

"It magnifies it."

"Sir?"

"Magnifies it — makes it large."

Ruby was lost in wonder. "Let Marian see now," he said.

Marian looked, and was astonished, but she could not forget what hand it was that held the glass, and could not breathe with perfect freedom. She reminded Ruby again that they must get off their things and be ready for tea.

"Yes, I expect we must go," he consented; "but we'll see you at tea, Uncle Rede."

The tall man did not say a word, but looked at Ruby with his gloomy eyes.

But Ruby did not wait for words. When he had washed his face and brushed his hair and changed his traveling waist for a fresh one, and Marian had fastened on his plaid tie, he went to the study door again and knocked. This time he heard a "come" that sounded far away, and he walked right in.

"I stopped to go down to supper with you, Uncle Rede. Are you looking at it yet?"

Uncle Rede had not thought of taking supper with these two children. He usually took his meals up here in his study, alone except for the creatures on the walls and the skeleton, and he did not like changes. But, like most people, he did not know how to say "no" to Ruby, so suffered himself to be led downstairs.

Marian was in the dining-room when they entered, hand in hand, Ruby talking. Mrs. Green was putting a plate of bread on the table. She had laid plates for two only; now she hastily placed a third and withdrew.

When they were seated Marian's father turned up his plate and passed the bread. Ruby did not take any, but looked straight into his face and said:

"Why, you are like father was once, Uncle Rede; you forgot something."

"Forgot?"

"Yes, sir; the blessing, you know."

Uncle Rede set the plate down and said. "Will you say it for us?"

Ruby bowed his head over his folded hands and said with sweet simplicity the words his mother had taught him to say over his little plate, when he was very small and ate in the nursery: "God bless our daily bread."

When the hot muffins were ready, Tabby, the cook, brought them in. Tabby was as like Pete as a smiling mother could be like a smiling son, and to her smiles she added courtesies and "yessum" or "yessur," and "now I do say," in season and out of season.

The dining-room was very pleasant - a front room and wonderfully clean. The dark mahogany furniture, the windows, the silver and china—everything, shone. It had always been so, and Marian had often wished there were some dirt somewhere; this cleanliness was painful to her, for it made her think all the time of Mrs. Green's straight back and bony face and spotless neckerchief.

Every time Ruby looked up he saw himself in the round glass over the sideboard, and he frequently adjusted his tie and pushed the short curls away from his forehead. He talked a good deal, expressed himself as pleased with everything, and asked many questions which his host found difficult to answer. When Tabby came in with the muffins, bobbing her white-turbaned head, he asked how she was. Tabby was delighted and came near dropping muffins along with courtesies. Then he took a muffin and said it was very nice, and the bread and milk were nice, too.

There is no telling what Tabby might not have dropped at that, had not a sudden change came over the face of the little visitor. Whether he had felt it all along and had been struggling against it, or whether the sight of these homely articles, bread and milk, brought a too vivid recollection of another tea table, I do not know, but a wave of homesickness swept through his little heart, and he broke out weeping:

"I want mother! I want mother!"

Prof. Rede rose hastily. Marian, wringing her hands and weeping also, ran to the door, calling Mrs. Green and Tabby, she knew not why, and then threw her arms about Ruby and begged him not to cry. .

"You shall go home to-morrow if you want to, Ruby — yes, to-morrow; Dinah will go with you."

Ruby did not say any more, but let Dinah carry him upstairs, and there in the great bed-room, by Marian's side, sobbed himself to sleep.

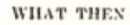

## CHAPTER XIII.

### WHAT THEN?

 HE next morning Ruby did not wake till Marian had gone downstairs, but Dinah was there and helped him to dress. He went down to the dining-room and found Marian there alone. Mrs. Green and Tabby were bringing in breakfast.

"You can pour the coffee, Miss Marian," said Mrs. Green, putting down the shining pot.

"Why, where's Uncle Rede?" asked Ruby, with a shadow on his countenance, for there were only two plates. Prof. Rede had taken breakfast in his study an hour ago. "And why don't you eat with us, Mrs. Green?"

Mrs. Green said she took her meals in the serving-room.

"But we will be so glad to have you; it'll be more like home." There was a hint of breaking in his voice, but he cleared his throat and stood up bravely. "There, now; Marian will sit on this side and you at the coffee pot, and it'll be all right. Here's another chair, and Marian will get a plate and knife and fork, if you will tell her where they are."

Mrs. Green was under the spell, and did as directed.

"This is real nice," continued Ruby, when they were seated. "Marian pours out the coffee very well, but I think there ought always to be a big lady at the table."

He asked the blessing again and they got through the meal well enough. Only Ruby

did not talk much, and his face was slightly troubled.

After breakfast, when he and Marian retired to the piazza, he asked: "Do you reckon Uncle Rede was worried about me last night, Marian? Was that why he did not come to breakfast?"

Marian thought not. "Father hardly ever comes downstairs to his meals; he takes them in his study."

"Is that it? But I wonder why he does? I think it is so much nicer to be with the others."

"Ruby," Marian began, "do you know what I told you last night? If you're — you're — if you want to go home, Dinah can go and take you."

Ruby bit his lip and winked very hard. This was his first experience from home and his first homesickness. When he thought about them all, especially mother and Aunt Sarah, he had to swallow hard and bridle up his head.

"No, Marian, I want to see them, and last night I just couldn't help it; but I've come here to stay with you, and I'm going to stay till you go back. I expect it'll be bad every night, 'most — you think more about it then than in the day — but I'm going to stay."

Marian put her arms about him and called him a dear little fellow. She said they could find some books in the library, and would have a nice time reading and looking at pictures.

"Yes, and I want to see all round the place," said Ruby.

That sun had not set before he had made a thorough investigation. He started with Mrs. Green; found out how early she got up in the morning and what she did first; learned which drawer was for silver and which for linen; carried the pan of meal dough and fed the chickens, and tried to count them as they fluttered round his feet; asked what they were going to have for dinner, and was delighted to be allowed to help Tabby pick beans. He cut up apples, too, on the back porch, while Tabby bobbed back and forth from the kitchen and blessed his "sweet little heart."

Pete hung around just to catch sight of the "jolly little chap," thereby meriting constant cuffs and reminders to "ten' ter his bizness" from his devoted parent, who, dissolving in good nature toward others, carried, seemingly, a most unnatural grudge against her offspring.

Pete's dog, Tony, a small, lean, yellowish

creature, with a pitiful face, came and sat on his haunches before the stranger, tapping his tail upon the floor and fixing upon him that begging look peculiar to his kind. Perhaps he was begging for his share of the affection which instinct told him was here, for, like some of us who think we have better perceptions, Tony did not realize the place he occupied in one heart.

Pete was his mother's own child: if some ill-conditioned youngster or any other prowling creature ventured to attack his pet, or speak in uncomplimentary terms of his breed or color, the boy would pounce upon him with unrelenting fury, while in the space of two minutes the pet might be sent yelping away for the slightest misdemeanor. Ruby thought Tony was hungry, and asked Tabby for a piece of biscuit. Tabby gave it, but said he was "plum' full," it was "jes' his everlastin' way."

When Pete went to curry and water the horses, Ruby got permission to go, too. He thought they were beauties, so black and sleek.

"What are their names, Pete?" he asked. Pete returned that "dey wuz Cut and Go."

"Did Uncle Rede name them?"

Pete showed the whites of his eyes. "Laws, no, Marse Rube! Misser Rede, he dunno dey got no names."

So Ruby found out about the place.

Uncle Rede did not come down to dinner, and as the afternoon wore away Ruby could stand it no longer. It was contrary to his etiquette to allow a day to pass without having some words with every person in the house, if every person were in a condition to be spoken to. So he tapped at the study door and was admitted. The recluse sat this time by the table, leaning his head upon his hand.

"You are not looking through the glass now, are you, Uncle Rede? I thought I would come up to see you awhile, we missed you so much."

"Missed me?"

"Yes, sir. Mrs. Green ate breakfast and dinner with us, but we missed you. You must get tired staying here all the time by yourself. Why didn't you come down?"

"I am very busy, child."

"Busy? Yes, sir. What do you do, Uncle Rede? Sir?"

"I read and write."

"And what are these?" — looking round at the creatures upon the walls.

"Specimens."

"Sir?"

"Specimens."

"Yes, sir; and what do you do with the spec'mens?"

"Examine them."

"And what then?"

"I find how they are made, and what they can do, and —"

"Yes, sir; and what then?"

"What then?" It was the question this man had been asking himself as he leaned his head upon his hand. "What good? What then?" All these years he had lived apart from his kind, all these years he had burrowed with the worms in the dark recesses of the earth. Searching for knowledge, what had he found? From the world of men, only a faint whisper penetrated now and then the walls of his prison-house, and that told of rapacity and strife. From the world of nature he heard loud voices that told of a relentless "struggle for life," a perishing of the weak and helpless, a "survival of the fittest." Was there not a break when man was made? Had not the Law, the nameless Force, working according to its own pleasure through all the gradations of Life, been suddenly possessed of a demon when the final chapter was written? Was it, then, final, and a survival of the unfit, or was it a digression, whose aim would be seen in the millionth year from ours? Whatever it was, he was weary of it; and whether his race were to pass away and leave only a few fossil remains imbedded in the growing rock, or whether the overthrow of his race were to make room for a higher, he felt now that he had no interest in the matter, and could gladly lay himself down where no haunting questions would ever come again.

"What then, Uncle Rede?"

How many times the child might have asked the question he did not know. His mind came back at last, and there was the earnest face before him, and the question, — his own question — in his ears.

"I wish I knew what then," he said.

"I wish you would tell me about things, Uncle Rede. I like to know about things."

And now the professor turns inquisitor. "What things do you like to know?"

"Why, how the water gets into the clouds and comes down rain and waters everything, and makes the wheat and corn and grass and flowers grow. That's the prettiest, I think, about the little seed. You put it in the ground, and it bursts and sends little green shoots up and little roots down, and they got bigger and bigger, and after awhile there's a trunk and leaves and a great big tree, and the birds make their nests in it. And I like to know about the pretty little eggs, and the tiny birds peeping out of them, and getting feathers and growing to be big mother-birds after a while."

"And what then?" asked the professor; "why do you like to know all that?"

"Well, I just like to know; I can't tell why. And then I like to think that God made them all."

"Why did he make them? Why did he make you?"

"Why, Uncle Rede, grown people know better than little children. Don't you know the catechism? I don't know much of it; Aunt Sarah wanted to teach me, but mother said I was too little. But I learned some questions, and one was, 'Why did God create man?' and the answer is, 'For his own glory.'"

"And what is that?"

"I never could tell; I thought I'd better wait till I got to be a man before I tried to understand; but I think God made us because he wanted something to love, don't you?"

The man of science did not say; he leaned his sallow cheek upon his hand.

"God would have been lonesome in this big world—I mean all round everywhere," describing a semicircle with one hand, "without any children to love. Just like father would be without Mabel and me and Ma—I mean, like you would be without Marian. Sometimes, when father comes from the store and we all tumble over him, mother says we'd better run away and let father rest, but he hugs us up tight and says, 'Why, Emily, I couldn't rest without the youngsters; I wish we had a dozen.' God is our father, you know, Uncle Rede, and I reckon he wants a heap of children to love. Oh, I hear Pete calling Cut and Go; he said I might go with him to water them. Good-by, Uncle Rede—I don't mean good-by, though; you won't be too busy to come to supper, will you?"

Ruby did not wait for a reply, neither did he stand upon the order of his going. In two minutes more he was on Go's back in front of Pete.

The professor came down to tea. He came down to tea every evening after that, and sometimes to dinner, but always breakfasted in his own apartment. He invited Ruby to come up whenever he felt inclined, and Ruby felt inclined every day. The scientist might be ever so busy, but he would lay aside his work to answer or ask questions.

Sometimes they took walks together, and Marian went, too; then the professor told about the birds—how they built their nests and why they left them. In his laboratory were many curious nests and stuffed birds which Ruby never tired of. The professor told them, too, about the trees, and how they drank in the rain and grew and flowered. To Ruby it was all the story of God and what he was doing every day; to the scientist it was the principle of nutrition and reproduction.

Marian listened, but spoke little. Ruby spoke whenever he pleased and what he thought, without reserve, and the man of learning was daily astonished at his questions no less than his answers. The professor was brought face to face with wisdom; that wisdom from which he had so long turned away that now he never heard her voice crying in the streets.

One day the three were in the woods. Marian had her book, the professor had his; Ruby had no book, but a lily which he had plucked from a cluster growing near the door. The professor soon became absorbed in his book, Marian in hers, so Ruby withdrew from them a little, stretched himself upon the soft grass, and contemplated by turns the lily, the great oak spreading above him, the blue sky showing where the leaves did not meet, and the sunshine peeping in here and there as through a lattice. Sometimes he "listened to the still," as he said to himself. After a time a little bird came and sat just over him and looked intently at the three silent folk.

"I wonder if he thinks I'm a babes in the woods," mused Ruby. "I'll just shut my eyes and see if he'll drop leaves on me." And so he did; but as no leaves fell, the pretended "babes" opened his eyes to find that the little bird was gone.

Ruby was sorry; it seemed an hour that he had been lying there, and it is very trying to be with people so long and yet not be noticed. By and by a gray squirrel ran round the great tree and peeped at him with his sharp little eyes. Ruby jumped up in his delight, and the visitor fled instantly, running into his hole in the tree.

Ruby was disappointed again. He sat up and looked at Uncle Rede and Marian, but neither looked at him. He cleared his throat twice. He waited another very long while, though not so long as before, then got up and went over to Uncle Rede, the lily in his hand.

The professor had probably come to the end of a chapter; he closed his book.

Ruby seized his opportunity. "Uncle Rede," — holding out the flower — "who does a lily always make you think of?"

"Who?"

"Yes, sir. Every time I see a lily I think of one person. It is Jesus; because he said, 'Consider the lilies; they toil not, neither do they spin; and' — what's the rest, Marian? I never can remember the long ones, but you always can. What about Solomon?"

"'Even Solomon in all his glory was not arrayed like one of these.'"

"Solomon was the wisest man and the richest man you ever saw, but he couldn't get anybody to make him a dress that would be as pretty as a lily. Because God made the lily. When I think of the One that made the world, and everything, and me, I say God, and he's like everybody's father; and when I think of the one that people could see, and that walked around like anybody, and made sick people well and said things to help folks along, I say Jesus, and he's like everybody's brother. But they're the same person, too. Now, here, Uncle Rede," laying his small hand upon the back of the scientist, "this that I'm touching is you, but there's a you inside that I can't touch and can't see. Mother says Jesus isn't away off in heaven. I used to think that, but he's all around, everywhere. That is one thing I was thinking about while I was lying over there. I think about it when I'm going to school; I say sometimes, Jesus is going along with me right down the street, and when we're playing ball at recess, and when I get up in the morning. But I believe I think more about Jesus being close when I'm out in the woods this way and it's still. Why, Uncle Rede, I never have sung my hymn for you, have I?"

And, putting his hands in his pockets, and raising his bright little head, beneath the blue sky, he sang:

"I think when I read that sweet story of old,
    When Jesus was here among men,
How he called little children as lambs to his
    fold,
    I wish I had been with them then."

And all the rest of it.

## CHAPTER XIV.

### "MY LITTLE DAUGHTER."

 RUBY did not neglect Mrs. Green, and that lady unbent, which was the extremest thing that she could do. She kept a jar of cookies in her closet and gave him one every day; in doing which she violated conscience, for she considered nothing fit for the digestion of a child but bread and milk. She told him about where she used to live, and about her son who never came to see her, he lived so far away, but wrote to her once a year.

Ruby visited the kitchen every day, and the stable yard. He remonstrated with Tabby on her treatment of her son, and with Pete on his treatment of Tony. Somehow Pete found out through the taciturn Dinah the story of Rover, and his respect for the "little un" rose higher still, and he began to be more tender with Tony. Tony repaid him with such slavish devotion that his master's heart was touched.

But Tony had a large place for Ruby, also. Ruby had never feared a dog, except it were Sim's Teck, and his whole spirit had been perverted by cruelty until there was nothing but enmity between him and mankind, which did not love him at first sight. The other children, and even his mother and Aunt Sarah, were sometimes afraid to approach certain dogs whose reputation was unsavory or manner menacing, but Ruby would walk right up, and, though there was in some cases a showing of teeth or low growling, it soon passed away beneath the charm of that voice and hand.

What was it? Some said it was because he was not afraid; no animal will hurt you if you are not afraid. But why was he not afraid? I think it was love, the love which knows no fear, that gave him this boldness of approach, not only to unreasoning creatures, but to higher creatures as well — and even to the presence of the Highest of all. He loved, and was not afraid.

The month was going by very rapidly, even to Marian. She wrote Mabel that Glenwood was a beautiful place this summer. Mrs. Green was no longer offensive to her, and she was not afraid of her father now, though she never approached him of her own will.

It was the evening of their last day and

Marian stood before the fire in the dining-room, for it was a cool, damp day, and Mrs. Green had had fires kindled more for health than comfort. Marian was thinking deeply and did not hear anyone enter, so was startled when a hand was laid upon her shoulder. It was her father who stood there.

"Marian," he said, "you are like your mother. Have you seen her picture?"

That was all, but it was a big book. He stood for a moment longer with his hand on her shoulder, then Mrs. Green came in with the tea and they sat down.

Yes, Marian had seen her mother's picture, as well as she could for the darkness of the great parlor. She could never make out that beautiful face as belonging to a real, live person, like Aunt Sarah, or even Aunt Emily. She had often wondered as she looked at it, if her mother would have taken her in her arms and kissed her as Aunt Emily did, or if she would have just touched her forehead as her father did, and never seemed glad.

Early in the morning Ruby went round to tell everything good-by. Tabby melted to tears, and Pete hung behind the door, and there was not a white tooth showing. He gave Ruby's sleeve a jerk as he passed out.

"Why, Pete, you're going to drive us, aren't you? We won't say good-by yet."

Pete motioned mysteriously toward the stable yard. Ruby followed him out. In the barn Pete fished among some fodder and produced a slatted box of rough make-up, and from it came sundry taps and whines.

"Dere! You take him, Marse Rube, los' yo' dog, an' he like you pow'ful;" and the dusky youth thrust the box upon the little boy. It was a heroic effort, and Pete felt his weakness; he was running away when Ruby realized the truth.

"Oh, Pete! Pete! Come back!"

Then he ran and caught Pete, who could not be persuaded to return, and held out the treasure.

"Why, Pete, I couldn't take your dog; he's yours, you know, and how could he ever be anybody else's? Tony is a fine dog and I like him, but I'd never take him from you. And then, Pete, let me tell you, I couldn't — I never could! Father told me one day, after — after Rover died, where there was a nice little puppy, and said I might go for him; but Pete, you know how it was. I love all the dogs, but I said, 'Thank you, father; you won't mind, but I'd rather not.'"

Then he grasped Pete's great, horny hand and handed him the box again.

"I will never forget you, Pete; we will always be friends. I will never forget Tony, either." He got out his handkerchief. "There must be smoke in here somewhere, Pete; it's in my eyes;" and he ran to the house again.

Mrs. Green secretly handed Ruby a bag of cookies, though there was a well-filled basket in Dinah's care. Uncle Rede helped the children into the carriage, and got in himself.

The train was coming as they drove up to the station, so there was no time to stop. The kind waitress, in her neat cap and apron, stood in the door, and Ruby called to her in passing, and asked how she did. Pete had to hold the horses some distance from the engine, but called, "Good-by, Marse Rube; good-by, Miss Ma'am;" and flung a kiss from the back of his hand at Miss Dinah, who paid no attention at all, but gathered up the luggage and mounted the car steps in the rear of her party.

Uncle Rede had lifted Ruby in his arms; he found a pleasant seat and placed him next the window. Ruby caught him tight about the neck and said:

"Good-by, dear Uncle Rede. You have been so good to me!"

Then the silent man bent over Marian, kissed her full upon the lips, and said:

"Good-by, my little daughter."

The conductor had called, "All aboard;" the train was moving slowly, there was no time to lose; the professor passed out hastily, and did not see his little daughter cover her face with her hands, and did not hear as she burst out weeping.

"Oh, Marian, what is the matter? Oh, Marian, don't!" cried Ruby, putting his arm about her. "Don't, Marian; we're going home."

"Poor father! He has no one to stay with him!"

"Never mind, Marian; we'll go back some day."

---

## CHAPTER XV.

### THE CHRISTMAS PARTY.

CHRISTMAS was just a week off.

"Oh, Marian, what do you think! Mother says we may have a party, a real Christmas party, for our class. We will have a supper and games and music and all sorts of things; and we'll send out invitations. Won't it be just nice, though!"

Marian assented with enthusiasm.

"But mother says we'd best not talk about it among the girls; we'll wait and surprise them. Now, just think how Josie and Madge and Nell and all of them will feel when they find a pretty little note on their plates — mother says she'll get tinted paper 'The pleasure of your company is requested,' and all that — and they're never heard a breath before."

The next thing was getting up the invitations. Mother got the tinted paper, the prettiest Mabel and Marian had ever seen, they said, and they were getting the list made out for her so that she might write a note to each little girl.

Marian was doing the writing because she wrote such a plain, round hand. She put down eleven names, then stopped and looked at Mabel.

"You know there's one more, Mabel; but we couldn't ask her, could we?"

"Nan?"

"Yes."

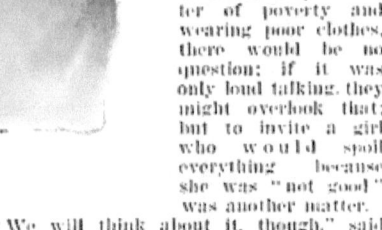

NAN.

Mabel shook her head slowly. "It wouldn't be nice to have Nan," she said.

When Aunt Emily came in, Marian gave her the list. She read it.

"Are these all?" she asked.

The girls looked at one another.

"Mother," said Mabel, "there is one other girl, Nan Larkins, but we don't think it would do to ask her."

"Why?"

They were silent for a moment.

"It isn't because she's poor, Aunt Emily, and wears rough shoes and coarse clothes too little for her, and lets her hair hang all round her face, but — but — she's not good."

"Not good?"

"No, ma'am; she won't study her lessons and talks right back to Miss Long, and — and sometimes she says real bad words

when we're playing. We won't any of us play with her hardly, now, and sometimes she comes up behind and shakes and spoils all the checkerboard just as we're going to get the game, and all such things as that; and when she sees she's spoiled our fun she points her finger and says, ' Ya, ya, ya!' and — well, she isn't good, Aunt Emily."

"No, she isn't good," said Aunt Emily, "and it's a pity, for she belongs to your class."

"Do you really think we ought to invite her, mother?" asked Mabel. "I think it would spoil everything, and not any of the girls would like to play with her."

"And she would just talk as loud, Aunt Emily! — she doesn't mind anybody."

Aunt Emily said it was a hard question. If it was only a matter of poverty and wearing poor clothes, there would be no question; if it was only loud talking, they might overlook that; but to invite a girl who would spoil everything because she was "not good" was another matter.

"We will think about it, though," said mother. "Poor Nan! She hasn't much help at home to make her good, I think."

Ruby had been curled up in the corner of the sofa, reading. Nobody thought of him, for he said nothing.

Uncle Alex was there to tea that night. He was still in the hospital, but was better and able to walk about some.

"And so you chicks are going to have a Christmas party — a real one, Mabel says, What's an unreal one, Miss Mab?" asked Mr. Vane, dishing the oatmeal.

Mabel didn't know, but she knew a real one was something just splendid.

"How many in your class?" asked Aunt Sarah.

Marian said there were fourteen.

"So there'll be twelve invitations to send. Now you'd best press each one to come, for if one should fail you'd have the unlucky number." said Mr. Vane playfully.

Mabel drooped her head a little. Marian went on eating oatmeal without a word.

Ruby sat on Aunt Sarah's left, and the two girls sat one on either side of Uncle Alex. Suddenly Ruby looked up at the girls opposite.

"Mabel and Marian," he said, "I think I'd ask Nan."

"Who's Nan?" questioned his father.

"Nan's in their class, and she doesn't always talk pretty; but, Mabel, it's to be a real Christmas party, isn't it?"

"Ye-es."

"Well, then, I'd ask her, because Jesus loves her. You know he must love every one."

There was a silence all round. The two girls looked at Ruby with sudden wonder in their eyes. Mr. Vane's playfulness vanished. Uncle Alex rested upon one hand his face, which was sad and weary still, and fixed his great eyes upon the little lad.

Ruby did not see that he was the center of attraction, but asked for some more cream and went solemnly on.

"That was in our last Sunday's lesson, and I learned it by heart; that's how I came to know it — 'Who loved me, and gave himself for me.' He must have loved Nan, too. I believe I'd invite her."

That night there was an amendment to the list, and when Mrs. Vane found it on the library table next morning, after the children had gone to school, there were twelve names — "Nannie Larkins" written plainer and heavier than the rest.

The tinted envelopes were to be posted, but Ruby said, "Mother, if you'll let me, I'll take Nan's round to her house."

"That will be a good idea, I think," said his mother; "it might not get to her through the postoffice until too late, as they probably do not get mail regularly."

So Ruby went to the tumble-down house where the Larkinses lived, and tapped at the door. A woman whose hair was as red and unkempt and whose face was as freckled as Nan's, whose forehead had deep up and down lines between the eyes, and who looked very cross, came to the door. A two-years child was hanging to her skirt.

"Are you Mrs. Larkins?" asked Ruby very civilly, taking off his hat.

"I reckon I'm that," was the answer in a shrill voice, with the jarring sound in it which made the resemblance to her daugh-

ter, and son also, complete. "You're wantin' anythin'?"

"I brought this to Nan. Is she here?" and he produced the missive.

"I say, you Nan, come 'ere!" And, thus summoned, the daughter made her appearance.

"Nan, Mabel and Marian are going to have a Christmas party, a real one, and this is your invitation. And you must be sure to come."

"My what?" cried the astonished Nan, taking the tinted envelope and touching it delicately as if afraid of breaking it; "my what?"

"Your invitation; it's asking you, inside, to the party. You'll let her come, won't you, Mrs Larkins?"

"Come! She'd be a putty 'un along o' you-uns with yer silks an' satins on. Yer ma'd not want the sole o' her shoes on her kearpet, and she'd be afeared her ole rags 'nd spile yer fine cheers."

"Oh, no, Mrs. Larkins, you mustn't think that of mother; she wrote Nan the note."

But Mrs. Larkins eyed both the note and its bearer suspiciously.

"The likes o' her 'nd best stay away from the likes o' you." Then, looking closely at the address, "Whose name's that on there? 'Tain't none o' hern."

In the past Mrs. Larkins had been able to write her own name, but ability to read and write had been lost by disuse; and Nan herself, accustomed to certain rough-hewn characters of her own, could not make out the delicate lettering; besides, she was not accustomed to hearing herself called or seeing herself put down as Miss Nannie Larkins.

"Ef Nan Larkins is been to school all this time an' can't read her own name, it's a po' case," continued the suspicious mother; "an' I jes' bleeve it's a make-up; yer want ter make er fool o' my gal, and git her ter yer party an' git er laff on her. An' if I knowed it I'd turn Teck on yer!" and the woman waxed vehement in voice and gesture.

Ruby looked up at her with his fearless eyes. "I don't know what you mean," he said; "but if you mean that you think the note is not for Nan, you are mistaken, and if you will take it to anyone they will tell you that is her name."

The young Larkins had let loose his parent's skirt; he made his way to Ruby's side, caught him by one knee, and cried, "Hi, b'y"

"How do you do?" said Ruby, trying to shake hands. "What's your name, baby?"

"Hi, hi!" shouted the youngster again, with something of the family voice.

"There, good-by," said Ruby. "Good-by, Mrs. Larkins. Good-by, Nan;" and he descended the tumble-down steps and went his way.

Ruby did not tell Mabel and Marian his experience, but had a long talk with his mother about it.

"Why would they think such things, mother?" he said.

"It is a pity; but, Ruby, the poor and ignorant have cause to be suspicious of those who are better off than themselves, for they are often ridiculed; but we must try to make poor Nan and her mother understand that we are in earnest and are their friends."

Nan was trying to make something out of the "letter," the first she had ever received, when Sim came in. He banged the door and knocked over a chair, shoved aside the Larkins of tender years, who upset and raised a series of yells—I cannot find a more agree-

SIM.

able word to fit—sat down on one side of the fireplace, vigorously kicking Teck and commanding him with no soft speech to "git frum befo' him." That misused animal showed his teeth in a snarl, whereupon his master wished to know if a beast like that dared to look ugly at him, and gave a more vigorous kick, this time with his heel, which sent the creature howling from the room.

The mother came in from the kitchen adjoining, and, as Larkins junior was still indulging him in a full exercise of his lungs, made at her first-born as if to cuff his ears, but desisted, picked up the child, shook it, tossed it upon a bed in the corner, with orders to "shet up," and turned upon her eldest again to know why it was he never could set his foot in the house without making a racket.

"When yer pa comes, I'll have him ter thrash yer, if yer don't mind." And Pa Larkins, with his weak wit and strong blacksmith's arm, could do that well.

When the youngest had exhausted himself and the mother had gone back to the kitchen, Nan went over to Sim and handed him the tinted envelope.

"Sim, you can read it. Is it my name?"

Sim, who was something of a scribe and prided himself upon it, spelled out the characters.

"'M-i-s-s'—you're no Miss. 'N-a-n-n-i-e'—Nannie, humph! 'Larkins.' Sho! Where'd yer git it. Nan?"

"Read the inside!" cried his sister, breathless.

There was some more spelling, but we will not lose time with it. At the conclusion Sim read it all as follows:

"The pleasure of your company is requested at our Christmas party, Christmas night.

"Mabel and Marian."

Sim gave a long whistle. "Ain't that a stunner! Yer'll look it at a Christmas party!"

"Sim, yer reckon it's ter poke fun at me?"

"Yes, yer simpleton! They'll set yer up in a chair and pint their fingers at yer berlin' yer back, an' giggle, an' say, 'Look at our fine yaller frock now, an' our clod-hopper shoes an' striped stockin's! And ain't our hair banged in style! An' yer keant see er freckle on our face now, kin yer?' Oh, yer'll jes' have er big time, now won't yer?" And Sim's laugh was loud, but not a pleasant one at all. "Here, take yer putty note, Miss Nan-nie Larkins, an' be gittin' yer white slippers on!"

Nan took her invitation with some despondency and sat down on the other side of the fire. She was disappointed, for she had hoped for something better from Sim. There was a sympathy between these two; such a sympathy as you sometimes find existing between two natures which seem antagonistic to the whole world besides. They were constantly pitted against their mother, and stood together loyally. Her scolding, her threatenings, they answered with jeers.

Their attitude toward the father was different. A man of few words, they had both felt the weight of his hand, when he was wearied of their contentions in his presence, or when the mother fulfilled her threats and told of their doings in his absence. When at home he would sit for hours, smoking his pipe and looking into the fire, never speaking a word. They always quieted down when he first came in, and slunk off somewhere. Gradually they waxed bold and bolder, and the noise of contention would be heard again. Sometimes he paid no attention until they almost forgot his presence, then suddenly, rising, without warning or without a word, would deal blows from that brawny arm with its muscles strong as iron bands. If Sim or Teck — for the master was held responsible for the doings of his dog — had been guilty of some aggravated misdemeanor, the mother was as good as her word and made a report; then the leather strap which hung over the fire-board was taken down and Sim was made to suffer.

Nan was just tucking away the invitation in her bosom when her father's step was heard at the door. Her mother might make complaint of her not helping with the supper; besides, she was glad enough to go when her father came in, so she hastened to the kitchen. Sim went to feed the pig.

The youngest was hanging about his mother's heels and irritating her spirit.

"Jes' yer take that youngun and hold him, Nan, an' I'll do the things an' ask nobody no odds. Yer pa'll be gittin' hungry an' raisin' a row."

Nan did as she was bid, for a row meant that her parent came into the kitchen to investigate, and most probably boxed her ears, judging her to be in some way at the bottom of the trouble.

The evening meal was passed through without personal encounters. The father, after taking one pipe and a mug of the vilest whisky and water, rolled himself into bed and soon the room resounded with his snores. Sim turned in early, also. The youth of tender age gave way at last, and only Nan and her mother sat beside the fire.

Nan fumbled with the bosom of her dress.

"Now, yer see what yer done!" was the filial remark with which she began. "Sim says it's er genuine note, er invite to the party, an' now who's to go, when yer done cut up about it and sassed Rube like yer done?"

The mother tossed her head. "Yer an' Sim kin make up all the tales yer want; yer'll not git the run on me."

"Well, yer can bleeve it, or yer kin not bleeve it, it's all one to me; but yer kin take it to the biggest school-teacher in the country an' they'll tell yer the same tale," was the daughter's rejoinder.

The next day Nan came in from a journey downtown, triumphant. Sim and her mother were both present.

"I'll tell yer what, Sim!" she cried, out of breath. "I seen the lady herself — Rube's ma — an' Rube was with her. They was in a store buyin' things. An' tereckly Rube be seen me standin' there — I was a-lookin' at the Christmas truck — an' he says, 'Here she is, mother; here's Nan.' Then Mis' Vane she turn round an' hole out her han', jes' so, an' she says, 'Howdy do, Nan? I'm glad to see yer. Me an' Ruby was goin' round to ask yer mother if yer could come to our party. Ruby said he thought she did not understand that I had invited yer.' Law! yer jes' ought ter seen her shakin' hands with me, like I was one! And she says, 'Yer ma won't object now, will she? an' I says, 'No'm, I reckon not.' An' I 'lows to go. You-uns can say what yer please. I 'lows to go."

"Go on. Miss Yaller Frock!" sneered Sim. "Yer'll have a larky time! I see yer now!" And his laugh was loud and not good to hear.

The days passed slowly, as the days just before Christmas always do, and then the best and brightest morning of the whole year dawned, bringing joy to thousands and thousands of homes where there were loving parents and happy children.

There were three stockings hanging on the mantel-piece in the room behind Aunt Sarah's; there were three pairs of eyes that found it very hard to close on the night before Christmas; there were three pairs of bare feet that touched the floor almost at the same instant in the gray of the morning, and three happy voices shouting, "Christmas gift!" and "Let's see mine!" and "Oh, look! look!" and all the other things that happy voices will shout. There was much talking and laughing, and much whispering and plotting to "catch" Aunt Sarah and mother and father and Janet and Dinah, and much trotting up and downstairs, and shouting and laughing and "catching" again, until the whole house was in a tumult.

Janet got up the best breakfast she could, and said it was "jes' too good to see them chill'en er hoorahin' that-er-way," and sniffled, which she never failed to do on all special occasions.

Nobody was forgotten in that household. Ruby came into the kitchen after breakfast, called upon Janet to be seated, blindfolded her, tested the totality of the blindness by holding up two fingers and hearing her say "it was six," climbed on her chair behind, and dropped into her lap, one by one, parcels, a gift from each member of the family. As each bundle fell Janet was to feel and guess what it was, and the guesses brought shouts of laughter. Janet was moved to tears and declared there "wa'n't never the like o' this," which she had declared for twelve years.

Dinah received her gifts without demonstration, but said, "They wus powerful putty, she thought, and she wus much oblige', Miss Sarah and Mis' Emily." And so on.

There was no little bustle and stir after dinner, for the dining-room must be got ready, the table lengthened and set, flower arranged, and numberless things must be done before the young guests arrived.

They came early — the invitations had requested that they should — Ellen and Floy and Madge and all the rest in their pretty evening toilettes, ribbons and laces and dainty shoes, and with curled and waved and braided hair.

They were all seated in the parlor, chatting merrily, when there was a ring at the door, and Mabel started a little nervously.

"I thought we were all here," said Lulu, looking round and beginning to count.

Three minutes later Mrs. Vane and Mabel came in, and with them the forgotten member of their class — Nan Larkins!

There was a flutter all round, and

ALL IN THEIR PRETTY EVENING TOILETTES.

smothered exclamations which Mabel did not fail to hear, then a sudden silence fell upon the merry circle. Mrs. Vane showed Nan to a seat near the fire and took one beside her. Then she tried to rouse an interest in conversation again, but her efforts were fruitless. Next neighbors whispered to one another, some giggled behind their handkerchiefs, while others sat bolt upright and stared.

Mrs. Vane's presence was needed in the supper-room, but she could not leave this guest, who was no doubt sensitive enough, alone in this oppressive atmosphere.

Mabel felt the situation painfully, and was unable to think of anything to say; Marian flushed, and, indignant at the girls' behavior, could do little better; but Ruby, either taking in the whole, or oblivious to the varying strata of society, left his seat beside Madge, the best-dressed girl in the room, and walked over to Nan.

"I am so glad you've come, Nan!" he said, holding out his hand. "You are a little late, and we'd almost given you up."

"Yer kin bet on me, Rube!" answered the unabashed maiden. "I told 'em I 'lowed to come, after I seen you and yer ma at the store."

"Now, I think a game would be real nice," said Ruby; "let's play thimble. By the time we play all round, mother'll have supper ready, and the time won't seem so long. May we play with your ring, Marian?"

Marian said they might, glad to have a break made in the ice, and Ruby asked them all to "Get round in a ring."

"Madge," he said, "you be thimbler;" and he gave her the ring.

Madge went round very deliberately. When she came to Nan she just touched her hands, and everybody knew that Nan didn't have the "thimble." When the secret was revealed they found that Ruby had it.

Ruby seemed very much pleased, indeed; he went round slowly, repeating at every hand, "Hold fast, till I go to London and back again," and no one could guess when he had parted with the treasure.

"Rise, thimbler!"

Nan looked round with real pleasure, showing the ring in her hand.

The other guests were very cool and indifferent as Nan went round, and, before another thimbler could rise, the summons for supper had arrived.

Mrs. Vane led the way with Nan, and there was some more smothered giggling and much confusion about getting paired. Everybody was clamoring to go in with Ruby, for they all loved the little fellow, and made a pet of him. In the midst of it, and when he thought his mother and Nan were out of hearing, Ruby said:

"Now, I'm the youngest, and I'll go with the oldest."

"Well, that's me," laughed Madge, catching his hand, "and we'll lead the way."

Then they formed in line. When Ruby, with his handsome partner, reached the door, he stopped and said:

"Girls, Nan never was at a party before in her life; let's try to make her have a good time."

A sudden silence fell upon the gay crowd again, but it was a thoughtful, not a painful, one.

Ruby sat in his father's place at the table. The supper passed off merrily, and everybody seemed to enjoy it. The hint of defiance which had crept over Nan's face when the girls looked indifferent about the thimbler, passed away entirely. And no wonder, for everyone seemed trying to please her. Madge sat on one side and Marian on the other, and they were so kind and attentive, and made her feel so much one of the rest, that altogether Nan was radiant by the time supper was over, and so was everyone else.

They had games again after supper. Mother went in and out. Father was there some of the time, and Aunt Sarah looked in once to see what they were about. They played drop-the-handkerchief, and Nan got it first one; they played "Smiling Angel," and Lulu asked Nan to be her partner. They spun the plate, and Nan could beat them all.

When they were tired of those things they drew up in a cozy semicircle round the fire, and had "nuts to crack," and in this fun Nan proved herself as quick-witted as any of them. Indeed, she enjoyed herself so well that she forgot all about her yellow frock which was too short, and her heavy, laced shoes, from one of which the tongue was missing, and her copperas-and-blue striped stockings.

When the clock struck half-past nine, the girls knew it would not be a great while before they were sent for.

"Let's have some music now," said Mrs. Vane.

They all gathered round the piano. Mrs. Vane played, and the girls sang in their clear young voices. They knew many songs, grave and gay; one was about the funny little boy who always laughed, no matter what happened to him.

"Let's have some real Christmas music now, mother," said Ruby; and they all decided that would sound better with the organ, so they went into the library.

When they had sung the Christmas songs, Madge said, "Now, Ruby, sing your hymn."

"Shall I, mother?"

His mother said, "Yes," and she played the air, and he sang:

"I think when I read that sweet story of old."

There was a knock at the door as he finished, and a general breaking-up followed, and the girls were running into Mrs. Vane's room for their wraps.

"Rube," said Nan, who had not many wraps to get, and who stood near Ruby, watching the others depart, "that was mighty putty."

"What, Nan?"

"Whut you sung."

---

## CHAPTER XVI.

### BACK INTO THE SUNSHINE.

 UBY was a general favorite at school, but from this time he had one strong friend who stood by him even though she must often take part against her brother to do so.

As for Sim, his contempt for the "swelled uns," a n d especially Ruby, increased from the Christmas party. Nan came in for her full share and suffered much from his ridicule, although she declared that she had never been treated so well in her life or had so good a time as at the party. She tried to convince Sim that Madge and the other girls who wore fine clothes were not so "powerful proud," and would have told of all their kind attentions, but he invariably broke into loud shouts of laughter or screeched at the top of his unmelodious voice:

"Oh, my—mo—mail!
Ther gawslin set on ther peacock's tail!"

and drowned everything.

One day Ruby brought his autograph album to school. Someone had given it to him Christmas.

"Nan," he said, "I want you to write your name in my album."

"Me, Rube? Why, nobody never asked me ter write in their album, I write sich a scratch."

"But I want you to write, because I want the name of every one in our school — in our room, I mean," he corrected himself, for he knew there was one name he did not want there. "Here is my pen, Nan, all ready."

"Rube," said Nan seriously, "I hate ter spoil your book with my name." She looked at the pure white page.

"It isn't just pretty handwriting that we want in albums, but people's names to remember them by."

"I wouldn't mind the scratchin' so much, Rube, but it's because I've got such a bad name; that's why I don't like ter spoil yer book."

"Bad? How, Nan?"

"Well, yer know I ain't no nice girl, an' my name oughtn't ter go down side o' nice girls' names."

For a moment Ruby was puzzled; he couldn't tell a lie and say that Nan was a nice girl, so what could he say? Then his love and truth spoke together.

"Nan, you've been mighty kind and nice to me here lately, and nobody is as nice as they ought to be, I reckon — I mean no children — and I like you. And Nan, there's just one person that can make anybody good, and He'll make you good and nice the same as anybody, if you like."

"Who's that?"

"It's Jesus," said the child, reverently.

The next day was Friday, and as Ruby was leaving the school-house alone — he had waited behind the others to have a little talk with Miss Long — Nan, who had been sitting upon the wood-pile, ran after him.

"Rube," she commenced, "would you-uns keare if I come ter yer Sunday-school?"

"Care, Nan?"

"I'd fix up the best I knowed, an' 'ud try to git the lesson. Yer reckon yer teacher would keare?"

"Why, we would be just as glad as we could be," said Ruby. "Now, you'll come next Sunday, won't you, Nan?"

"It's mighty near by, an' I ain't got much clothes."

"Don't mind; come anyway, Nan. You've got the dress you wore to the party."

"It's a mighty po' do, 'side o' Madge's an' Mabel's an' all of 'em, but I ain't akearin' much 'bout that, if ther folks want me ter come."

Ruby talked with his mother about it. "I wonder why I never thought of asking Nan to come to Sunday-school, mother. I thought everybody went to Sunday-school, though, I wonder if they don't go to church either."

The next Sunday was Easter, and there were to be special services in the Sunday-school. Ruby was on the lookout for Nan, and when she came in, with her "yaller frock" on, sure enough, he went back and asked her to his class.

The teacher was a very pleasant young lady. She gave Nan a catechism, and paper with reading and pictures in it, and asked her to come every Sunday.

"Won't you stay for church, Nan?" said Ruby in the intermission. "Come and sit in our pew."

"Will yer folks not mind?"

"Oh, they will all be glad."

Mrs. Wyman saw the shabby-looking child in the Vane pew and guessed that it was some of Ruby's missionary work. She came up after church was over, shook hands with her little favorite, and then with the stranger.

"What is your little girl's name, Ruby?" she asked. "Did you bring her to Sunday-school? That was very nice."

"No'm; she asked me if I thought our teacher would like to have her, and I said yes. Her name is Nannie Larkins."

"Ah, yes—yes," panted the lady in her new, tight Easter costume. "Where do you live, Nannie?" she went on, tapping the back of the pew with her silk fan. "If you will come to see me this week, I will give you a dress."

"I've got a dress!" said Nan shortly, flushing up to the roots of her red hair; "I didn't come here a-beggin'."

"Oh, no, no—I didn't mean that." But Mrs. Wyman was really set back by this spirited creature.

Ruby caught Nan's hand and said they would go and catch up with Aunt Sarah.

Nan's independence was of the solid kind. She was charmed with Sunday-school, and was determined to go back, but she felt her differences. Having been made to understand by her mother that, Sunday-school or no Sunday-school, she would have no new clothes, she made up her mind.

Late one afternoon in the same week she went to "Rube's house," and knocked at the back door. Dinah opened it and asked if she wanted anything. That was always Dinah's question when people came to the back door. She had never learned that usually knocks at the back door were more important than those at the front.

Nan wanted to see Mrs. Vane.

"Why come in, Nan," said that lady, when she saw who it was; and she led the way to the library.

Nan sat down and looked at the rows of books and wondered if anybody ever could read them all; and at the picture over the mantel of a fine-looking old gentleman with a very high collar on and something red thrown over his shoulders.

"Mis' Vane," she said, when she had taken in all at a glance, "I come ter see if yer would let me work for yer."

"Work, Nan? Don't you go to school?"

"Yessum; but I gits out at two o'clock, and I could do lots after that. I don't want no money, but one of Marian's dresses that she don't wear; it 'ud fit me."

So Mrs. Vane made the arrangement. Nan was to come for four afternoons, and on Saturday would receive her dress.

Each time Mrs. Vane gave her employment, and Nan was like a new person. There was cleaning silver, polishing the brass andirons, redding the hearths, and rubbing up the furniture.

"You have earned your wages, Nan," said Mrs. Vane, as she handed her the bundle.

Nan went home with a triumphant heart. That night when she spread her things in the attic, she saw that the dress had been altered till no one would know it was ever Marian's. There was a hat, too, and black stockings and gloves. Nan almost shouted. She did not know that Aunt Sarah had made over the dress and bought trimming for it, and had bought the hat, too, and gloves, and had produced the hose from her own bag.

Ruby knew; he had watched with eager eyes, every evening, Aunt Sarah's needle going in and out, in and out, and the shiny scissors ripping and cutting.

Mother said Nan must know who her good friend was, but Aunt Sarah was very positive. "She's worked well and deserves it, so let it go as her wages. She's got spirit, but if you begin by giving people things, right out, you'll make beggars of them."

When Nan came to church next morning in her well-fitting dark blue dress and sailor hat, and with her stringy red hair neatly brushed and tied with a blue ribbon, the girls did not know her at first.

And Nan did not know herself. She knew she was happier than she ever had been in her life, because she felt like somebody.

The lines on her mother's face softened, and, though she turned away with a would-be contemptuous "humph!" was secretly proud.

Uncle Alex was going away; that was a sad blow to Ruby. Almost every day he had seen Uncle Alex and every time they loved each other better. For two months Uncle Alex had been staying with Father Paul, and now he was so strong that he was able to go away. He was going far out West, where he had lived a long time, mother explained to the anxious little fellow; he was going to teach the children out there, the children of the miners. He had lived among the miners and knew how they went away down into the dark places of the earth, and knew, too, how sometimes they never came back. He had seen the wives and children standing at the mouth of the pit, calling those who would never hear them again, and crying and wringing their hands. And he knew some who led wild lives and whose children had no one to teach them to be good men and women.

"I would like to go with Uncle Alex, if you could go, mother, and Aunt Sarah and father and all of us, and everybody I like."

"That would be a large party of emigrants, I think," said his mother.

On the last evening Uncle Alex and Father Paul came to tea. They two and Ruby were alone in the library a while after tea.

"Ruby," said Uncle Alex, "you must sing your hymn for me;"—he was going to add "for the last time," but his voice failed at the thought.

Then Ruby lifted up his bright head and sweet voice:

"I think when I read that sweet story of old."

When he got through, he went and laid his little hand on Uncle Alex's knee.

"You look so much better, Uncle Alex. You're 'most well, now, aren't you? And you don't look sorry all the time."

"No," said Father Paul. "Do you remember, Ruby, how you used to tell your uncle about God's love, and how he loved us even when we did wrong? Your uncle used to know that once, and then he came to think that God did not love him any more; that was the reason he was sad. But now he knows that God loves him and has loved him all the time."

"Paul, Paul! I dare not speak or think of what has been, but this is enough—I have come again into the sunshine of His love."

Everybody kissed Uncle Alex that night when he left, even mother and father—everybody except Aunt Sarah, and she took his hand and, looking into his pale face, said, very low:

"Good-by, Alex."

## CHAPTER XVII.

### ALSACE.

THE glad spring and golden summer passed. Marian did not go to see her father this summer, for he was in Europe. Sometimes he wrote to her, and his letters were longer than they used to be, and always began, "My dear little daughter."

Marian and Ruby read several books that summer. Mabel was not so fond of reading as they were. Sometimes she would join them, but oftener sat with her mother, learning to do embroidery, or practiced new pieces on the piano, or painted wild roses on scraps of silk for pincushions and toilet bottles.

It was sweet in the twilight to gather round the piano and follow Mabel's clear soprano, and sweetest of all was it on Sabbath evenings when they sang the hymns that brought Aunt Sarah down from her solitude, and made their father lay aside his paper and lean his head upon the mantel.

One Sabbath evening when Ruby went up to Aunt Sarah's room, he carried a well-worn book. "Aunt Sarah," he said, taking his accustomed seat, "I want to read you a story in here. It is a book of different stories; mother read it to us this afternoon, and I want to read you the one I like best. It is a Sunday-school book, but I think you will like this story." Then he found the place and commenced, and his voice was as sweet in reading as in singing.

### "ALSACE; OR, THE CUP OF WATER.

"The great battle was ended, and men lay all over the plain, wounded, dead and dying. The sun blazed like a fire upon the poor soldiers who lay bathed in blood and moaning in their great pain.

"Alsace was but a youth, yet he had fought very bravely. A spear had pierced his side, and he was dying; but he did not know that. He thought if he could get water, if it were but a drop to cool his burning tongue, he could live. 'Water! Water!' he gasped. But no one heard.

"He was very faint. He could scarcely raise his head. He felt his life-blood trickling away. He thought of his home on the mountain side; the vines clambering over the cool porch — it was purple with clusters now — the birds singing in the trees, the apple tree growing by the door. He thought of the spring gushing out of the rock, just below the door-step; he could hear its gurgle, and see the water as it flowed down and sparkled in the sun. Perhaps his mother was sitting there now in her low chair, knitting — knitting stockings for her soldier boy and praying for him; or perhaps she was singing with her voice and praying in her heart.

"And the two little sisters — they were making crowns of roses and saying, 'When Alsace has won all the battles, he will come back, and we will put a crown upon his head.' And the little brother was paddling his feet in the sweet stream and shouting, 'Alsace will be king! We'll crown him king!' And he is dying! dying! Dying for one drop from the spring!

"He hears a tinkle, tinkle; and the goats come down the mountain and drink, and bound away. The little brother leads the white cow from the stall, and, while the sisters crown her with roses, she drinks her fill. He sees and hears it all, and moans again, more faintly, 'Water! Water!'

"Some one is passing that way, though he does not know it — some one who thought the poor lad was dead. But when the passer heard the call, he bent and placed upon the ground a cup. 'Here is water,' he said; 'it is only a few drops, but all I have,' and hastened on, for there were hundreds lying on that battle-field, and few to care for them.

"When Alsace heard that word he gained strength, and, raising himself a trifle, grasped the cup. If he had been a little stronger he would have swallowed the water in another instant and there would have been no story to tell; but, as he lifted the cup to his lips with a feeble hand, a pitiful groan broke upon his ears and he heard his own cry repeated: 'Water! Water!' All around him had been quiet before. The men were dead except this one, and he had but just aroused from a deep swoon.

"The rim of the cup had touched the parched lips of the youth.

"'Who are you?' he asked.

"'Baldac.'

"Then a sudden flame more terrible than thirst shot through the heart of Alsace. This was none other than his mortal enemy; not the honorable enemy of battle — with him the generous youth could have shared his cup even with joy — but the enemy who fought side by side with him, who had lifted up his hand against him and made his hearth-stone desolate. Why did he see no father coming to join the little group at the spring? Why was that look of sadness always upon the mother's face? Because this enemy, this Baldac, had lifted up his hand in jealous rage and slain the man who had never harmed him.

"'Water! Water!'

"Then like a whisper from heaven, Alsace heard his mother's voice, and it was telling him how, when he passed beyond the mists and the sun's rising, he would reach a great gate which was but one single pearl; and the Master would be there with the light about his head, and when the gate had swung open and Alsace had knelt at his feet, the Master would lay upon his head a hand, in which was the print of nails, and would say, 'What dost thou bring me, Alsace?' And then every kind word, every good deed, even the giving of a cup of cold water in love, under the Master's touch would form into a glowing jewel, sardonyx, or chrysolite, or beryl, or amethyst, and all together would make a crown. Then the Master would take the crown and place it upon Alsace's head, saying, 'Thou hast brought me these; now wear them for me.'

"Alsace could not divide his cup of water; there were but a few drops, and one must have it. He felt the blood trickling still, but he was a youth and high of hope; he thought, 'If I might but cool my tongue, I could see my home, my mother, my little sisters.'

"And what if Baldac died! His father had died, and he had sworn vengeance. Was not this his time? Had not the Lord delivered his enemy into his hand? Yea, it was his time; the Lord had delivered his enemy into his hand — to heal or to destroy?

"What had he done in all his life that he could rejoice to lay at his Master's feet? 'I must die,' he said; 'and he who took the father's life will also take the son's.'

"Then his spirit gave him strength, and, crawling a little way, he reached over and held the cup to the parched lips.

"Baldac drank, and opened his eyes. 'Who saves me? Who saves me?' he cried. 'God reward you.'

"Then he saw the pale face of the boy whom his hand had rendered fatherless, and he raised himself and cried with a bitter cry, 'Keep it! Keep it! Do you give me to drink?' and thrust the cup away.

"But there was no drop left for the youth. He fell back, and a great glory filled his soul. All the hate which had poisoned his young life for those years was gone. His face was as the face of one who saw a vision. 'Mother,' he whispered. 'the Master has but spoken; I do not want the crown.'

"Then a cloud came over the sun, and breezes, as if angels swept their wings over that bloody plain, cooled the burning brow of Alsace."

Ruby shut the book and was quiet a long time.

"Do you know why I like it, Aunt Sarah? I haven't said anything to you lately about one person, but I have not forgotten, and I do not love him yet. When I read that, I thought if I could do something kind to him I might feel better. I have always just tried not to mind and not to do him any harm, but now if I could find some real good thing to do for him, I might feel it pass away."

But Ruby was disappointed a week later when school commenced. He went and told Aunt Sarah about it.

"He doesn't come to our school now; he has a job on the railroad, and won't be here any, hardly, so I can't do anything for him."

---

## CHAPTER XVIII.

### THE ACCUSED.

IT is two years since Uncle Alex left. Ruby is ten, and is growing tall. His hair still curls round his forehead in bright ringlets, just a shade darker than they were. His face is not so round nor so rosy, and you might not know him until he looked up at you; then you would see the eyes and could make no mistake. Just as full of grave questionings is he, just as full of the love in which there is no fear.

Mabel has shot up like a white lily with a golden crown. Her head and shoulders are inclined to droop, and Aunt Sarah says she should wear braces; but mother prefers that she take daily walks in the fresh air.

"Count the stars when you're walking, Mab," said her father.

"And fall into the ditch!" retorted Aunt Sarah; "besides, who's going to see stars in daylight?"

"Correct, Sarah; you are more practical than I am. But remember how seldom I have time to see the sky."

Marian is shorter and thicker-set than Mabel. Her dark chestnut hair is braided, but short curls still cling around the forehead. Marian carries a high head — she has no need of braces.

Mabel and Marian are in the higher room at school now, but Ruby is still under Miss Long. Miss Long's hair is turning gray, and there are lines about her mouth and eyes, but the children love her better than they did when she first came, ten years ago, when the roses were in her cheeks.

One day after school Mr. White, the principal, came with a flushed face into Miss Long's room. He was several years younger than Miss Long and had not a tenth of her experience, and if he had recognized her superior wisdom and come to her at times for counsel, if he had found the secret of her self-control, he might have made fewer mistakes and censured himself less often for rashness when it was too late for repentance.

"Miss Long," he said, "I wish to examine every drawing-book in your room."

Miss Long saw his excitement and felt that harm was coming, yet she could do nothing but give him leave. Then she waited, drawing on her gloves.

"You need not wait," he said, in a tone which meant, "I prefer that you do not."

Miss Long was troubled. She had a loving faith in her pupils which was not shortsightedness. She had had pupils who, she sorrowed to own, could not be trusted, but they were not with her now. She was a good reader of children; she studied her little flock closely, and taught them by her words and inspired them by her own example to love the truth better than life. If only Mr. White had told her what was wrong! If one of her children had fallen into temptation, she was sure that she could find out the truth. So she was troubled.

Mr. White, left alone, went straight to a desk next the wall, in the front row. There was a look upon his face which said, "I know, but have come for proof." His was the dangerous position of judge having power to pass sentence and inflict punishment upon the offender, and there was no jury of reason and calmness and self-control and unprejudice and love to deliberate upon the case; but haste and passion and wounded pride clamoring, "It is he! It is he!"

With a shaking hand the master turned over the leaves of the drawing-book; yesterday he would have said, "What a neat little fellow, and he has talent!" To-day his heart was burning, and he saw nothing until he had gone through—then he saw a ragged edge where a leaf had been torn out. "Ha!" he cried, and one would have thought him well pleased. Then he took from his breast pocket an envelope, drew out a leaf which he unfolded and laid along the ragged edge. It fitted exactly. The last page of the book was marked 24, this was 25, and, to make proof positive, in one corner were the two letters, written in a small, round hand, " R. V." No doubt the owner of the book had written them there some day when he had nothing else to do. "And," said the school-master, "forgot it."

Then he looked through the book again. The drawing was true, so was that upon the sheet in his hand; too true, in fact, the latter was—that was the reason it hurt so. But here—here was evidence enough! About the middle of the book was a grotesque figure, a school-master; the same long legs as in the torn-out picture, the same flat feet, the same old coat dangling from the lank shoulders. There was this difference between the two sketches: The one in the book had a cadaverous face, with stringy hair falling into the eyes; the one on the torn sheet had upon the lean body a round, florid face—for it was colored—a wide mouth, out-standing ears, and red hair that was bushy and stood straight up from the forehead. Mr. White had seen his own reflection too often not to recognize the likeness. If he had been an artist he might have detected a difference in the character of the two drawings, but he was not, and that the same hand had produced both pieces, Mr. White did not doubt. That the hand was that of a caricaturist he was equally certain.

That morning Mr. White had found an envelope upon his table addressed to himself in a small, round hand. He had broken it open at once, thinking to find a message from some parent—a message of complaint

most probably—and found the sketch! His florid face turned scarlet when he saw not only the likeness, but some doggerel below, which rhymed very well, bringing in "White" and "fright," and certain other words which we will not reproduce. If it had not been in the face of the whole school it would not have been so bad, but there was not a pupil but noted his confusion and some caught sight of the drawing. But not a word was said then.

There was one other thing—the handwriting. Mr. White now drew from the desk the owner's copybook. He opened it and compared the writing with that upon the envelope. It was the same style; the round characters, a certain little twist to the " W " which was uncommon.

When Mr. White folded the drawing and put it in his pocket there was a kind of triumph in his heart. And why?

This was his second year at Greenville. At the close of the first year, when an election was held, Mr. Vane opposed him and candidly gave his reasons. " Mr. White, as a gentleman, I like," he said, "and in some respects as a teacher; but he acts from impulse more than judgment; I have found that to be so in a number of cases, and cannot consider him a guide for youth."

Had Mr. Vane been a poor and uninfluential man, Mr. White would probably have passed over his opposition with contempt, as the majority, taking his occasional violence for discipline, upheld and re-elected him. But Mr. Vane was his wealthiest patron, and Mr. White was not free from that pride, the most dangerous of all, which makes the poor man hate, because he fears, the rich man.

"Mabel," said Ruby that evening. "some one has torn a leaf out of my drawing-book—the last one."

"Why, who could it be, Ruby?"

"I don't know. I'm sure. I must tell Miss Long to-morrow, for, you know, she has told us never to tear out a leaf, and she will not understand that I did not do it."

## CHAPTER XIX.

### CONVICTED.

THE next morning Mr. White opened school with the self-satisfied air of a man who had come to a decision and made up his mind as to his course. After roll-call he said he wished to see Ruby Vane in the cloak-room.

Ruby rose up in some wonder, but without a shadow of suspicion followed the school-master. Mr. White had not cultivated the acquaintance of his pupils, and had never passed a dozen words with Ruby. Ruby, who usually opened conversations with whom he pleased, had not felt drawn to Mr. White. This pupil, then, was a stranger to him.

The first thing Mr. White did was to produce the evidence — the drawing-book with the missing leaf, the torn sheet that fitted exactly into the ragged edge, and the copy-book written in the neat, round hand.

"Now, sir," said Mr. White, "can you explain this?"

Ruby could not.

"You know nothing about this drawing and these idiotic verses?"

"No, sir."

"And yet the leaf has come from your book; can you deny that? And the drawing is partly a copy of one here," — showing it. "I am sorry, Mr. White, that you think I would do such a thing, and I am sorrier that you think I would tell a lie."

Mr. White was almost ashamed under that steadfast gaze, and his passion would have cooled had Ruby been the son of any other man. But there were Mr. Vane's words rankling in his bosom, and there was the unworthy thought, "The child has learned from his father's example that money gives him privileges, and supposes that it places him out of the way of punishment. They shall find I am no fawner."

"And this," he went on, though in spite of him his assurance was melting under that truthful gaze, "and this," — holding up the envelope addressed to himself — "can you deny this?"

Then a gleam of triumph shot over his florid face and all his vindictiveness returned, for Ruby's cheek flushed, and, though his eye did not fall, he stammered:

"N-o, sir, I cannot deny it."

Ruby felt sick and wanted to catch hold of something, not from fear — for he had not thought of punishment — but from the thought: Who was plotting against him? Surely not —

Mr. White did not ask for further explanation and Ruby was too dazed and overcome to give any.

"You may return to your seat," said the school-master; and Ruby obeyed sadly.

As Mr. White and Ruby walked down the aisle, there was one boy on the right whose freckled face was diffused with pleasure, if we may call it such, and when the door of the cloak-room was safely shut he made sundry noises, as loud as he dared, and grimaced with all his might to attract the attention of a fair, flaxen-haired youth on the left front row. But the fair youth, who seemed to feel the fire from behind, only dropped his head lower and lower, and his deskmate wanted to know why his knees shook.

The well-pleased boy was none other than Sim Larkins, who had been discharged from railroading for going to sleep out of season, and whose father had sent him back to school until more profitable employment could be found. Sim had been back a month, and, strange to say, the ardor of his hatred for Ruby had not cooled in the least by many months of absence. Perhaps Nan's having grown into such a quiet, decent girl under Ruby's influence, and her devotion to the little lad, enkindled the brother's jealousy. Perhaps it was the silent reproof of Ruby's eyes which fanned the flame of rage.

Ruby had not forgotten Alsace, and was glad when Sim came back. "I may find some way now," he thought.

Sim was fifteen. He had grown a great deal, and was more formidable than ever to the "little chaps." He was developing his father's arm, too, and there were some who had found it out to their sorrow when they told tales. The fair youth on the left front row had seen evidences of Sim's power, though he had never felt the heavy hand himself. He was almost as old as Sim, but of a delicate constitution, and had been petted and coddled until he was "weaker 'n any girl," as Sim said with contempt. And his will was not stronger than his back. This youth with the shaking knees was George McPhail.

Ruby was by turns flushed and pale, hot and cold. He missed his lessons; that was very strange, and Miss Long, who knew nothing of the interview in the cloak-room, asked if he were not well.

At drawing time Miss Long showed him the ragged edge which she had discovered.

"Yes'm, I don't know who did it, Miss Long;" and the child looked so very sick that Miss Long felt his pulse and thought he might go home. But he was not sick, he said, and stayed till school was out.

George McPhail looked white all the time, and he, too, missed his lessons, for which he was well scolded by the school-master, who was very irritable that day, and also kept in. At length he pleaded sick; and Mr. White relented and let him go. He had avoided Sim all day, and when he took up his books and started for home, would not look to the right of the aisle.

Mabel and Marian were quiet at home that evening. Ruby did not tell what Mr. White wanted in the cloak-room, and they thought it best not to mention it, but to leave Ruby's affairs to him, confident, at least, that he had done nothing wrong.

## CHAPTER XX.

### NAN'S AFFECTION.

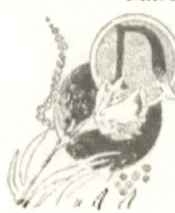

NAN was really glad when Sim came home. Though a genuine Christian, she breathed an atmosphere which was not upbuilding to the new life. Then the old temptations caused her hard struggles at times, and she had not "grown in grace" as Dr. Caruthers might have expected after eighteen months of church membership. Though less turbulent, the family life was not one of harmony yet, Nan often plaguing her mother, and her mother often threatening her. The relations between father and daughter were almost as strained as ever, except that Nan felt along with her old fear a certain reverence for this strong-armed man who, in contrast to the scolding and yielding mother, acted, and without words. She felt, too, a kind of pity for his weak wit, and struggled to keep down the vengeful feelings that were awakened by the iron hand.

Nan was glad when Sim came back, for the old sympathy was strong between them. Stronger on her side than on his it had ever been, and now that she was seeking to cultivate the good within her, it had grown to a real affection in which there was little of selfishness. When she said her prayers she sometimes forgot her mother's name; when her heart was hot she sometimes left out her father's knowingly; but Sim's was never left out, never forgotten.

That evening when she met Sim coming in with two rabbits thrown over his shoulder and a gun in his hand, her face was perplexed.

Sim set the gun in a corner and prepared to skin the rabbits. Nan was making out a batch of biscuit for the oven on the hearth.

"Sim," she said, "what was the matter of the teacher and Ruby to-day?"

"Matter, yer simple! Didn't yer see the putty picter ther ole coon foun' on his desk yistiddy?"

"No, I never."

Then Sim went on to describe with great relish the likeness to the school-master, and repeated the uncouth doggerel with loud and harsh laughter.

Nan's face grew white. "And what did Ruby have to do with that?" she asked.

"Because he done it!" Sim cried, rising and shaking his fist in his sister's face, all the boasting hilarity giving place suddenly to threatening, his own face ashy with rage and evil to look upon. "Because he done it, an' it's prove on him."

Nan did not flinch; she held her white lips together, trying to steady them.

"He didn't do it!" she said, "and you know who did. I saw that picture here, night afore last, in your gography, and them rhymes, they was there, too, in your own handwrite!"

Sim caught the neck of her dress and shook her till she could not speak. She was getting purple in the face when a heavy step was heard at the door. A heavy hand pushed it open, and the mother called from the shed-room to know if "them biscuits was done."

Sim let go his hold, but not without some muttered threats, took up his rabbits, and went out.

That night Nan was racked with so many conflicting emotions that she knew no rest. To tell on Sim, her own brother! And yet to see any innocent one punished when she could prevent it — was she not guilty, too? And Ruby! Her very soul cried out, Ruby! Ruby! "What will he do to him?" she asked. She knew nothing of Mr. White's prejudices, but she knew something of his quick temper and almost childish sensitiveness, and she knew how the sins of some had been visited upon them. But Ruby! Surely nobody would touch Ruby. Nobody could look at him and raise a hand to hurt him. Besides, how could they prove it on him, when it wasn't so?

So she tried to comfort herself. And yet she could not be comforted. Round and round and round went her arguments, always coming back to the starting-place. Ruby was falsely accused and must suffer for what Sim had done. She did not sleep more than an hour all night, and that hour was full of dreams which were worse than lying awake. She would get on her knees and try to pray, but could not say a word of her nightly prayer; it wouldn't come. She could only cry, "Oh, Lord Jesus, don't let 'em touch Ruby!" over and over again.

She did not see Sim the next morning. "He'd eat a snack an' gone by light," the mother said.

Nan's vigils had not brought her to any plan of operation; only this was she determined upon—Ruby should not be touched, not if she must match her arm against that of the school-master. Perhaps if Nan had been older and wiser, if her education had been more thorough, she could have thought of some prudent course. To her there were but two things in view. Sim must be told on or Ruby punished. Either was too much for her affection.

## CHAPTER XXI.

### SHAME!

R. WHITE was determined that no charge of haste should be brought against him in this matter. Wherefore, though, as he said, fully convinced of the guilt of the accused, he let the punishment lie over till the next day. In fact, he was by no means so eager for the performance of this duty as he had been previous to the trial in the cloak-room. He did not sleep well that night, and yet was sorry to see the first streak of day. He felt himself growing irresolute. Still, the offence had been proved; the culprit had been forced into confession after having sought to lie out of it, thereby adding crime to crime. He must uphold the majesty of the law, the majesty of his person, though he could have wished to pass the matter over in silence. So, like poor Nan, he argued in a circle, and ever returned to the starting-point: The guilt was proved; the offender must suffer.

The school-house had three rooms—the primary room, which was Miss Long's, adjoined Mr. White's; the main room, in which the large boys sat; while the large girls, under Miss Withers' supervision, sat upstairs, coming down at times into the main room for recitations.

At roll-call the whole school assembled in Mr. White's room. Nan's face was pale still, and she waited with a heavy feeling upon her heart all through roll-call for what might come next. Sim was there in his usual place; and Ruby was there, looking sad still and having dark rings under his eyes, but not fearful. Nan only looked to see if Sim was in his seat, then she would not turn her eyes that way again.

But to her great relief there was not a word said by the school-master. The classes were dismissed to the different rooms as usual. Nan's first thought was that her prayer was answered, and she was radiant. But this joy was short-lived.

Nan, though she had done conscientious work for the past two years, had not been able to attend school regularly, and was behind the class with which she had enjoyed the Christmas party. She still sat in the primary room, while Marian and Mabel enjoyed the privileges of "upstairs."

The first lesson in Miss Long's room was the fourth reader. The class was in its place, Nan had been called upon for the first paragraph, when Mr. White came to the door and asked for—Ruby Vane!

Ruby got up and passed through the door without a change of countenance. Miss Long, who, strange to say, was entirely ignorant of the whole affair, was not moved.

Nan was wading through a sentence, had stopped when Mr. White came in, commenced again, and all the time was saying to herself, "He won't do it! He won't do it!" not knowing what she read, when through the thin partition there came the sound of a quick, sharp blow.

Nan gave one short cry, dashed Appleton's Fourth Reader against the opposite wall, cleared the space to the door in two bounds, and, rushing into the main room, sprang toward the school-master, grasping his arm as it would have brought down the rod again upon the innocent back. Nan's grip was like iron; her eyes like coals of fire.

"Don't you do it again! Don't you do it!" She did not scream. Her voice was low, but so full of passion that every boy in the large room heard and rose to his feet.

"Shame! Shame!" she went on, fixing her burning eyes upon the school-master, who trembled. "Shame! to touch that child, as wouldn't harm a fly! Shame, I tell you! And he didn't do it — you know he didn't do it!"

Mr. White was trying to regain his ground, but in vain; he could not find a word to match with this avenger.

"Yes, you know it, because you know he wouldn't! And I know it." Here she turned and faced her brother, whose countenance was ugly to see. "I know it, because I know who did it!"

The school-master's arm, which had never resisted the clasp, fell down limp at his side.

"You knew?" he said. "Why did you not tell?"

"Tell!" She was giving way. "Tell! No, I won't tell neither!" Then she broke into pitiful sobs.

And Ruby, who had stood through it all as one in a trance, reached his arm around her neck, and said soothingly. "There, Nan, never mind! And do not tell!"

Then Nan's sobs grew wilder; she caught Ruby in her arms and cried over him, letting the tears stream over his bright curls and pale cheeks.

"Ruby! Ruby! I didn't think they'd touch you! If I'd thought so, I'd 'a' told!"

In the confusion that attended this scene, the tall youth on the right of the aisle passed out, while one on the left front row, whose face was like cotton, could hardly stand, his knees shook so. He tried to speak; he wanted to ask to be excused because he was sick, but could not say a word.

Miss Long, who had at last found an explanation, went through the open door, laid her hand gently upon the shoulder of the still weeping Nan, whispered that she would better return to her room, and passed silently by the impotent school-master, who either did not seek, or was not able, to restore order.

Nan would not let go Ruby, and when they came in together, Miss Long said it would be as well for them both to go home for that day.

Ruby went home and straight to Aunt Sarah's room; he thought he would be alone there. He laid himself upon the bed and tried to get his thoughts together. Everything had been like a dream, a bad dream, that morning. He did not cry nor make a sound.

After a while Aunt Sarah came in and found him there, perfectly still, upon the bed.

"Why, Ruby, are you sick? When did you come home?"

"I don't think I'm sick," he said. "I came home a long time ago, I think."

Aunt Sarah went and felt his pulse; it was quick and irregular.

Then she opened the blind and saw his face. It was pale, with a bright spot in either cheek. His eyes had a strange glitter, and his lips were dry.

"You've got fever, Ruby. Did Miss Long send you home?"

"Yes'm, I think so. But not because I had fever."

Aunt Sarah was alarmed. She went straight for her sister-in-law.

Mrs. Vane said the child was feverish; he had been far from well for some days; they would put him to bed.

But an hour later, when Mabel and Marian came in from school, the tale was told.

Marian had to tell it, for Mabel could only sob, and throw herself into her mother's arms. Marian's face was fairly blazing; she told the whole in a few excited words and disjointed sentences. Then she fell to sobbing, too.

"Where is he?" she cried. "Where is Ruby?"

There was little dinner eaten that day except by Mr. Vane, who had only been told that Ruby was not well. Mabel was in bed also. The others sat and played with their forks, and could hardly keep the tears back.

When the plates were removed and the servants gone, Mr. Vane grew serious.

"Tell me what this means?" he demanded.

It was left to Marian again to explain. The mother could not trust herself. Aunt Sarah could not, either, for that matter, though no one knew it.

When Philip Vane got up from the dinner-table, his face was white and stern.

---

## CHAPTER XXII.

### RUBY'S ILLNESS.

BY night Ruby's fever was high, and for a week it raged. Sometimes he talked incoherently. "No, Nan, I wouldn't tell." and, "I'm sorry you think I would tell a lie, Mr. White. It was the handwriting. George asked me to write the name on the envelope. I am sorry he thought I would do that. It must have been a mistake; George wouldn't have done it. Nan said, 'I know'; yes, yes, Don't tell, Nan."

Sometimes he talked of Rover. "Where can he be, mother? I haven't seen him this morning. There he is, whining at the door! and I can't open it. Aunt Sarah, please help me. He wants his breakfast, poor fellow! Why can't I open the door?"

When the thing became known, there was a general coolness toward Mr. White, and Mr. White was burning with remorse. It was not the first time he had found a long leisure for repentance, but it was the first time he had reaped such bitter fruits. He went to see Mr. Vane, but that gentleman heard him in silence more cutting than any reproach.

Miss Long sent in her resignation on the day of the trouble, but the trustees refused to accept it from one who had served them so faithfully. Three days later Mr. White sent in his; it was accepted.

But Mr. White could not go away with that great load upon him. He would make another effort. He went to Mr. Vane's residence. Aunt Sarah met him, and the fire from her eyes burned up his remaining courage.

"May I see Mrs. Vane?"

"I think not." That was all she said. It was Ruby's worst day.

Mr. White stood a moment, miserable, helpless. "Miss Vane," he pleaded, "if I might see her but for a moment! Let me see her, in the name of humanity!"

"Humanity!" The fire scorched him deeper than ever.

But Mr. White did not go.

"Be seated," said Aunt Sarah, pointing toward the open door of the library. "Mrs. Vane has a sick child, and does not care to receive visitors, but I will speak to her."

That was a deep thrust, ignoring his knowledge of the child and his sickness.

The wretched man sat down and waited. He did not wait many moments. There was a footstep upon the stairs. It was not the same that he had heard go up. All his courage was needed now; he raised his eyes to meet the pale, lovely face of the mother of the innocent child. Mr. White said afterwards that he did not believe there was an angel in heaven who would have met him with more gentleness.

Then the weak, the strong, the proud, the humble man, weeping like any woman, tried to speak. He tried to say that he did not come to excuse his haste nor to ask for pardon; he only came to say that he despised himself.

It was not a long interview, but when Mr. White went away he found a heart to pray again.

Everybody who knew Ruby came or sent to inquire, for everybody who knew loved him. There was one visitor who came twice a day, one who knocked at the back door and would not be content with Dinah's say-so, but waited till a member of the family came to tell her how he was. "You are a friend I will never forget, Nan," said Mrs. Vane, and she kissed the astonished girl upon the lips.

That kiss helped Nan to a long stride on her upward way. "Mrs. Vane, a lady like that, to kiss me! I never want to wash my mouth, and I never want it to say nothin' that's a harm. When it draws itself up to say a wrong word, I'll say, 'Mrs. Vane kissed you; keep quiet!'"

As for Sim, he was in an incorrigible mood. All day long he was away, no one knew where. He came in at night and sometimes for meals, and was so savage that everybody let him alone. He seemed, like his own dog Teck, to consider the hand of every man against him, and he kept his hand against every man. He was strangely sensitive, also, and would take up the slightest remark as a reflection upon himself, and would break out fiercely and unexpectedly in his own defence.

Nan wept much, and at night when, in the attic room, her petition went up for Ruby, Sim was not forgotten.

After a week Ruby's temperature lowered. Some days it was almost normal, then he would say he was hungry and would like some milk toast, but when it came he only nibbled a tiny bit and asked to have it put up till next time, it was so nice.

In another week he had no fever, but lay weak and white. One day, when he had finished trying to take the soup, he reached out his hand and laid it in Aunt Sarah's, for she sat by his side.

"I'm sorry for one thing, though, Aunt Sarah."

"What?"

"I'm sorry I never had a chance to give the cup of cold water."

"Why, Ruby, what are you talking about,

child?" Aunt Sarah felt his forehead in alarm; she thought the fever was coming back.

"Don't you remember Alsace, Aunt Sarah? And you know I wanted to be kind to some one, but never found how I could."

"There, now, Ruby, you mustn't talk!" and Aunt Sarah drew the blinds closer. "You haven't slept any this morning."

"No'm, and I'm tired;" and he closed his eyes.

Aunt Sarah watched him a moment, went out with the soup-bowl, and came back again. How still he lay! Was he breathing? The long, curling lashes swept the pale cheeks. A heavenly peacefulness sat upon the little face. One small hand, smooth and white, lay outside the covering. Why did he say he was sorry he had never had a chance? Did he mean he would never have a chance again? Aunt Sarah bent her ear to the parted lips and heard the light breathing.

Then she stood and watched him, and every emotion of her whole life, every hope and every disappointment, every joy and every grief, every feeling of pride and every sense of humiliation, seemed to surge within her, and it was as if she lived again her fifty years in that half-hour.

And now, she thought, if this child should die, all the past, that had seemed so bitter, would be as nothing to the bitterness of that loss. And her heart crystallized. Once she had poured out her soul before the Lord; now she could not pray.

It went abroad that Ruby was lying between life and death. There were so many who wished to see him that Dr. Matthews said at first he could see no one; but when Ruby himself asked that certain ones might come in, the kind doctor yielded. No one must stay long or talk much, however. Aunt Sarah was on guard and there was no danger of her giving in to anybody. Father Paul came, and Miss Long, and Nan. Mrs. Wyman, who joyed and sorrowed in fancy, shed real tears.

"Mother," the sick child said, "ask Mr. White to come."

Mr. White came; he could not speak, neither could Ruby, for he was very weak that day. He gave Mr. White his little feeble hand and looked into his face.

"On the borderland," said Dr. Caruthers, as he bade the mother good-by, "'Of such is the kingdom of heaven.'"

That evening all the family were in the room, and Ruby asked Mabel and Marian to sing. "My hymn, all of it," he said.

"'Shall crowd to His arms,'—yes, there'll be so many of—us," he said when they had finished.

The others went down to supper. Aunt Sarah sat in her place by his side.

"Aunt Sarah," he said, feebly, opening his eyes suddenly, "it has all passed away; there is not a shadow;" and he laid his little hand upon his heart.

## CHAPTER XXIII.

### SIM.

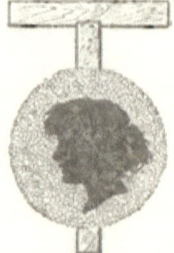

THAT night and the next day Ruby lay in a stupor; many times they thought he did not breathe. Aunt Sarah sat beside him and scarcely spoke.

In the evening Mabel and Marian were in the east room, which was theirs now. Mabel had wept until she could weep no more, and had fallen into a troubled sleep.

Marian had wept little; all day she had been about the house, filling gaps everywhere. Aunt Emily never gave up, but she was like a shadow, and, Marian thought, like a flower on a slender stem which a sudden blow might snap.

Marian sat by the south window. The twilight was gathering and the moon rising over the housetops. She could see down by the back gate, where Dinah was talking to some one. After a while there was a knock at the door and Dinah entered.

"Miss Ma'am," she whispered, "there's a boy down yon'er—he's pow'ful quare; he wants ter see you."

"What can he want with me, Dinah?"

"I dunno 'm; I done all I could ter git him off, I 'lowed he wus a-wantin' sumpthin' ter eat, an' tole him I'd git it; but he jes' ack like er plum' crazy loon an' say he wa'n't a-beggin', an' he wanted ter see you."

Marian was not timid and said she would go. At the gate she found a slouching figure, but could not see the face, for a torn hat was pulled over it. She asked the stranger if he wanted her, waited a moment for a reply, and when the boy lifted his head, discovered beneath the ragged hat-brim a face pale and unspeakably wretched.

"Why, Sim!" she said.

Sim caught the gate-post with both hands. He tried to speak, but his voice was thick and the words stuck in his throat.

"Why, Sim!" repeated Marian. "Is anything the matter at home? What is it?"

She felt very sorry for him and laid her hand upon his sleeve.

"Don't tech me! Don't tech such as me!" he gasped. "Ef yer knowed whut I was, yer'd not 'low me in yer sight. Yer'd sooner tech a rattler; fer I done it, Miss Marian, I done it! But I couldn't stay 'way no longer. I heard by Nan how he was a-layin', an' sumthin' driv me to come and tell you."

"What do you mean, Sim? I can't understand. What do you mean that you did?" Marian was pale, too, and trembled.

"Why, don't you know? I made the picter, an' I made it a-purpose to fix it on—him!"

The painful incident on Ruby's last day at school had almost passed from Marian's mind in the face of other distresses. Now she saw Sim's meaning, and understood his conscience-stricken misery.

"But, Sim, how could it be? You did it on purpose? I thought every one loved Ruby. What could he have done to you?"

"It was whut I done to him that made me hate him!" the boy groaned, leaning heavily against the gate. "You know whut that was."

"I? What?"

"Didn't he never tell?" Sim looked at her as if such a thing were beyond his comprehension. "Didn't he, though?"

"No."

"Why, it was me," he spoke under his breath, "it was me as—as killed his dog!"

No one but Aunt Sarah had ever heard that tale, and she knew no names.

"Yer know how sick he was about it, an' yer've seen me a-devilin' him, ain't yer? An' 'cause he tuk it all an' didn't hit ner git mad, I got wuss; an' ever' time I thought about whut I done to his dog I was madder with him. An' I done it! God 'a' mercy! Ther was another feller in it, but he didn't mean no harm. I tole him whut I was doin', 'cause I knowed he was skeered to tell, an' I says, 'Go git some uv the little chaps ter write the teacher's name on the envelope, 'cause he might know our hand.' An' I

sent him to—to him a purpose, and he writ it."

Here was the whole story—and was not that last cruelty the cause of Ruby's sickness? And even now, while he spoke, that gentle heart might have ceased to beat! it seemed to Marian afterward that the sweet spirit lingering in the little tenement must have flitted down and whispered to her. She would not have believed that she could feel so much pity for anyone so cruel and one who had brought such sorrow upon them all.

"Yer and yer folks is erbliged ter hate me," Sim said.

She reached out her hand and laid it upon the arm of the conscience-stricken lad.

"No, I do not." She tried to think of something else to say. He raised his miserable face. "Ask God to forgive you, Sim."

But Sim's gaze had wandered from her face, where, in wonder at her voice, it had rested an instant. The back gate was near the garden fence, and on one corner of the garden the moon was shining full, lighting up a little mound and a white, wooden slab, on which he could read, "Rover."

He turned back to her piteously. "Ef yer was a man and would do sumthin' to me—send me to jail or sumthin'."

His face seemed to plead for punishment, as some faces plead for pardon.

Marian tried again to think of something to say. "Sim, I must go now. Mabel will want me, and Aunt Emily may, too. I am sorry for you—so sorry! Go home and ask God to forgive you."

She left him, and went back into the house. The boy stood and watched her in a dazed way.

"Why didn't she git mad? Why didn't she order me off? Why didn't she call me names? What made her look like that? That's the way he used ter look. I used ter see her git mad with Nan an' me when we was up to meanness, and she could talk fast, too."

---

## CHAPTER XXIV.

### NIGHT WATCHES.

AUNT SARAH had never suffered Ruby to be taken from her room since the day he had thrown himself across her bed, saying, with parched lips, that he thought he was not sick.

On this night she sat in her usual place by

the bedside. She had commanded every one to leave, and not even Dr. Matthews had the nerve to disobey. There was no danger but she would call if they were wanted. Aunt Sarah had no hope; it had all passed away in that moment when her heart had crystallized and the voice of prayer ceased.

Marian, when she had helped Janet and Dinah through with supper and dishwashing, and had taken a cup of tea to Uncle Philip, who had not tasted food nor left his room all day, and had induced Aunt Emily to lie down, and had found from Mabel's breathing that she slumbered deeply, clothed herself in a light wrapper and went to the silent room. The night-lamp was darkened and the moon was not shining through the windows, but there was light enough for Aunt Sarah's keen vision, and when Marian had stood a moment in the doorway there was light enough for her to see the motionless form upon the bed and the figure beside it, erect and just as motionless. In that moment every particle of antagonism towards her austere aunt, which ever since she could remember had lodged in her heart, melted away. It seemed to her that for Aunt Sarah this loss which they were preparing to meet would be greater than for anyone, because she, who lived so much apart from people, would lose all that she loved. A great pity and tenderness filled Marian's heart.

"Aunt Sarah!" she said, softly, and took the rigid figure in her arms.

It was rigid no longer and upright no longer. Aunt Sarah's head bowed upon Marian's shoulder as if glad of a resting-place, and tears, which had not moistened her eyes for many a day, flowed freely. Marian's tears flowed also, and she fondled her aunt and kissed her as if she were the woman and the other the child. And to Aunt Sarah it seemed that the tears flowed inwardly more than outwardly, and reached her heart and dissolved it little by little, until she no longer knew it for her own. They did not speak a word, and in that silence a sympathy was born between these two who had never cared for one another.

When Aunt Sarah lifted her head, Marian slipped to the floor and leaned against her knee. "I want to tell you something," she whispered softly.

"Well?"

The little ear would not be disturbed.

Marian told in few words of the visitor at the gate, his confession and evident mis-

ery. Her heart was burdened and Aunt Sarah was the only one she could tell.

Aunt Sarah listened in silence. She remembered well how, on that Sabbath evening three years ago, Ruby had sat at her feet and told of the bad feeling within him toward the person who, in cruelty, had taken Rover's life, and how he had wished to forgive and do good to his persecutor, and how his last words had been, "It has all passed away; there is not a shadow — nothing here," as he laid his hand upon his heart. But Aunt Sarah could not tell all this to Marian; she could only ponder it in her heart. So they sat a long time.

Aunt Sarah never closed her eyes, but, before the library clock struck one, Marian's head drooped until it rested upon the knee against which she leaned, and Aunt Sarah, looking down upon the fair face, thought how good it was to be young. For the young can forget.

All through the night watches the woman sat alone, yet no longer lonely, for new thoughts were springing up within her, new hope, new love. Deep down within a voice was speaking; a voice her quickened ear knew, a voice she had thought awful, but which now sounded unspeakably gentle, and it called her by her name. "Lo, I am with thee." She was not alone.

When the dawn was breaking, after the short June night, Marian opened her eyes and found she was still leaning against Aunt Sarah's knee. She was not cold, though the night was chill, for a shawl was wrapped about her.

"Why, I dropped asleep! I must have tired you, Aunt Sarah. I will not sleep again." But Aunt Sarah sent her to bed.

Marian thought the brightness was from the moon still shining, but when she entered the room where Mabel lay, the glowing east told her that she had slept all night. "And left Aunt Sarah to watch alone! I am like Peter," she said.

Marian had hardly gone when Ruby stirred, yawned feebly, and said quite distinctly:

"I am so hungry!"

Aunt Sarah went across the hall and called Dr. Matthews, then downstairs, and soon returned with the bowl of soup. Ruby took what they gave him, yawned again, and dropped into a sound sleep.

Dr. Matthews bent over him, heard his deep, regular breathing, and saw the color coming into his lips and cheeks. Then he knelt by the bed, great tears rolling down his cheeks.

"He will live! Let us thank God, Miss Sarah."

---

## CHAPTER XXV.

### WHAT MANNER OF MAN IS THIS?

IM did not follow Marian's advice; he did not go home, neither did he ask God to forgive him. The rising sun found him moving slowly down the street, his ragged hat-brim over his eyes, heeding nothing. He wanted to ask people he met if they had heard from Ruby, but dared not.

At a corner he brushed against a boy turning it, who gave a nervous cry. "Oh, is it you, Sim? Where've you been?"

Sim looked at him a moment in silence. "Last night I was up—yonder," pointing behind him. "I don't know where I've been sence."

"Not up there!" The boy's teeth chattered as if it were a December and not a June morning.

"Yes, George McPhail, and I told 'em all about it, and—"

"Told them! What did you tell them? You know I didn't mean anything—you know I was just—" He was growing weak.

"I never spoke yer name, George McPhail. I told Miss Marian what I done, and 'lowed for her to tell the balance of 'em. It's bad enough with me now, but I tell you I wouldn't have the feelin's I had yistidy and the night afore for all yer could give me in the world."

"Sim, I would tell, too, if I had really done anything; but I didn't, you know. I didn't think once of getting him into trouble. And then—you and I are—different. You can confess, and it will not be thought so much of, but I—if I were to say anything—"

"Folks would talk. But I'll tell you, George McPhail, I'd 'a' outened with it if I'd been the President's son."

At his own door Sim met Nan, who had just come in. Her face was all in a glow. "Oh, Sim, have you heard? I met the doctor, and he says he's better, a heap better!"

For three weeks Sim had searched the town; he was determined to work if anybody would have him. But people who did not know him well asked for a "character," which he could by no means produce, and those who knew him shook their wise heads without inquiries. At length he told Nan he would strike out to-morrow; cotton-hoeing wasn't over, and he might get a job in the fields; he thought he'd get on best on a farm anyway; it was open, like.

But the next morning early he met one of Mr. Vane's clerks, who said that gentleman wished to see him in his office. Sim went straight there, pale but not cowardly. He thought of but one thing: Mr. Vane knew now the story of his baseness and had sent for him.

When he entered the office Mr. Vane was at his desk, a pile of papers before him.

"You are Sim Larkins?"

"Yes, sir."

"Sit down, Sim."

Sim obeyed, though wishing rather to stand.

Mr. Vane went on writing for a few minutes, then he pushed back the papers and laid down his pen.

"I have something to say to you, Sim."

"Yes, sir, Mr. Vane," said the boy, rising, "and I won't think nothing strange, no matter what yer say, because I know I deserve more'n anybody can say er do."

"You mistake, Sim. I want a trusty office boy, and yesterday some one told me that you were hunting work and suggested that I try to engage you."

"Trusty office boy!" "Some one" had "suggested" him; "try" to engage him! Poor Sim's expression of blank astonishment would have been ludicrous to one who did not know the circumstances.

"I—I don't quite make yer out, Mr. Vane," he said. And when he did make it out, he stood turning his ragged hat round and round in his hands, looking upon the floor. Then he raised his head and asked:

"Don't yer know, Mr. Vane? Didn't Miss Marian tell yer?"

"Miss Marian did not tell me, but I know what you mean, Sim, and we will not talk about it now. Would you like the place?"

"I'm ready, Mr. Vane. What must I do first?"

"Take this to Mr. Owen," handing him a note. "Go over to old Mrs. Clarke's, where the clerks get dinner, get yours there, and come back at two o'clock."

Sim was back promptly at the hour, clothed—by Mr. Owen—and with a new countenance. When Mr. Vane told him at night that he had done well, and gave him instructions for the morrow, the boy said:

"It ain't no use fer me to try to thank yer, Mr. Vane, but I 'lows to show yer that I mean it, and that I'm goin' to do different as fur as I'm able."

"You are not the only one of us who has need of repentance and new resolutions, Sim," said Mr. Vane, as he locked the office door.

In a few days Sim asked permission to visit Ruby.

"You are not busy, so may go now," said Mr. Vane. "He is weak, and we do not let every one see him, but I can trust you to talk little and quietly, Sim."

Sim understood. And Ruby's father could trust him! This being trusted was keeping Sim in a state of continual wonder at Mr. Vane and all his house, and at himself. "Is this me?" he sometimes asked, waking in the middle of the night.

He found Ruby upstairs in a big leather-covered arm-chair, with pillows at his back, looking very white, "but as glad to see me as if I was his bes' frien'," thought the humble youth.

A tall lady with black hair and eyes that could see through you, sat by the window sewing. She "spoke kind," he told Nan, and gave him a chair, then she said she would let him take care of Ruby while she went downstairs.

He remembered his trust and spoke quietly and in few words.

"I wouldn't worry about it now, Sim," Ruby said, laying his tiny hand in Sim's great one, "because it's all over and we're friends."

"And seeh a look in them big eyes! I wanted to git down on my knees, Nan."

Ruby asked him to come back real soon; the tall lady asked him also.

The next time he went was on Sunday, and Ruby asked him to come every Sunday, which he did as long as Ruby kept the house. Once he staid while Aunt Sarah went to church. Ruby gave him a little package. "It's Aunt Sarah's present, Sim, but she said I might give it to you. Aunt Sarah's always thinking of something. Don't you like her, Sim? You needn't open it till you get home."

At home he found it was a little book, bound in morocco, "Gospel of St. Mark" in gilt letters on the cover. He read in it at night and on Sundays. He had never read a whole chapter in the Bible in his life. He had never thought it was like this. What sort of a man was this that his little book told about—this Jesus? Sim had heard of him; he had been to church sometimes and heard the Bible read and the preacher preach, but never had paid much attention. He had heard this name spoken in seriousness, but more often in vain; he had some kind of a vague idea as to this Jesus. He was a man or spirit or something that people preached and sang about. Sim had seldom troubled himself with the spiritual; he did not believe in "ha'nts."

But he was reading now about a real man who lived and walked about and talked like any other man; only he was not like any other man either, for he could do things that no one else could do, and—he was different. Sim wondered much when he read how Jesus made the sick well and the blind see and the dead rise up and walk, but the wonder at these things was as nothing to that which Sim felt when he came to the place where he was spit upon and struck, but struck not back nor even answered, and allowed them to lead him to death. "He could have killed 'em all, jes' by his say-so, a man like that, and could have come down from the cross, too, as easy! Why didn't he?"

Then in re-reading he found these words: "For even the Son of man came not to be ministered unto, but to minister, and to give his life a ransom for many."

At church—for he was now a regular attendant—he heard now and then something that gave him new light. "Christ died for us," was the text one Sunday; he could understand the text better than the sermon. After a while the light broke upon Sim's darkened understanding. "He done it a-purpose; he let 'em do him so and kill him, because he loved 'em, and this was such a great chance to show his love! And now they say he's a-wantin' us all, good and bad, fur—he died for us. Even for me—Sim Larkins! That's what they say—fur the wust one."

And Sim began to understand what manner of spirit Ruby and his household were of.

## CHAPTER XXVI.

### THE YOUNG AND THE OLD.

WHEN the train stopped at Greenville one October afternoon a slight, gray-haired man alighted. He passed swiftly through the ranks of eager porters and hackmen, who had considered him an easy prey, and walked rapidly up the street. But when the station, with its hurry and noise, was left behind, he slackened his pace. He walked more slowly still when he reached the side streets, mere lanes, some of them, with their rows of poplar and sweet gum, gorgeous in their apparel.

But though his hair was thin and gray and his shoulders stooped slightly, and his face was deeply lined, it was not from age, and his step, though slow, was not heavy, neither was it uncertain; he was as one pressing forward to something ever in sight.

Every little gust blew down the golden shields of the poplar and the gold and crimson stars of the sweet gum, and they fell upon his shoulders and clung to his hair and made a royal carpet for his feet. He seemed to see the beauty around him, yet never to lose sight of the beauty or hope or purpose, whatever it was, always ahead.

Aunt Sarah had finished her work and was folding it before going down to lay the table for tea, when there was a knock at the front door, and a moment later Ruby's voice rang out, surprised and joyous:

"Uncle Alex! Oh, it's Uncle Alex!"

Aunt Sarah's scissors dropped, and, when Ruby bounded upstairs with the glad tidings, she was leaning over the railing.

Ruby did not stop longer than was necessary, but was away to his mother's room, to the dining-room, kitchen, everywhere, with the same good word:

"Uncle Alex! Uncle Alex's come, and we didn't know!"

"And you have forgotten your politeness," said mother coming out, "and have not asked Uncle Alex in."

"Why, Uncle Alex's at home, mother. He doesn't have to be asked in. But then, I suppose I ought, as he's been away so long. Only, I was so glad I didn't think."

Aunt Sarah, though called again by Ruby, did not come down to lay the table until Uncle Alex was safe in the east room.

It was a happy circle that gathered round the tea table. Mabel and Marian were almost as joyful as Ruby, who was bubbling over. Mabel whispered to him when they went in, that he might have her place, which would be at Uncle Alex's left, but he thanked her and said no, he always sat by Aunt Sarah.

Aunt Sarah said little and did not ply Uncle Alex with questions, yet she looked happy, too. After supper Mrs. Vane touched the silver bell, and the servants came in; they bowed, and Janet hoped Mr. Alex was well, and sniffled, either being reminded of his past sufferings, or calling to mind her own ever-present infirmities.

When every one was seated, Marian and Mabel on either side of Mrs. Vane, Ruby by Aunt Sarah, his hand in hers, Philip Vane read from the Bible that Marian had placed beside the shaded lamp, and when they knelt it seemed to the traveler that the weary years had folded back, and that it was "Uncle Reuben's" voice he heard uplifted to God in the old home.

It was a happy circle which gathered later in the library, and there they learned the reason of Uncle Alex's visit. A distant relative, of whom he knew little, and who, it seemed, like himself, had been alone in the world, had died recently and left to him his property. The kinsman had lived in Philadelphia, and through some acquaintance had heard of Alex Harmon's work for others.

"It is not a large sum, but sufficient for my needs for the rest of my life," Uncle Alex said.

But Ruby's radiance was the radiance of tears on finding that Uncle Alex must be gone on the morrow to Philadelphia.

"To-morrow, Uncle Alex? Couldn't you stay just a little while?" And the others echoed it.

But he must attend to the business at once; it might occupy some weeks, and he had so little time to spare. He must be at home.

"Home, Uncle Alex? This is home, isn't it?" and Ruby looked aggrieved.

"Yes, Ruby, one of them. But I have two; this is my resting-home, that is my working-home, and you know we must work while it is day."

"'For the night cometh,'" said Ruby, slowly. "Yes, Uncle Alex, I see."

But they got Uncle Alex's promise to stop on his return, at least for one day. They told him Father Paul's health was failing, and he could not go back without seeing him again.

Before the lights were out Uncle Alex heard a soft tap at his door. He knew the sound well; he had waited to hear it.

"I could not let you go away, Uncle Alex, and not have a talk with you in here," said Ruby, seating himself after the old fashion on the low stool. "I love this room so much. Many times I come in here and think about you and remember the things you and Father Paul used to talk about. Uncle Alex," after a pause, "what did it mean once when Father Paul showed you five letters on his breast? How could they get there, and what did they mean? - 'T—H—I—E—F.'"

"Ah, Ruby," said Uncle Alex, with a sigh, "that is Father Paul's secret, and we will let it be buried. Perhaps every one has a secret, my child, which we should not try to touch."

"Yes, Uncle Alex. If I had known it was a secret I would not have asked." Ruby looked up with some wonder in his eyes.

They were both silent awhile. Uncle Alex was watching the rosy, grave little face, when Ruby suddenly roused,

"I was thinking about what you said, Uncle Alex. Now, do you suppose Aunt Sarah has one?"

"One what?"

"One — I mean, a secret."

"Aunt Sarah?" Uncle Alex's thin hand dropped from his cheek, which had rested upon it. "Aunt Sarah? Why, Ruby?"

"I don't know, sir, only you said perhaps everybody has some secret, and I wondered if Aunt Sarah had."

Silence again.

"Uncle Alex, you looked sick then, and dark under the eyes, and your hands could not hold anything hardly; you don't look so much fatter now, but you don't look sorry. It seems to me you are thinking of something all the time and it makes you glad."

"I am, Ruby." Uncle Alex bent and stroked the bright curls. "I am thinking of how the dear Lord loves me, and of the time when I shall see him face to face."

"Oh, yes, I know how that is, Uncle Alex! You know when I was sick last spring I thought I was going to—to meet Him. And the others thought so, too, I know. One evening, after Marian and Mabel had sung

for me, I felt sure of it. I laid my hand here" — on his heart — "and told Aunt Sarah there wasn't a shadow, and went to sleep. She knew; that was my secret. Why, I have a secret, too! But we were talking about something else. I woke, though, and then commenced to get better. I believe I was sorry at first. I was so sure, that I had lain and thought about it every day. I know they all thought I was sleeping, but I was only thinking with my eyes shut. How would Jesus look, and what would he say to me? What would I do? When mother and Aunt Sarah and father and Mabel and Marian and Miss Long and everybody came, I would be at the gate and would be so glad as they came in. Once Father Paul said, 'Sticketh closer than a brother, Ruby.' I knew what he meant. I never thought of being afraid. Every night I would think, 'Maybe the door will swing open and He will shine out in the dark to-night,' and every morning I would think, 'Maybe to-day I'll feel Him lift me up and hear Him say, "Ruby."' But I'm not sorry now. I think of what Father Paul said, and I know He sticketh closer than a brother now just the same as then. And then, I don't want to die, Uncle Alex. I don't want this" — he held out one hand — "and these" — pointing to his feet — "to have to lie still in the grave, and I don't want all of me, my head and body and all, to go to dust. No, no!" shaking his head. "I want to live, I want to be a man."

"And it is right that you should, Ruby; but for myself I feel that to be with Christ is far better."

"But you are with him now, Uncle Alex."

"Yes, but not free; free from this weak body." The man seemed to forget that he was talking to the child.

"I must go now, Uncle Alex;" and Ruby rose and kissed the thin lips good-night.

---

## CHAPTER XXVII.

### T—H—I—E—F.

UNCLE Alex came back in three weeks. It was late Friday afternoon and he could stay only till Monday, so when they told him Father Paul had been quite ill he started at once for the cottage. Ruby went with him. But Ruby came back at nightfall alone. Father Paul was glad to see them, he said, and was lying very quiet, but Uncle Alex was going to stay with him all night. Ruby was disappointed. "And he's going away Monday; we'll hardly see him. Aunt Sarah, why don't you beg him to stay? Everybody does what you say." Then, after a period of no response. "Uncle Alex looks happy, but he looks sad, too. I'm sure he must want some of us, away out there. And he doesn't have anybody to take care of him and mend his clothes and everything. Why, Aunt Sarah, that's his coat you're mending now; won't he be glad! But who'll mend his coats and make his tea and put his chair and slippers by the fire when he goes away from here?"

Something bright fell on the well-worn coat-sleeve, and Aunt Sarah, with averted face, hastily gathered up her work and was about to rise, when Ruby put his arms about her.

"Now, Aunt Sarah, why should you mind me? I want to cry, too." And they did cry together.

When Ruby was in bed an hour later, he thought how strange it was. "I never saw Aunt Sarah cry before, not in my whole life; but I never thought about it till to-night."

Uncle Alex saw what he did not tell the child. His old friend was not only very ill, but the sands for him were running low. He told the neighbors who came in as usual to attend the sick man, that he would remain all night, and when they were gone sat by the shaded lamp and tried to read. But his eyes turned again and again to the sleeper upon the narrow bed, and his thoughts wandered over the checkered career of this life that was drawing to a close. His own burden, the harvest of tares which would never be lifted entirely from his shoulders in this world, seemed light compared with this that his friend had borne with fortitude and calmness. Those who say that there is no virtue in bearing patiently the evils which we have brought upon ourselves, know nothing of repentance. The sharpest pang of loss, of failure, of shame, is, "I might have done otherwise." If I have failed because of a hindrance that I could not control, that hindrance, in whatever form, is to me the hand of God; but when I remember that it was my own willful hand that put aside the good and seized the evil, then are the penalties a hundredfold harder to bear.

On the table was a Bible, old and worn,

and as Uncle Alex turned the leaves he read not only the history of repentant sinners of olden time who were transfigured till their faces shone as the light, but, in here and there a much worn page, a marking, a blotting such as sudden drops of joy or grief leave, the history of that one slumbering upon the narrow bed; that one who had entered the kingdom of God through much tribulation.

The sick man's slumbers were light. He opened his eyes often, but his spirit seemed never to awake till the day was breaking. Then, as Uncle Alex bent over the couch, Father Paul pressed his hand and bade him sit beside him. His voice was not strong, but distinct.

"Alex, I thank God that you are here, for we have loved each other long, and you only, of all the world, know me. Of all the world," he repeated, slowly. "I did not seek to deceive or hide my crime, Alex, God knows, but when I left the scenes of my shame and came here where no one knew me, I did not see that it was God's will that I should proclaim my past, but I sought to leave the things that are behind and press forward as one of the redeemed. But now that I am departing I am glad you are here; you will fulfill my request." He laid his hand as he spoke upon his breast. Uncle Alex remembered the inscription there. "I can't shall not reveal your secret, Paul; I will guard it."

The dying man had closed his eyes; he opened them. "You do not understand, Alex. I do not mean that. I mean I am glad you are here, because you must tell them. When they lay me to rest, have only 'Dust to dust' said over me; then you must tell to those who have come, all—you know —all. Tell them of Him! Him! A broken life, and 'Jesus Christ maketh thee whole.'"

It was well that the message was delivered. When the sun was shining high in the heavens, and Uncle Alex left the cottage, Father Paul was lying neatly arrayed for burial.

---

## CHAPTER XXVIII.

### THE GULF.

UNCLE ALEX went back to the cottage after dinner, and later Aunt Sarah went, taking the children, for they wanted a last look at their old friend.

Father Paul's neighbors were going in and coming out, some weeping, all sad; for he was a friend to each.

As Aunt Sarah was starting back home, Uncle Alex asked her to remain and go with him later, so the three children were sent on alone.

It was growing dark before Uncle Alex was ready. He took the path that led by the river side and walked slowly. When they had left the houses and no one was in hearing, he commenced to tell her about Father Paul's life. It was a sad story. Then he told the dying request and asked what she thought. Should he tell? Why not bury his secret with him? What would be the effect upon these people who reverenced him? When they found that he had once been a common convict, would not all the influence of that unselfish Christian life be lost upon them? Awhile ago in the cottage he had heard Judge Lander say to Dr. Matthews, who was telling of Father Paul's kindness and good works among the poor, "But it is his integrity that will live when his good works are forgotten." Must he blot the fair name of his friend?

Aunt Sarah did not answer at first. They walked on slowly by the river, rushing over its rocky bed, now in the light of the young moon, now in shadow. After awhile she said:

"Yes, you ought to tell, I think; it was his request and he trusted you to carry it out."

Uncle Alex gave a long sigh. "I knew you would give me a plain answer," he said. "It is natural to come to you for counsel, Sarah; it used to be the sweetest thing in the world to me."

Then he began to talk of his own life, of the dark years that yawned like a great gulf between him and his youth, swallowing up in its blackness his strength, his ambitions, his hopes, and, he had once believed, his very soul.

"But the very greatness of that gulf makes it possible for me to talk freely to you now, Sarah, for I am no longer the Alex Harmon that you knew, but another person; an old man, who can talk of that hot-headed youth, holding royal treasures in his hand and flinging them away. I can even talk to you of the last time we sat together by the spring. I can see you now, going up the path; then the grapevine hid you from my sight — forever. Yes, forever, for I never saw that Sarah again."

She faced about and demanded:

"Who is this, then?"

They were crossing the bridge.

"You are not the same, as I am not. Though you are not old; you are strong and your hair is black. But I am very old."

He took off his hat and passed his hand over his thin gray hair. They were in the middle of the bridge, where the young moon shone full. Aunt Sarah faced about again, and stopped with her hand upon the railing.

"I am as old as you."

"A calendar does not tell how long we are living, Sarah. There are times when one day is a lifetime, and —"

"And where have I been all these years that you talk of? Asleep?"

"You have been living your quiet life of Christian charity."

"Quiet life! And how do you know but there have been times for me when one day was as a lifetime? Christian charity! How do you know anything of the pride that kept me far off from my Lord? He is meek and lowly in heart — what have I been? But God has been merciful to me and shown me myself."

She walked on then, and so did he.

"Yes, it is true, I am not the same, Alex, but —"

"But what, Sarah?"

I do not know what, for they passed into the shadow at the further end of the bridge, and stopped again. I only know that when they came out into the light they were no longer old, for all the dark years had slipped away out of the calendar, and they stood as they had stood a quarter of a century ago, hand in hand, upon the threshold of life.

Nobody understood exactly why Aunt Sarah had such a wonderful smile that night. For nobody had ever seen her smile like that, not even Uncle Alex; there was a whole lifetime in it.

When Ruby went to say good-night, Uncle Alex held the rosy face between his hands and said, "I have something to tell you, Ruby, and I am afraid you will not love me as well as you do now."

"Why, Uncle Alex!" Ruby looked grieved.

When Uncle Alex told him, he did not say a word, but went softly to his own room and sat down in the dark. Aunt Sarah always lighted his lamp, but she had not to-night. He was not jealous, oh, no; it was because she had expected him to come to her room first for the "going-to-bed" talk. He was not jealous, oh, no; only so miserably lonely and homesick he did not know what to do. He sat perfectly still in the dark. Last night he and Aunt Sarah had cried together because Uncle Alex was going away alone. Was it only last night? Oh, how selfish he was! He had so many, and Uncle Alex had nobody.

After a while Ruby went and opened Aunt Sarah's door softly. She was in her high-backed chair and had her Bible open in her lap, but was not reading; she was looking in the fire.

And she did not hear him! She had always turned around so quick when he opened the door! No, no, he was not jealous, and he loved Uncle Alex just the same, only — only, he didn't feel right, and there was a sore place all around his heart. He tiptoed over the carpet and stood behind her; he looked over her shoulder and saw the Bible was open at Isaiah. There was a heavy black mark around one verse, and he thought she had just made it there, for the pencil was in her hand. He read: "And the desert shall rejoice and blossom as the rose."

All this, and she did not know he was there! It used to be he could "catch" any of the others, but he never could catch Aunt Sarah.

The place around his heart kept getting sorer, and his throat was sore, too, and "dry-feeling." Then the little lad laid his hand on Aunt Sarah's shoulder and scared her half out of her wits.

She saw how pale he was and how large and troubled his eyes looked. She put her arm around him and kissed him.

"Aunt Sarah," he said. "I know."

"Oh, Ruby, I can't leave you! And I won't if you say the word!" She hugged him tight with both arms.

"But I won't say the word," he said, when they had had it out.

Ruby did not say any more for a while, but stood looking in the fire. Then:

"I used to think you didn't like Uncle Alex, Aunt Sarah, when he first came here, and I was sorry, because I liked him so much. One day I found a picture lying on your bed. I went and asked him if it was his, and he said he thought it was. It must have been taken when he was a young man and staid at grandfather's house and was like father's brother. His mouth was red and his cheeks, too, and his hair was so pretty. I thought at first it was a lady's picture. He doesn't look like that now; he's

old and has hollows in his cheeks and his hair's gray, but you like him better than you did then, don't you, Aunt Sarah?"

"Yes," she said.

---

## CHAPTER XXIX.

### "LITTLE DAUGHTER" AGAIN.

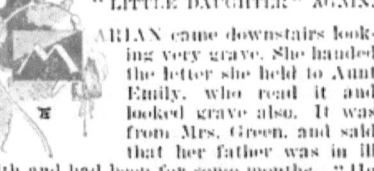

MARIAN came downstairs looking very grave. She handed the letter she held to Aunt Emily, who read it and looked grave also. It was from Mrs. Green, and said that her father was in ill health and had been for some months. "He don't complain," it ran, "but I think you ought to come here." That sounded like Mrs. Green.

It was decided that Marian should go, but Aunt Emily was troubled; the child was young for the duties before her, if her father's illness should be serious. Marian, though sorry to leave them all and to miss school, felt glad to think that she might do something at last to cheer her lonely parent. And the more Aunt Emily spoke of the responsibilities that might await her, the more important she felt. Yes, there was so much that she could do! She loved to nurse sick people. She would make her father's tea and toast and soup, and arrange his waiter as daintily as Aunt Sarah herself could. Then she would sit and talk with him and read to him if he wished. She would not be afraid to talk to him now; she laughed when she thought how foolish she used to be. She was such a little girl then! Everything had been different since the time Ruby went. He had opened the door, as it were, and brought in the light.

It was serious enough, though, on the last night. It was serious for everybody, for not only Marian, but Aunt Sarah, left on the morrow — Aunt Sarah and Uncle Alex, to begin life over again.

They were all gathered in the library and nobody talked much. The clock ran so fast! When it came to tea they had prayers. Then Ruby got up. "I'll have to sing for you once more, Aunt Sarah."

When he had finished every eye was wet but his, and then they said good-night.

Marian clung to Aunt Emily when she came to see them into bed.

"I think father will be better soon—in about a month—and I can come home. Don't you, Aunt Emily?"

"I hope so, I will miss you, and I know you will miss us; but you are a brave, patient and thoughtful child, Marian, and—God is with you."

Marian felt very lonely when Aunt Sarah and Uncle Alex left her. How fast the train was moving! And the farther it carried her from Greenville and the nearer it brought her to the end of the journey, the more lonely she became. Her enthusiasm was spinning quite out. Aunt Emily was right; she was very young—and what if her father were sick a long time?

The big red-brick house looked more gloomy than ever, with the leafless trees waving their long branches, like ghostly arms, around it. Her courage was spinning out, too, and there was hardly a thread of it left by the time she had ascended the great, dark stairway.

When she knocked, a young man opened the door. He was not tall; his hair was dark and close-cut, his eyes were blue-gray and very keen, and his mouth was a thin, firm line, which gave you the notion that his words were few and to the point. He was the kind of person that you cannot help seeing, and Marian saw all this before she asked where her father was. He was in his bedroom; not in bed, but sitting by the fire, taking his evening meal.

Where was the daughterly caress Marian had thought to give him? She could only take his hand, touch her lips to the sallow cheek and hope he was better, and stand there without a word more to say. He said he did very well and that she would better go and rest.

Why did he not take her in his arms? Why did he not call her "little daughter" again? Surely he did not love her. Surely all her plans for helping and cheering him were come to nothing. She went out ready to overflow.

But it was no time for weeping, for Tabby was in her room to welcome "Miss Ma'am," and tell her how "she'd growed" and how sweet she looked. And Pete came in with a fresh supply of wood for her fire, and chuckled and dropped his hat and said, showing every white tooth, "Miss Ma'am hadn't brung no waitin'-maid this time." They both had so many questions to ask about Ruby, and Marian had so many mes-

ages to deliver from him, that she was almost herself when it was over. Almost, but not quite, for she was swallowing the tears back as she went down the stairs.

The young man was at the front door, putting on his hat, but when he saw Marian he came to meet her at the foot of the stairs.

"You are Prof. Rede's little daughter?"

"Yes."

"And you're going to live with him?"

"Oh, no!" Marian swallowed harder. "I have only come to spend a while—a month, I think. I will have to go back then, and—be at school."

"Yes," he said, looking at her with his keen eyes; and she knew that he saw she was homesick and miserable.

"I am going to stay to tea, if you don't object," he said, hanging up his hat.

She was glad; she liked the "straight" way he had of looking and speaking.

They had a pleasant time. Marian quite forgot herself, for Mr. Waring talked of so many interesting things. He had traveled over the world; he was a great scholar, Marian thought, like her father, and he could say so much with so few words, Marian was glad to know that he came almost every day.

## CHAPTER XXX.

### WHAT SHE COULD.

HE next morning it was raining, a chill, November rain, and when Marian arose and went to the window there was the heavy gray sky and the prospect of a day's rain—or a week's. She thought of how she had planned to make the dreary house cheerful by her own cheerfulness, and her lonely father glad that he had a little daughter. And in the first advances how utterly had she failed! She thought of how, when her aunt had been serious about her responsibilities, she herself had been well pleased. She did not feel fit for any responsibilities now, but cried out in her heart to be at home with Aunt Emily. She turned away from the window, against which the rain was beating thicker and faster, and was about to throw herself upon the bed again to indulge in tears, when the words came to her, "You are a brave, patient and thoughtful child, Marian."

She was not brave, oh, no! for was she not giving up? She was not patient, for there was one consuming desire within her, and that was to run away. And how was she thoughtful? Yet Aunt Emily had said it with her own truthful lips that never spoke lightly, and Aunt Emily ought to know something about her — more than she knew about herself. If she was brave, she must stand up; if she was patient, she must wait; if she was thoughtful, she would find many things to do.

"And God is with you." She remembered something Dr. Caruthers had said once. If one followed Dr. Caruthers through the deep mines of theology, he was often rewarded with nuggets of pure gold that he might carry home and keep.

"Your noble scheme may come to naught, but be not discouraged. Let it alone, if need be, and lay your hand to the homely tasks that surround you, of which there is no lack, and know that thereby you are a laborer with God, working out, bit by bit, a sublimer scheme than your puny intellect could ever conceive."

All through breakfast Marian was trying to make up her mind how to approach her father. She thought of one way and of another, but nothing suited. She was beginning to worry, when the thought came, "I will not think beforehand what I shall say."

She read in the Bible Aunt Sarah had given as a parting gift. Mabel had one like it, and they had agreed to read in the same place and at the same hour each day. Then she went to her father's door.

There was new boldness both in the knock and in the voice that greeted the silent man good-morning. He was in the study, by the long table, with a book before him.

"Father," said Marian, "I would like to sit with you, if you don't mind."

He said, "Yes," looked at her as if not knowing what he said or what she had said, then went on with his reading.

Marian took a chair near the window and sat watching the rain. The wind had risen, beating the drops against the pane, and adding its dismal note to the world's dreariness. From time to time Marian turned to her father; she did not feel shy, as on yesterday, but thought that if a conversation were opened she could talk freely.

But there was no opening. There sat the scientist, and there in arm's reach sat his little daughter, silent, waiting. He, lost in thought, was totally oblivious of her presence; and she knew it, but still sat and waited, if something—her mother's voice, perhaps—might whisper to him that she was there, and that she was his child. She noticed that the book, which was heavy, lay upon the table, and that the hand which now and then turned a leaf was tremulous. When she got up and went quietly out, he did not seem to know.

It was a sorry way to cheer a father's heart, she thought, but it was the best she could do, the best she knew of.

Downstairs Marian learned from Mrs. Green that her father took a light lunch at twelve. She asked leave to take it up, and Mrs. Green made no objection. Prof. Rede received it without a word, as if she had brought it every day, crumbled the bread into the soup, and ate in silence.

Mrs. Green was getting out the table linen when Marian went down with the tray.

"May I set the table, Mrs. Green?" she asked.

Think of setting the table for herself only! When the housekeeper came in with the golden butter and cream, Marian said, "I have laid two plates, Mrs. Green; shall we not take our meals together?"

Mrs. Green said yes, if Miss Marian wished.

It was a solemn occasion, but Marian was gaining power. She talked about household matters, complimented the pie, and asked questions which Mrs. Green answered in monosyllables as far as she might.

When dinner was over Marian wanted to know if there was not something that she might take for her daily task. Mrs. Green consented to her laying the table for meals and keeping the silver in order. She might arrange and take up her father's meals also.

Marian spent the afternoon in the library. It was behind the great, dark parlor. Here were none of the works of science that her father read upstairs, but history and the choicest literature. There were books of which Aunt Emily or Miss Long had told her. "Sesame and Lilies" she seized eagerly, and read till there was no longer light enough coming through the great window.

The next morning, was dark and rainy, also, but Marian did not wake to weep.

"A worker together with God," she said, as she took up, one by one, the homely tasks,

When she went up to her father's room she carried her work, and, sitting in the same chair by the window, sewed in silence, glancing now and then at the silent man, who read as before, or gazed at nothing, immersed in his own thoughts.

After awhile there was a quick step on the stair, and before the door opened Marian knew it was Mr. Waring. He entered without knocking, said good-morning, and, going to the other end of the long room, seated himself at a table strewn with books and papers. There he sat reading, sometimes writing, and Marian wondered if he were as much absorbed in his world as her father was in his. It was strange company. She felt almost as if she were in a graveyard; there was the dead stillness, and yet that indescribable feeling of being surrounded by life.

When she folded her work and left, neither seemed to notice.

And so every day it was the same. Marian's shining needle went in and out, while the elderly man and the young man sat, each bent upon his own pursuits. Yet Marian never felt in the way. She did not feel lonely after the first day, and she came to look forward with pleasure to her two silent hours. It was a good time to think.

But although Mr. Waring had nothing to say in the study, he was sociable enough downstairs. He often staid to dinner, sometimes to tea. Mrs. Green never ate with them when Mr. Waring was there, so he and Marian were much alone and came to know one another very well.

---

## CHAPTER XXXI.

### THE OPEN DOOR.

HE month was nearly at an end. It had passed much more rapidly than Marian had supposed it could. Yet she was not free from homesickness, and now wrote to Aunt Emily asking what she should do.

"Father is not worse, though I can't see that he is any better than when I came," she wrote. "Tell me what you think best for me to do, Aunt Emily. If I thought father needed me in any way, I would not leave him."

And in her heart she added, "If I thought he would miss me."

It was pitiful, anyway, to think that she had sat with her father from day to day and from week to week, because she was his daughter and wished to cheer him and could find no better way, and now that she was going he would scarcely know she had been there.

Aunt Emily's letter came very soon. She thought Marian would better come home. She knew her thoughtful Marian would not leave her father if there were real need for her at his side. She should return for school, if nothing more.

"I will go next week," Marian said. But she had not set a day for her departure, and no one knew anything of it.

One morning she woke with a sore throat. It did not get better all day. Mrs. Green came up herself that night and gave her pepper tea. But next morning the throat was only worse, and by midday the housekeeper saw that a more experienced hand than hers was needed. But Prof. Rede had no physician. He thought he knew his own frame perfectly.

Mrs. Green's face had a real expression on it when she met Mr. Waring on the stairs. She laid the case before him.

"Let me see the child," he said.

He looked into the red and swollen throat, felt the quick pulse, and went out.

"Let Pete go for Dr. Worth; I will see Prof. Rede."

Prof. Rede sat resting his elbow on the table, his head upon his hand. The open book was before him, but unread. He had been strangely alive that day to the sounds without, the footsteps on the stairs, the frequent opening and shutting of the door across the hall. When Mr. Waring came in he did not turn his head.

"Prof. Rede, your daughter is ill, and I have sent for Dr. Worth. I did not wait to consult you, as the case is urgent; she has been neglected too long already."

The professor looked at the young man without changing countenance. "Neglected?"

"The housekeeper has been attentive, but her remedies do not meet the case."

Prof. Rede said no more, neither did Mr. Waring, who took his accustomed seat and resumed his studies.

Later, two persons came up the stairs. Mrs. Green was one.

Then the father spoke: "When the man

comes out, find what he thinks of the child."

Mr. Waring was ready when the doctor left the sick-room and had a short consultation with him on the stairs.

The case needed prompt attention. Dr. Worth said, and careful nursing. Did Mr. Waring think the housekeeper could do the work? Mr. Waring thought the housekeeper could follow instructions strictly. He himself would remain at the house all night.

When Mr. Waring reported in the study Prof. Rede made no reply, neither did he seem to notice the keen question in the young man's eyes: "Are you a father?"

Mrs. Green did not leave Marian's room that night, and Mr. Waring went in often to note any change of temperature and assist in carrying out the doctor's directions.

After midnight Marian slept a while. When she opened her eyes and looked about in the dim light, it was not Mrs. Green sitting there, nor yet Mr. Waring, but her father. When he saw that she was awake, he came to the little table by the bed, poured out her medicine, and held it to her parched lips. She swallowed with difficulty; he raised her head and laid it back upon the pillow.

"Sleep, my child," he said.

There was no tenderness in his eyes, no lightening of the settled gloom, but there was a note in the voice that Marian had never heard before, not even when he had kissed her in the cars and called her "little daughter."

Was it the note of kindness, of gentleness? She knew that already; this was something more. It was the note of fatherhood!

Marian was better next day. Every evening and morning her father came in, took her hand and asked how she was. And each time Marian felt that he missed her presence in his room. But why should she think so? He did not say this, he did not say a word more than I have told.

In a week Marian was able to leave her room. She and Mrs. Green were getting quite sociable. That lady never failed in attentions and Marian saw that they were not mere mechanical duties.

As soon as she might, Marian went to her father's room, at the usual hour and with her work. He did not say he was glad to see her, nor did his countenance change. He looked at her a moment, returned to his book, read a little, closed it and laid it upon the table.

"Marian," he said, "I should like to have you remain here if you wish to do so. Your education is incomplete, but you shall have every advantage of study. I will provide a tutor and teachers of music and whatever else you may desire. I do not ask you to stay against your will; you may consider, and answer when you choose."

He took up his book from the table and in a moment seemed not to know that she was there.

Marian sat and looked at her father, her hands lying idle among the folds of her work. Did he catch the flash of pain that ran along her open face? It was well that he did not ask an answer then — she would have betrayed herself; it was well that he sank into his own world again and left her alone.

She did not sit her time out, but, gathering up her work directly, left the room.

That very morning she had taken out Aunt Emily's letter and read it over. How sweet it was to think she would soon be at home with them all! Had it not been for this sudden sickness, she would be there now. Yet she had thought of that illness with gladness, and not regret, because of what it had brought her.

Marian went to her own room and fastened the door. "No, no, I cannot stay! I cannot! How could I live here, without Aunt Emily or anyone to help me or tell me what to do? Why, I am only a child. I could not take care of myself. And I must go to school. I do not want any teachers but Miss Long and my dear Aunt Emily. Oh, I must go home! I must go home!" Then she burst into a flood of tears.

Tears are good to purify the vision. When her eyes were well cleared she could look into the heart of things.

"Poor father! He has lived here all alone ever since my mother's death. He is more alone than anybody else would be. He scarcely ever speaks to anyone. How terrible it must be to be so alone! And I am his daughter, his only child; there is no one else that I know of in the whole world who is anything to him; and he wants me, he wants me to stay! It is different with me. I have Uncle Philip and Aunt Emily and Mabel and Ruby and Aunt Sarah, besides some who are no kin to me. But father has none, not one, but me; and I — I want to go home!" She buried her swollen face in the velvet cushion.

After awhile she sat up. "I will write to

Aunt Emily. I will write now; she will tell me what to do. Or, suppose I write to Aunt Sarah?"

Aunt Sarah did not like her to be here; she knew that very well. There was a note of uneasiness in all her letters, and there were constant reminders that the world was spread with snares for youthful feet and that there was need of unceasing watchfulness and prayer. Marian understood.

Yes, she would write to Aunt Sarah. She got paper and pen, but her hand was shaking.

"I will come and stay with father when I am grown," she kept saying, as if explaining to someone. "I think it will be better. I do not know anything to do for him now, but then I will. I will try to learn a great deal. Aunt Emily will teach me, and then —"

And then if he should not be here?

She took up the pen again and tried to write, but threw it down. There was a Counsellor nearer than Aunt Sarah. She kneeled down before the chair.

"I will not shut the door; come in and let me hear but Thy voice, dear Lord," she said.

---

## CHAPTER XXXII.

### THE NEW MINISTER.

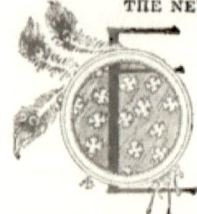

VERYBODY was alive about the new minister. Dr. Caruthers, who had ministered to the Greenville church for a quarter of a century, had not been requested to retire to promote the prosperity of Zion, neither was he pensioned as a compensation for holding his peace. But the good doctor felt the weaknesses of increasing age, and, wishing to write a commentary upon the Prophecies of Jeremiah, begged that the church would relieve him and call a younger man, fitted by his strength of body, as well as spirit, to fulfill the obligations resting upon him.

Mr. Elder, the new minister, was taken into the Vane household. He did not like boarding-house life. It was at Ruby's suggestion that he was given Aunt Sarah's room. "I think Aunt Sarah would like a minister in her room, mother," he said.

Mr. Elder was pleased with his room, the more when Ruby told him some of its history. He bestowed his goods there, and in the one across the hall which was to be his study, and then made himself at home all over the house. He was cheery and had for every one the good word that doeth good like a medicine.

Ruby talked with the minister a great deal; told him about the town, about the church, about his friends, especially Sim and Nan.

Ruby wrote to Aunt Sarah about the changes and said he liked the new minister and liked his sermons, too; they were just like every-day talking. "But I suppose I'll always love Dr. Caruthers best, for he brought me up, you see. I think Dr. Caruthers is a great man, Aunt Sarah."

Mr. Elder was not long in finding out Sim and Nan for himself. He visited them in their own home. Poor children! It was a sad time they had trying to make that home better, and they needed all the help there was. The father was dead and the family's support was upon them. Sim was making good his word to Mr. Vane. Nan was in a small shop.

Indeed, Mr. Elder found out everybody. The ranks of the Sunday-school were swelling, the congregations were increasing.

Mrs. Wyman was delighted. She cornered the minister on every occasion and had ever a new scheme; and the minister always listened politely and generally did some other way.

But Mrs. Wyman was delighted. "We're going to get out of Dr. Caruthers' ruts," she said.

Old Dr. Crews, creeping on to eighty, a retired physician, the pillar of the church who, in spite of professional duties, had seldom missed a sermon in fifty years, who had been loath to give up Dr. Caruthers — for what does a young man know? — listened for four Sabbaths, then he went to see the minister.

"You are drawing crowds, young man, but — beware of popularity. These people come with itching ears. I fear you try to tickle them. You have not yet told them of their souls' danger."

"Dr. Crews," Mr. Elder replied. "I am a young man, and value your advice. I know there are many times when we must speak not only of righteousness, but of judgment. But Jesus opened his ministry by saying, 'The Spirit of the Lord is upon me, because he hath anointed me to preach the gospel to the poor; he hath sent me to heal the broken-hearted, to preach deliverance to the captives, and recovering of sight to the blind, to set at liberty them that are bruised.' When I was a little boy and my mother read that to me, I said, 'Mother, if God calls me to preach I want to begin as Jesus did, and preach the good news to the poor and deliverance to the captives.' I hope you will come to see me often, Dr. Crews," the minister said, handing the old gentleman his hat as he rose to go.

On his way home Dr. Crews met Dr. Caruthers. "I think the young minister will be acceptable to the congregation in time," he said; "he is conversant with Scripture and willing to take advice."

Mabel liked the new minister very much. "I can understand every word in his sermons," she wrote to Marian. She liked to talk with him, too; he never seemed tired of listening, and nothing was too small for his sympathy. Sometimes she forgot she was not talking to Marian. Then she would tell him so, and tell him about her cousin who was like her twin sister, but who had gone to live with her father in that great, gloomy house.

One Sunday afternoon Mr. Elder went with Mabel to the Sunday-school in Father Paul's cottage. Mrs. Wyman said the cottage ought to be kept sacred and had rented it; the idea of the Sunday-school came later. A small organ was placed there, and Mabel was teaching the children to sing.

Late that Sabbath evening Mr. Elder found Mabel in the study, sitting by the window.

"Don't you think the children sing sweetly, Mr. Elder?" she asked.

"Yes."

"And didn't you think it was nice, and that they are learning a great deal?"

"You mean didn't I think you and Mrs. Wyman are doing a great work?"

Mabel flushed and dropped her head. "I didn't say that, Mr. Elder."

"No, I know it. Mabel, do you ever think what wisdom one needs to teach?"

"Why, Mr. Elder, I am not wise, I know, but I thought I might teach those little children something; they are so ignorant."

"And so need the wisest teaching. If they all had mothers and fathers taught of God, there would be little need of you and Mrs. Wyman or any of us; but because they know so little, they need most careful guidance.

To-day I talked to your class while you were consulting with Mrs. Wyman about the hymns. I asked, 'Can any of you tell me about Jesus?' But they did not seem to know much about him."

"But, Mr. Elder, they haven't been studying long, they haven't gone far in the catechism; if you had asked them some questions they've been over, you would have seen what they really know." And Mabel looked as if this were not fair.

Mr. Elder seemed not to notice. "Mabel," he said, "Jesus is the first and last. He is the one your children should know about. It will not matter very much if these little ones never know in how many days God created the heavens and the earth, or what was created on the first day and what on the second and the sixth; nor if they never know who was the strongest man, or the meekest, or the wisest, or who was swallowed by the whale; but it will matter very much indeed if they do not begin now to learn and keep in mind, from day to day, who it is that not only created them, but so loves them that he gave himself for them."

"Oh, Mr. Elder, I must not teach any more; I do not know enough, I am not good enough. I told Mrs. Wyman so, but she said it would be so lovely, and insisted that I should come and help them to sing anyway, and then she wanted me to teach the catechism, too. You think I ought to give it up, don't you, Mr. Elder?"

"No, Mabel. If there is a spark of love for Jesus in your heart you are able to tell of it, and that spark makes you wiser than the wisest teacher who has it not. No, I would not back down, nor would I shed tears and think meanly of myself. But now I would get up and go down to tea, for the bell is ringing."

---

## CHAPTER XXXIII.

### AT HOME AND ABROAD.

MABEL grew up tall and fair, but too delicate. Dr. Matthews said she must stop school for a while and take exercise. She did all they told her, but to little purpose. That dread disease which no one who fears its approach wishes to name, had carried off more than one of Mrs. Vane's family, and the mother's heart sank as she saw one sign after another developing in her child. They took her to the mountains, to the seashore, and brought her back with a tan on her fair skin and a hacking cough.

Mr. Vane had a consultation of physicians; they said she should travel  cross the ocean.

It was hard for Mrs. Vane, almost an invalid herself, to start out upon a trip like that, but at last everything was arranged; the whole family would go for a year at least. Mr. Vane had no fears about leaving his business affairs. Mr. Owen could attend to everything as well as he himself, and Sim was every day making good his word.

About that time Mrs. Wyman got into her carriage and drove hither and thither. The banker's wife was on fire. It was the thing now for a minister to travel; she had heard say that no theological course was complete without a journey through the Holy Land. "It gives one such a name, and Greenville is growing and our church should not be behind. Then think of the lectures we should have, a series in Mr. Elder's fascinating style, and everybody would flock to hear." She would head the list with a hundred dollars.

It was not a hard matter to get others to follow the fashion thus set, and a few days later a committee of ladies, Mrs. Wyman chairman, knocked at the door of the minister's study. Mr. Elder could hardly believe it; he was surprised into speechlessness.

When he recovered he tried to thank them. But how could he spare the time for this journey? And who would serve the church in his absence?

Oh, they would miss him, but there was Dr. Caruthers, and neighboring ministers would come in. Mr. Elder must go for his own sake and theirs.

When the rustle of the committee's garments had died upon the stairs, the minister leaned upon the half-made sermon and wondered if he had not dreamed; but no, there on the floor was a red rose which Mrs. Wyman had worn, and dropped as she assured him it was his duty to go. Was he then to stand where Moses had stood? Was he to walk in the earthly footprints of his Lord, to pluck the rose of Sharon, to hear the plash of the waves along the shore of blue Galilee?

That afternoon the young minister heard Dr. Crews' step upon the stair.

"I suppose," said the old gentleman when he had seated himself, resting his hands upon the head of his cane, "that you will go in a straight course for Jerusalem."

"I expect to travel with Mr. Vane's family through France and Switzerland," said Mr. Elder. "Then I will leave them in Italy and sail for Palestine."

"Young man, you are a minister of the gospel, and I hope you will not visit that godless city, Paris, or waste your precious time sightseeing, like any worldling. The Holy Land is the place for you."

"Dr. Crews," said the young man as if he were speaking to his father, "to me every land is holy where the footprints of its Creator are seen, and everything holy which bears the mark of his hand."

In November letters bearing foreign postmarks came to Glenwood, and were brought upstairs to Marian sitting, as three years ago, in her father's room. Had the home people seen her they might have thought that she also needed the salt sea air. They had not forgotten her. When their plans were made they had each one written, begging her to join them. Uncle Philip had inclosed a letter to her father; this she read, but did not deliver. Her father was feebler and, if that were possible, more melancholy. Marian had planned more than once to visit them all, but the right time had never come.

Though he sat silent, still she knew that if she were sick and kept from him but a day, or if she were hindered and was not in her place at the usual time, her father missed her. Yet this was the chance of a lifetime. Once she had thought of consulting Mr. Waring. Mr. Waring had been her tutor ever since her father's house became her home. He told her a great deal of his own travels. "'Home-keeping youth have ever homely wits,'" he would say. "We need to stretch ourselves by seeing the bigness of the world."

But Mr. Waring was so much interested in her improvement that he might seek to overrule her objections entirely, and his arguments were so clear and strong that she had never been able to resist them. He might at least make it hard for her to do what was right. She must stay with her father.

For Marian did not sit in silence in the long room. She had received the best reward of well-doing, which is higher service. One day the scientist laid down his book and sighed. His daughter had never heard anything like that from his lips. She watched him awhile as he sat with closed eyes.

"Father, does it hurt you to read?" she asked.

"Yes, my eyes, and here;" laying his hand upon his chest.

"Father —" Marian began, and stopped.

He opened his eyes.

"Might — I mean, I would be glad to read aloud, if you like."

He looked at her a moment, then handed her the book, naming the page. Marian summoned all her courage to the task. She did not understand much of what she read; some words were new to her and she stumbled over them. But her father did not seem to mind; sometimes he corrected her, sometimes said nothing.

When she had read an hour he reached his hand for the book, and when she came the next day he handed it to her opened at the right place. Every day it was the same, and Marian felt that she had not waited in vain.

Mr. Waring was usually at his table, and at first Marian was afraid her reading disturbed him, for she often found him looking at her. But he said no, he never heard unless she wished.

Sunday came, and Marian awoke asking herself, "What shall I do to-day?" Should she go as on other days and read the books which, though they had little meaning for her, were not Sabbath reading? Should she stay away? She had never stayed away on Sundays, but had sat her time out with empty hands.

Then a bold spirit seized her. She took the Bible, Aunt Sarah's gift, and went to her father's room. Without waiting for the book to be placed in her hands, she began:

"Father, I always read this on Sundays; may I read it to you?"

"Sundays?" But he made no objection.

Where should she read? She had been learning the 103d Psalm, and turned to that.

"Bless the Lord, O my soul; and all that is within me, bless his holy name. Bless the Lord, O my soul, and forget not all his benefits; who forgiveth all thine iniquities; who healeth all thy diseases." And on to "Like as a father pitieth his children, so the Lord pitieth them that fear him."

Marian read on, psalm after psalm, and when she closed the book her father reached his hand for it.

"Where did you get that?" he asked.

Marian started. Was he displeased?

"Aunt Sarah gave it to me," she said.

He examined the title page, turned the leaves slowly, stopping now and then as if to read a few lines, then closed the book and handed it to her.

The next Sunday Marian, with new boldness, opened her Bible without apology. She chose the Sermon on the Mount this time. And every Sabbath morning it was so. Marian read aloud from the Scriptures, sometimes selecting beforehand the place, sometimes reading where her eye fell first.

Mr. Waring spent his Sundays in town, but one Saturday evening it was raining, so he remained. The rain continued next morning. Mr. Waring was in the library when Marian went up to her father's room, and she found herself hoping he would stay there.

But he did not. She was reading a series of miracles — Jesus stilling the tempest, casting out the legion of devils, healing the woman who touched his garment, and raising the ruler's daughter. If Mr. Waring knew that she was reading any other than the usual volume he made no sign.

"And he put them all out, and took her by the hand, and called, saying, Maid, arise. And her spirit came again, and she arose straightway; and he commanded to give her meat. And her parents were astonished; but he charged them that they should tell no man what was done."

Marian closed the book, and, raising her eyes, found Mr. Waring's fixed upon her. She flushed and dropped her own, for there was something in his face which was not contempt, but a certain pity very near akin to it. It was such a look as she might have bestowed upon a poor, ignorant, little Chinese girl, born and bred in superstition, burning incense at the shrine of her grandfather, and believing with her whole soul in the efficacy of the offering.

There was to Marian more in that look than many of us can understand. Mr. Waring was her teacher, and an inspiring one. Her studies were a delight. Every day his strong hand opened up some new and higher path and she pressed on, wondering. He did not delve, like her father, in the bowels of the earth; the stars were his study. Marian did not think he was a religious man, though he had never spoken a word against her faith. Yet she had not expected this.

What did her father and Mr. Waring believe, anyway? Did they think there was no God, no Christ? Were the wonderful stories of the Bible fables to them? Did they never think of anything beyond this life? Of heaven? What was the good of living, if they were right? Everybody must die and everything come to an end sometime; that is, everybody and everything would be lost — lost! It were better not to have lived at all if we must be lost! And what if they were right? How could she know the Bible was true? Her father, was very learned; he went to the root of things. And Mr. Waring — he was learned, too, and always looked things squarely in the face and reasoned. Could his logic be so clear and strong on all points but one?

All this brought to Marian's young face a thoughtfulness that deepened into a shadow. It was partly her lonely heart crying for sympathy, partly the agreement with Mabel that made her ad her Bible daily.

Marian was plunging through these deep waters when the party left for Europe. She felt as if an anchor had slipped away.

The letters from abroad were very sweet, but far apart. Mabel wrote of the strange places and people she saw, wishing on every page that Marian was there, and breaking out between times with, " Mr. Elder." " Mr. Elder." — how strong he was and how good; how he helped her up the mountains and rowed her upon the lakes. How he made her feel all the time that God was everywhere.

And Ruby? He made himself at home with everybody, just as he always did. The ladies called him "cute," though he was such a large boy now, and the gentlemen liked to talk with him. The peasants at work in the fields and vineyards knew him, and he liked to go with them and help bind wheat and gather the grapes.

" People are just people everywhere, mother." he said one day. " I used to think that when we came across the ocean, everybody would be strange. But then, all the world is one big house, and God is the Father."

## CHAPTER XXXIV.

### NEW EXPERIENCES

IN a year Mr. Elder and Ruby returned. Mr. Vane was advised to keep Mabel longer abroad. In January Ruby was to enter college.

New Year's day was crisp and clear, and Ruby's spirits were high enough as he descended the steps of the omnibus and entered the college campus. But when he entered the room that the porter showed him, and found a group of loud fellows, he felt, which was unusual for him, strange. They greeted him kindly enough, but he had little to say, and was glad when they scattered.

One remained, a tall young fellow, who sat with his heels upon the mantel. He was smoking a cigarette; giving a long puff, he turned toward Ruby.

" What name, eh?"

" Ruby Vane."

The youth shrugged his shoulders, nodded knowingly, and puffed again.

" I'd advise you to give your surname only when a fellow asks the honor of an introduction."

" Why?"

" Well, it's the custom in college for a man to be called by his surname, and — well, if he's got a girl's name he'd best not mention it. I'm an old fellow here, you see, and you're — just from home. You won't mind a little advice from your room-mate."

" I'm willing to be called by my surname," said Ruby, " but you don't call Reuben a girl's name, do you?"

" Oh, well, Reuben; but you said Ruby."

" That's what everybody calls me, and I never thought of saying anything else."

" You saw that tall fellow, with light blue eyes, who was singing when you came in; that's Thomas, and he can run things high, I tell you. So you'll do well not to say anything about what everybody calls you."

Ruby was glad that the porter came in then with his trunk. He busied himself with opening it and finding places for his books and other things. His room-mate puffed awhile in silence, watching proceedings, then he gathered himself together, yawned, stretched, and whistling " Yankee Doodle," took himself out.

Ruby was relieved to be left alone. He was thoroughly homesick by this time and thoroughly disappointed with his new surroundings. Were all the college boys like this? If so, whom should he talk to? He could do without going to college, but he couldn't do without father and mother. Mother! How could he keep the tears back! Yet he must, for his room-mate might be in at any moment, and the others, and Thomas; and besides, he must be a man. Thomas could " run things high." Ruby didn't understand exactly, but thought it would not be pleasant to be run high.

Ruby thought he knew what it was to be away from home, but found how little he really had known about it, when the supper bell rang, and, mingling with the crowd, he entered the long, low, basement dining-room and took a seat at the end of one of the tables. It was a confusion of tongues all around. Everybody seemed in good spirits except himself, but there was no one to talk to him or care that he could not eat. Thomas, on his left, was the center of a group discussing base-ball, and on his right was a sallow-faced young man arguing with a mild-eyed one on the comparative merits of Demosthenes and Cicero.

But Ruby knew it would not do to give up to this. He tried to talk to Carter, his room-mate, that night, and succeeded better than he hoped, and the next day went to work. And work is the best thing in this whole world to make us forget that we are homesick and lonely.

He joined the base-ball team, and Carter, who had shied off from him a little at first, grew quite proud of the "kid," — for Thomas, seeing his first play, slapped him on the back and said he "would do." And after a time Ruby, though he had never realized that his ruddy face and soft curls and serious eyes and gentle ways, together with the name by which everybody called him, combined dangerously to make him a target for the wit of the schoolmen, came more in sympathy with his mates, and reproached himself that he had at first thought them so little worth cultivating. Not that he admired all they did or agreed with all they said. In fact, he never hesitated to differ when occasion required, nor to put in a word for the right when he saw it abused; but so straightforward was he, and so fearless, and so free from conceit, that nobody thought of getting angry. Often they referred to him matters which had caused dispute. "He's such a long-headed little chap," said Thomas; "he thinks more in a minute than Hollis does in a year." Hollis was the honor-man, who studied till the cobwebs grew across his eyes. (That is the way they told it to me.)

## CHAPTER XXXV.

### COLLEGE LIFE: THOMAS: CARTER.

ONE night Carter wriggled, puffed and looked at Ruby by turns; he had something to say. But Ruby, who was reading, did not notice.

"I say, Ruby," — Thomas had introduced the name, so it was the thing — "I say, Bible-reading and saying prayers is all right, but it strikes me it would be better to have all that to yourself, when there are no fellows about."

"I would much rather be alone, Carter," said Ruby, earnestly and quietly; "but I cannot leave it off, and when the others come in there is no help for it."

"Couldn't you sit up till they're gone?"

"No, I promised mother to go to bed before eleven."

Carter ran his fingers through his hair, making it stand upright. He suggested that in bed was as good a place as any to say your prayers, and was about to cite his own experience, but, remembering that he had long since ceased the under-cover exercise, concluded that that experience might not prove anything to this young lad who had a way of searching out all things.

Ruby did not say anything. He was thinking. Once when he was a "little fellow," Aunt Sarah read to him the story of Daniel. When she finished he asked, "But Aunt Sarah, couldn't Daniel have prayed just as well with his window shut?" He could see now the bright look in her eyes. "Well, if Daniel had shut his window then, when every time before he had opened it, what would you say about him?" "That he was afraid."

So Ruby went on his own way, and Carter, though he squirmed over it, was loyal to his mate, and, when he saw that Thomas never even smiled, took courage. He grew so bold at length as to show the door to a certain one of the baser sort who, as Ruby knelt one night, broke out loudly and mockingly with, "Now I lay me down to sleep," set to a tune whose associations made this use of it seem even to Carter blasphemous. There were a half-dozen in the room, but only one attempted to laugh at the great jest, prepared beforehand, and he soon slunk out after his ally.

That was the last of it. Daniel had conquered.

Ruby spent the summer vacation partly at Glenwood, partly at home with Mr. Elder.

To Marian it was a continual feast to have Ruby with her. Prof. Rede did not take walks in the woods now, and he said little, but Ruby spent hours every day in the long room, and the weary scientist always laid aside his book, or whatever occupied him, and listened.

Tabby couldn't get over it that "dat little honey chile" was "growed mos' a man," while Pete couldn't get through blacking "Marse Rube's" shoes and "toting" water and saddling Cut, for the college youth was as fond of a gallop as the "little un" had been, and he didn't have to ride "double."

Mrs. Green was as glad as anybody, if she didn't say so, and made quantities of cookies, which were devoured straightway, sometimes with apologies — nobody else made cookies like these. But Mrs. Green never tired making them and asserted that she was glad he was "hearty."

Ruby stole into the library often when Mr. Waring and Marian were at their studies. He thought he had never heard anybody make things plain like Mr. Waring, and sometimes asked questions.

Mr. Waring taught little out of books. One night, when he had been pointing out some of the constellations and telling of the great number of the heavenly bodies and of the appearance and journeys of the planets, Ruby said:

"It is wonderful; it seems to me God is sitting at the center, watching and keeping all the worlds right. You make things so real, Mr. Waring."

It was one night in the fall term that Thomas came in and found Ruby alone by the fireside. Carter had been restless since the vacation; declared that he had had enough of school, wanted to go into business, wanted to travel, wanted to settle down on his "estate,"—here he would give a long puff and watch the smoke curl above his head, meanwhile placing his heels higher upon the mantel-piece — wanted to see the world; in short, wanted no restraint. He was out every night and often crept in long after Ruby had closed his eyes. Sometimes he would be sick in the mornings, pale and unsteady, and Ruby was solicitous and wished to consult the president or matron; but to this Carter objected so seriously, urging that he would be all right directly, and begging Ruby, as "a good fellow now," not to mention it, that Ruby gave in, and, as Carter usually did rally before noon, and seldom was too far gone for the class-room, Ruby concluded that it was only loss of sleep, and advised Carter to that effect. But his room-mate laughed and sometimes patted him on the back patronizingly. "There are more things in this world than are dreamed of in your philosophy, Ruby, my dear."

Which was the only attempt at classical quotation that young Sophomore ever made, and at which he seemed mightily pleased with himself.

"The fellows" did not frequent the room as formerly, which was a relief to Ruby; and yet he was sorry, when he thought that Carter might be where he ought not.

Ruby was thinking of these things when Thomas came in. Thomas sat down and was silent for some minutes, his head resting between his hands. Ruby read on and said nothing either, for he and Thomas saw much of each other and stood on no ceremony.

At length Thomas raised his head suddenly, "I wished I roomed with you, old fellow."

"Why, Thomas?" Then, fearing he had been abrupt, "I'd like it, too, you know, only Carter and I have always been together, and he's been very good to me."

Thomas kicked the fire-irons, and Ruby, who understood people pretty well, waited for what he had to say.

"Now, if I roomed with you, I could be a different fellow, I think." He glanced at the open Bible, "Do you know what my mother cut me out to be? Why, a preacher! Her father was one, and she started with me from the first. And I took to it, too; you needn't pretend you're not surprised— you know I haven't got a thimbleful of religion. But when I was at home I used to like things that I never think of now, Ruby; and I'm — a member of the church." Thomas sat and rested his face between his hands again, gazing into the fire, "I don't play the hypocrite, though, any more than I can help. I asked Mr. Bland, the pastor at home, to take my name off the book, and it isn't my fault that he wouldn't. I don't go to the com — I mean I don't make any pretensions, you understand. But sometimes I wish it was all different; I wish I had never come to college, but had staid at home and grown up with my mamma, a good little boy, and had been a minister to point to brighter worlds and lead the way."

At this picture of himself, Thomas ended with a laugh; but it was not hearty, and soon died away.

"Serious, I never think of being a preacher now, but I'd like to be a better fellow." He looked again at the open Bible. "I used to do all that, when I came here, and thought I would be a sort of evangelist and turn every fellow's mind to religion in a month by my good example. But I didn't keep it up long; this house wasn't built upon a rock, so it didn't take much of a flood to smash it. I thought I could say my prayers under the covers just as well, and read the Bible on the sly. But you know that won't do. It's show your colors, or nothing. If I roomed with you, now, I think I might get a sort of footing again. I'm not hankering

Then he looked at Ruby awhile.

"But there's nothing long-faced about you, though you're not noisy and noise doesn't count; and you go into what we do, pretty much. You're the third best player on the ground. Your religion doesn't keep you from enjoying yourself; it only keeps you out of messes. Well, how is it, anyway? They used to tell me that as I professed being a

"IT'S ALL UP WITH ME, RUBY," CARTER SAID.—SEE PAGE 76.

to be a saint, only—I'd like to be a better fellow. It's all right for you to do these things; but I—I couldn't plunge right into it; it would be—well, noticed so. And then, if I'm religious at all, I must be consistent. I've no use for half-way folks. I must take religion everywhere with me, and give up some things that I own I like mighty well. I don't believe I could do that, and be happy."

Christian, I must be always on my guard and steer clear of temptation, and give up so-and-so and so-and-so. Then when I came here I found I liked so-and-so so well that I let religion go by. But there! I'm going to bed. I'm trespassing — I know your rule."

Ruby smiled. "Never mind the rule to-night, Thomas; this can be the exception. I can't talk to you as some people could about it, but I'll tell you what mother said once when Mabel — that's my sister — asked her if it was right for Christians to play games and have pleasure like other people. Dr. Caruthers had preached that day about doing all things for the glory of God. Mother asked if we ever felt happier and kinder after our romps and games. I said I always did, I thought. Mabel said she did, except when someone didn't do right and fair. 'But when none of you are selfish or unfair do your plays make you feel happier?' 'Yes,' we both said. 'Then remember,' said mother, 'this that a great man has said: "Whatever makes you happier, makes you better." '"

But this was bringing up a home-scene too vividly for the hour of the night, and Ruby felt himself weakening; and when Thomas said heartily, "No wonder you're a good fellow: I wish I could see your mother," he replied:

"I wish so, too." After which ambiguous sentence he laid his face upon the open book.

Carter did not come in at all one night. Twice Ruby woke, and, hearing nothing, looked over to the bed by the window. The moon was shining upon it; it was untouched. Just as Ruby rose, his room-mate came in, very pale in the rosy light, and with dark rings under wild-looking eyes. He was not in a mood to be spoken to, and went to bed without taking off his clothes. Yet Ruby was sure he was not sleeping, though he never moved, not even when the breakfast bell clanged outside. He was still there, and with the cover over his head, when Ruby returned. Nothing passed between them, and Ruby saw him no more that day. He was not at roll-call, nor in the class-room, nor at dinner, nor on the campus in the afternoon.

But after supper Ruby went up and found him before the fire, leaning upon the table, his face downward. Ruby sat down quietly to his books, but his mind was not on them, and every now and then he looked across the table to the figure that did not move. He felt very sorry, but asked no questions.

After a long time Carter raised his head and showed a face that was quite pitiful, with signs of tears upon it.

"Well, it's all up with me, Ruby," he said, trying to speak clearly, but with no attempt at bravado. "All up. They've dismissed me and written to my father. I'm to go to morrow."

"Carter!"

"You're such an innocent, Ruby!" said the youth, running his fingers through his hair. "Here I've been acting like the mischief all fall — I was tamer last term, though there was many a time that I played my tricks in the dark — and if you ever suspicioned a thing I didn't know it. The fellows in my set wanted me to change quarters and go over and room with them, and if you'd ever been uppish and preachy as they thought you were, I'd have gone; and maybe you'd have liked it better, for I'm no companion for you. But somehow, after I found you out, it did me a power of good to find you here every time I came in, and it made me homesick to think of sleeping in that mess over yonder, as much as I liked to stay there — worse luck!

"Well, it's no use for me to tell you the whole of it; it's not a pretty tale, but the end of it is — I'm up. And I knew it was coming, and I blame nobody — nobody but myself, and I've got no excuse to make except that I'm a born fool."

He kicked over the chair upon which his feet had been — they had not aspired to the mantel-piece to-night — and stared gloomily into the fire.

Guileless as Ruby was, he had not been without his suspicions, which grew more and more serious as Carter's retiring hour became later and later, his headaches more frequent and severe, his class-room record marking zero except when some unusual luck came his way. Ruby had trembled many a time as to the ending.

But his heart was full of pity that his room-mate was brought to disgrace, and visions were tumbling through his brain all the time Carter was talking, of himself rushing at once to the president, of calling together the professors, the trustees, and, if they remained obdurate, of seeking the president's wife, who, though in appearance cold and distant, could not fail to be moved by Carter's genuine repentance, and would surely intercede in behalf of the erring youth, whose motherless estate, of which they might be ignorant, would awaken sympathy. It was not usual for Ruby to think in a jumble like that.

But Carter only shook his head mournfully when he heard the outline of the plans.

"Sit down, Ruby. That would do no good. Now listen: This is the third time I've been up, and every time it was for worse doings. My father had to come and get me out of the second mess, and he wouldn't ask a pennyworth of patience for me now; the last was such a bad case, and he was so outdone himself he promised them that if they'd try me once more he'd never ask them to stave off again. I was on trial, you see, and had had experience enough, which they say is the only thing a fool can learn by. But I'm such a fool I couldn't even learn by that.

"And I'm to go to-morrow," the wretched lad continued, after awhile. "And go to what? It's not the expelling that's so hard on me, though that is bad enough, but it's going home and taking what I'll have to take there. For father'll be so mad he won't give me a penny, so that I'd as well be in prison, and the Madame will not lose her chance of looting me and making me a toss-ball for the crowd of them. I tell you, you don't know what it is to be brought up as I've been. I've never had a mother or sister or anybody to look after me or care what I did. And people never thought it, I know, but I always wanted somebody, and many a night when I was a little chap I've cried myself to sleep under the cover, because nobody told me good-night or tucked me in bed. My aunt, who lived with us then, took good care of me, people said—and switched me for everything I did and didn't do, but seldom said a good, kind word to me, as I remember; and father, he was in and out all the time and never noticed me if I kept out of his way.

"Then they told me he was going to bring a wife home and she'd be my mother, and some of them laughed and said I'd catch it. But I was glad. I made up my mind to be a good fellow—I was eight or nine. I thought any sort of a mother would be something.

"And she was so good to me! She kissed and hugged me, and called me her darling boy, and put me to bed, and gave me everything I wanted. And that lasted till—she found out."

"Found out what, Carter?"

"That she was poor and I was rich; that I was master of the house." He laughed harshly.

Ruby wondered.

"You see, it was this way. My father passed for a rich man; and so he had been, but somehow got swamped in debt. I had money from my mother, and my uncle was the trustee. My father got it to pay off, but had to mortgage to my uncle, for me, the plantation. Of course he couldn't redeem it

—he never can—and when I'm of age it will all be mine. Well, when she found out, she shook me off like a wet spaniel. I was a child, I didn't know anything about it; I didn't know why she hated me and dogged me till I wished for my old aunt again, and wished I could run away; and I did run away from breakfast to dinner and dinner to supper, with the little darkeys. I didn't care where I went so I got away from her.

"She has four children, all girls, now, and I loved them every one. I stood by the cradle of the first one and wanted to kiss it, but she started up—she had been asleep—and cried out, 'Take that—that—boy away! Don't let him touch my baby.' I don't doubt I was dirty and ragged and looked like a little ruffian, but whose fault was that?

"I used to play with them when they were little, and she was not there to see; and they loved me, too. When she found out they loved me she hated me more and tried to turn them against me. Then she had my father send me away to school. She would tell them all sorts of things, so when I came back for vacation, which wasn't often, they had forgotten all about me except that I was a bad, wicked boy that they must not play with.

"Well, I came here three years ago, and had a good enough time, except those two times when they ran up on me. I didn't do much rising in my classes, and caught it from my father for that, but I've managed along very well. Just before Christmas last year was my last case, so I slacked up and was on good behavior when you came. But of course that couldn't last; I had to lapse back sometime. But I might have kept up appearances, anyway, till I was of age—just two years; but here it is—I'm done for, and you don't know, and nobody else knows, the life I'll lead those two years." Carter laid down his head again and sobbed like a child.

Ruby's heart was full of pity. Such a revelation as this, of Carter's own heart, of his unhappy childhood, was amazing to him. Truly, there were some things in this world that had not been dreamed of in his philosophy. He thought of his own home, of his own mother and father, and wondered how such things could be.

At dawn Carter left. He did not wish to face his old chums or anyone. He leaned over Ruby and shook him lightly. Ruby rubbed his eyes and sprang up.

Carter grasped his hand. "Good-by, old chap! You won't forget me?"

"Oh, Carter! Oh, Carter!" Ruby wanted to say so much, but knew not how. "I wish you had a happy home like mine!" and the tears rose in his eyes.

But Carter's season of weeping was over. "There, there, go back to sleep, little fellow! Good-by!" he cried, quite merrily, and fled.

---

## CHAPTER XXXVI.

### THE KEY.

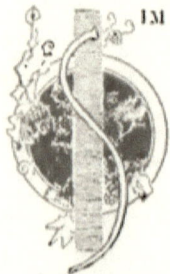

SIM was the last to leave the store, as usual, for Mr. Owen had been suffering with rheumatism since the cold weather began, and Sim was second in command, as he proudly said laughingly, and proudly, too, to Nan. Mr. Owen was driven round every day that it was possible for him to venture out, for his responsibilities in Mr. Vane's absence weighed heavily upon him. Overwrought nerves from illness, coupled with a not trustful nature, made him wary, suspicious of the under-clerks, and especially of Sim. He had never approved of Sim Larkins, knowing the stock, yet if Mr. Vane chose to promote him and trust him, he could do nothing—but watch! And if there is one thing above another that a youth is quick to detect, that he feels before he sees, it is that watching eye; and if there is one thing above another that he resents, it is that same eye. An evil brood of thoughts naturally hatches in a hot-bed of suspicion; that is an old story.

Mr. Owen had been unusually severe, even unjust, that day. Sim was thinking over these things as he securely fastened doors and windows; thinking how hardly life had gone with him since Mr. Vane left; thinking moodily.

The front of the store was locked and bolted first, then the back. When all was done he went out, as was his custom, through Mr. Vane's office, which was at the rear, but opened on the side a few yards from the street. Sim lingered a moment, turning the key slowly, and started when a fellow-clerk, who had been home and got his supper, called out from the front street,

"Hullo, there, Larkins! You're slow to-night!"

He answered surlily that he was minding his own business; at which the young fellow thrust his hands into his pockets, faced about, said he couldn't see as that was anything to fire up about, and went his way.

Sim drew his soft hat down until it almost covered his face, and walked slowly. He had the appearance of a man with something on his mind, but no one regarded him, for there were few abroad that cold December night, and the street-lamps that lighted the little city were not brilliant. He still held the office key in his hand, fumbling with it and thinking of Mr. Owen's words, and of his look which said more, when, at the beginning of his illness, he had given Sim the key to keep. "You could bring it to my house after closing up, but I prefer that you be responsible." If Mr. Vane had given him the key to keep, it would have been an honor borne proudly; but from Mr. Owen, with that insinuation of voice and eye, it was a grievous burden. It meant: "If anyone—anyone, no matter who—should enter the store before daybreak, you know where suspicion will rest."

So Sim had carried the key for four months. He was so absorbed to-night that he collided at the street corner, where it was dark, with a slim young man carrying a cane. Sim started, and for a moment forgot his sullenness when he saw who it was. He remembered vividly how he had collided with this same person, at the same corner, one morning at sunrise, nearly six years ago.

But the meeting with George McPhail, when the first shock was over, only served to deepen Sim's discontent and sullenness, for he despised his weakness as much as in their school days, and to-night he chose to compare himself and his hard life with this elegant young man about town, who had nothing to do but draw money and twirl his cane and be driven behind fast horses. The young heir was much admired by people generally, and petted by the ladies, but he never appeared to be quite easy about the collar, and always seemed undecided on reaching a street corner whether to go up or down.

"Oh, I say, Sim, is that you?" he cried, when he had recovered breath and position. "Wait! I'm going that way."

"I thought you were going up," said Sim shortly, drawing his hat down closer.

"I was — but — it wasn't anything important; I would rather walk with you."

Sim wished George had kept on his first course and chosen more cheerful company. For a time both walked in silence, then George ventured:

"You're doing well now, Sim, I hear."

His companion growled something, then stopped short as if struck a blow, gave a quick exclamation, and ran back.

George stopped, too, but did not follow; he was afraid of Sim in this mood. But he watched, and saw Sim, when he reached the corner where they had crashed, stoop, looking closely upon the ground and feeling about. Presently he came back, and did not seem pleased that George was waiting, yet the latter saw by the dim light a look of intense relief on his face. Later he saw in Sim's right hand a big brass key. George was not smart, as the saying goes, yet he thought it would be as well not to ask Sim if it was the key he had run back to search for.

At length George took up the thread again. "As I was saying, I think you're a lucky fellow to get into such a position with good wages and—and—to be so—trusted." He glanced at the key.

Sim pretended not to notice.

"Now, I know what you're thinking. You think because I dress and have no work to do and go into society, that I'm the lucky fellow. But there's just the trouble of it. I must dress and drive and spend money in a thousand ways that you can't imagine, and —I haven't got the money."

Sim was roused out of himself into genuine surprise.

"Oh, you think I'm rich and could get all I want, but you don't know. You see, it was my aunt that managed for me, and while she lived I did get enough. She would not allow me to be checked up nor scolded, either; but she's dead now, you know, and it's all different. Father holds a close hand; he gives me so much—why, it wouldn't keep you in clothes, Sim,—and after that I daren't even ask him for a dime. So you see my fix; I'm poorer than the poorest fellow in town who only has to live on his wages, with no calls from society."

Sim knew as much about society as about the planet Jupiter, yet he knew something about the price of clothes such as George wore, and of the cost of hiring the best horses and carriages with a sleek groom to drive. He could not understand at all how

these things were necessary to anyone's existence, yet he could see that giving up some of them might be a source of annoyance to a young man like George McPhail.

"Well, why don't you go to work and make your money to spend?" he answered surlily.

"That's what my father says," and the young man plucked at his collar uneasily. "But what could I do, Sim? If I'd been brought up to it now— But you see, my aunt — why, Sim, I never washed my own feet till she died!"

A most contemptuous grunt from under the soft hat.

"And then, I'm not strong, you know, Sim—anybody can see that. My dear aunt watched me so carefully." He coughed, and it did sound hollow.

But he got no sympathy from Sim.

"Well, I'll tell you—I just could not help it. I've overrun my allowance four hundred dollars!" He dropped his voice to a whisper and cast fearful glances around. "Four hundred, Sim, and what to do about it I don't know. They're pressing me all round, and there's only one thing I could think of doing."

"Well?" Sim showed some interest.

"There's the Rhodes' place. That is mine; it came from my aunt. It's a fine place, everybody says, and I suppose that's the reason father is so close with me. He thinks I ought to manage it and live on the revenue. But he doesn't understand. I'm no farmer, and they impose on me terribly. When they say they haven't made a half crop, for the rain or the drought, I can't press them. And so it goes. But if somebody had it who could manage it would make a tidy sum."

"But I don't see how you're going to sell it now. You're not of age yet," growled Sim.

"I'll be of age in just four months, and I can make a deed of it now that will be all right then. Only, I don't want father to know. I wish I was of age now, then I could get twice the money for it easy enough. I would make you a deed to it if you would get me the money, and you could keep the matter to yourself."

"And you'd sell the place for four hundred dollars?"

"Anything to get out of this scrape now. What good will it be to me? Only, I wouldn't have my father know of it; now that's the reason I don't go to a regular money-lender. I want to get help from somebody who would be a friend—who would keep quiet, you know."

"So you are coming to me for four hundred dollars, are you?" Sim burst into a harsh laugh.

George squirmed, and twisted his long, white fingers together. "You've been working five or six years; haven't you anything deposited?"

Another laugh, harsher and louder. "Oh, piles of it! I have a safe bank for depositing my wages—victuals and clothes—which cost something, as you know."

"But—but—" The wretched young man squirmed again, his long fingers clasped convulsively together around the gold head of his cane, his lips were pallid; he stole a side glance at the brass key shining in Sim's hand. "You are in a position of—influence."

Something like an electric shock passed through Sim from head to foot; it seemed to pass through his soul even, making it quiver. He understood.

A year ago, perhaps even last night, he would have turned upon the coward and spared him not. But— He had met with some things of late that were hard, unjust. And—

Something had happened that evening. Now it came to him like a flash. Mr. Crawford, a young civil engineer, had come in hurriedly just before six o'clock and after Mr. Owen had gone, "I have a sum I want to deposit, Sim. The bank is shaky; I'm afraid to risk those fellows now. I've got a job in New Mexico and will be gone eight months at least. I didn't know till this morning, and must be off now for the train. Just receipt it, will you? I've deposited with Mr. Vane before."

And it lay now in the cash drawer, in the same envelope in which Sim had received it — five hundred dollars. And no one knew!

"Eight months at least." Sim reasoned that he could make some arrangement in that time to pay the money back.

Are we surprised that the evil spirit should return to his house from whence he had gone out, and seek to enter, to pollute again what had been swept and garnished? There are ten thousand avenues of approach for that spirit, and, if we leave one open, he is sure to find it.

The Rhodes' place! The Rhodes' place! Sim had worked faithfully in the store, but never liked the closeness of it. Many a time he had said to Nan, "When I save up enough I'm going to buy a farm and we'll

all settle down; that's the life I hanker after. The Rhodes' place now, with its fine bottom-lands."

Now, if he had four hundred dollars, the Rhodes' place was his!

---

## CHAPTER XXXVII.

### "BUT DELIVER US FROM EVIL."

NAN was worried, for Sim was sullen and silent. He looked sick, too, and pushed away the supper she had prepared and saved so carefully.

His mother was anxious to know what ailed him, but he was short and almost fierce in his commands to be let alone.

Nan knew when to be silent. This was a mood she had never known Sim to be in since that time when remorse was sore upon him, and she felt a strange and unnamed fear. It was not unusual that he should come home out of humor and, sometimes, he was even disagreeable, wishing no questions. Nan understood and asked none, and when she had gone up to her attic room for the night he was almost sure to creep in from his and tell her the whole story. He got her ready sympathy and clear, strong counsel, which had saved him many a time. Sim often wondered how Nan, a young woman, had so much worldly wisdom and was able to take in his troubles, to stand in his shoes, as it were, and at the same time could so firmly counsel patience in the midst of unkindness and even injustice. How little he knew of Nan's daily life!—of the unkindness and injustice that she bore, besides household cares, her mother's complaints, and her younger brother's waywardness. Neither did anybody else know, for Nan was not one to tell.

Nan hoped to hear the whole trouble to-night when they were alone, for the more serious it was the more sure was he to come. So she finished as quickly as possible the week's mending which always awaited her, and went up to her own room. She lighted the little lamp, bright and clean like everything else there, and sat by the table, her book open, her thoughts with Sim.

Sim did not come. The town clock struck nine—ten—eleven. Then she put out the little lamp and sat by the window.

Surely he would come. Her listening ear had not caught a sound from the other room, though Sim went up directly after supper. Now that her own room was dark, she looked under the loose door for the streak of light she had often seen coming from the other side, but it was not there. Surely he had gone to bed. But she could not go.

It was very dark. The raw, cold wind was a forerunner of sleet or freezing rain; the clouds were thick; yet she sat by the window as if she could see out until the clock struck twelve. Then she knelt where she had sat. When Nan was sorely troubled she had never been able to find words of her own. Then she had always repeated, "Our Father which art in heaven," slowly, weighing every word. She had never failed to feel quieter at the close. To-night when she came to "but deliver us from evil," she stopped a long time. It seemed that she could go no further.

She finished at last and laid herself down, without undressing, upon the bed. Involuntarily she went back to the petition, and again and again found herself unconsciously repeating it: "But deliver us from evil."

She began to realize that she was cold, and wrapped the quilts around her. But she did not sleep.

One! Nan was shivering still. Then she began to wonder at her anxiety. Sim was no doubt sleeping off his vexation. Why should she lie awake?

Two! She rolled herself up snugly and turned over, making up her mind to sleep. She was nearly dozing when a door creaked. Unshod feet tipped cautiously upon the steep stairs. Nan was up and in the entry when the front door opened and closed softly.

"But deliver us from evil! Deliver us from evil!" she cried aloud and almost hysterically, for night-watches and cold feet are not good for young women who have stood all day behind a counter.

"Deliver us from evil! I believe that Thou art able."

But believing did not mean that there was nothing for her to do. She caught up an old shawl that hung by the bed, and, with less noise even than Sim, she passed quickly down the stair and out through the door. At the gate she listened for his footstep, then followed. It was dark enough to hide

her, yet her heart quivered as she thought. "Suppose he finds out, and turns on me?" It was not fear for herself, but for him. This evil mood, whatever the cause, might render him desperate if he found himself pursued.

She had to run at times not to lose the sound of his footsteps, for he walked very fast. Finally he turned into a narrow, crooked little street of unsavory reputation. Nan shuddered and clasped her hands over her heart, through which a sharp pain darted. Would he stop here? And when he stopped, what would she do? What could she do?

No! He walked slower through this place, but leaped a fence, at length, crossed a deserted garden in whose midst stood the blackened ruins of a burnt house, and was in the open street, near the depot. Nan followed. But on the street he was very cautious; she could hardly hear his light step.

What was it? Was it guilt? A hundred visions swam before her—visions of crimes of which she had heard. She was unstrung, and suddenly realized it. She laughed at herself; then turned hot with shame, because Sim had come home in an ill-humor—which was not unheard of—because he had not come to talk it over with her, because he had left the house in the middle of the night—what then? She had distrusted him who was a true and affectionate brother; she had suspected him of—she knew not what; and when had she ever known him, at least since the repentance that changed his whole life, to lie or show the least taint of dishonesty? And as to anger, she would not trust him so far on that, but anger would not call him out in this way; he would have struck while the rage was on him. What if he found her, sure enough, hounding him down in the darkness, because something had called him out? He might be walking off his vexation and sleeplessness; many a time she had wished she could do that at the dead of night.

Nan had turned on herself. The footsteps ahead were no longer heard. "I will go back." Then the thought of where she was gave her a creeping chill. Alone on the street at this hour! Suppose someone—suppose Yanks— She covered her face with her hands and hardly kept from crying out.

It was well that she had stopped. Something like a low growl sounded just ahead. Was it a dog, and would he seize her? The growl came again, and following it a low-muttered curse. Then she saw what Sim had seen already—a narrow stream of light. Yanks, the night police, had turned a corner not far ahead, and he was coming straight on, in the dark himself, his searchlight turned now this way, now that.

The stream of light came on, but slowly, for the night watchman seemed in a watchful frame of mind. On Nan's right where the buildings were close together there was no escape; to turn and flee was desperate, with that long, bright stream upon her track and Yanks in pursuit. There was but one chance—to slip across the way when the light was turned upon the buildings and hide behind the bales. She might be discovered there, but it was the only hope.

Evidently Sim's conclusions were the same, for Nan heard his footstep, cautious as it was. Now there was double danger, but her quick ear told the direction Sim was taking, and she avoided a collision. She felt along the barricade of bales, found an opening, and scarcely had she crept through it, wedging herself between two bales farther on, when the light flashed along the way she had come. Yanks had stopped; he left the buildings and crossed the street. "Blame me if I didn't see sumthin'!" he muttered.

The light was so bright that Nan knew he held it at the very opening, and but for this crevice there had been no hope for her. She squeezed farther in and was almost choking. Would he come into the narrow passage and discover her?

But those were too close quarters for the bulky night police. "Some plaguey dog!" he muttered again, "but it's gone."

Nan almost shrieked from the reaction, as the light was withdrawn and she heard his heavy tread. Cautiously she drew herself out; it was stifling in there, and then, since that muttered curse, her forebodings had returned. She would follow again.

Across the street, on, on; silence again.

Nan knew pretty well that she was not far from Mr. Vane's store; she felt along the wall and concluded she was in front of it. Then Sim must have gone around the corner. True enough, as she turned the corner, she heard a key grate in the lock, the door opened and shut. Sim had gone into Mr. Vane's office!

Again reaction set in with Nan. Did not Sim hold a position of responsibility in the Vane establishment? Did he not keep the key, which meant that he had liberty to enter at any hour? Not Mr. Owen himself had

a better right. Yet at this hour? What of that? Perhaps he remembered something he had left undone, some window unbarred, and could not rest. Why did he avoid the police? Then she remembered having heard that there was a town ordinance which allowed no one to be upon the streets after midnight without good reason. There had been evil doings in town that winter, and the mayor and council had roused themselves. But Sim could have given his reason.

There was no love between him and Yanks, as she well knew; and her cheek grew hot. Though it was not like Sim to be afraid. And the curse? She had never heard that from Sim's lips since he became a member of the church. Sim had drifted away from church during Mr. Elder's absence. The other ministers preached away over his head, he told Nan. He had left off Sunday-school altogether. Nan was not slow to see how things were going. Yet she knew his repentance had been true and deep, and she believed the Good Shepherd followed the straying sheep till he brought it back. And she was praying for him night and day.

God did not forget to listen. Nan would gladly have gone back and let Sim attend to his own business, but there was Yanks somewhere down the street with his searchlight. No, she would wait and follow Sim back, and if he discovered her she would confess how nervous she had been and could not sleep because he was worried, and how loss of sleep and all had upset her, and—she was afraid when he crept out of the house.

She found the door Sim had entered and drew away a little distance, waiting in the darkness. She heard the night train come in—it was three hours late—and wondered if there would be much light about the depot as they went back.

She had not waited long when she heard footsteps on the street. Someone was coming from the train. But Nan felt secure in her covering of darkness. Whoever it was evidently stopped in front of the store, then came on and turned the corner. Had Nan not been a quick thinker, or if she had had less courage, she would have screamed out to warn Sim, for that was her first impulse. But like a flash the argument framed itself: If Sim were but doing his duty, no one had a right to interfere; if she cried out, he would be suspected, for she would be discovered; if—if it were possible that anything was wrong, a warning could do no good, for the person was right there.

Yes, and opened the door. As he entered the office, and the light, though dimmed, of the wall lamp fell upon the strong, boyish figure and ruddy face, she recognized Ruby.

"Sim!" she heard him say. Then her heart stood still, for someone rushed into the light, struck Ruby to the floor, and kneeled over him, clutching his throat.

Was it Sim with that livid face and eyes savage with fury? Nay, more than savage; the evil spirit had brought with him seven others, more wicked than himself, and it was they who glared through the eyes of Simeon Larkins upon the face of his friend, the friend for whom that very day he would gladly have cut off his right hand.

When Nan came to herself she was rushing with outstretched arms toward the light, and she remembered afterward that as she crossed the threshold, Sim, with a fearful cry, leaped past her into the blackness.

## CHAPTER XXXVIII.

### FAITHFUL.

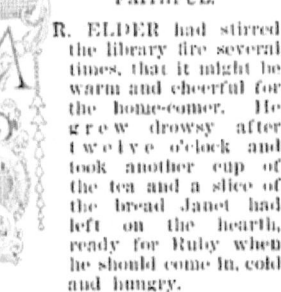

R. ELDER had stirred the library fire several times, that it might be warm and cheerful for the home-comer. He grew drowsy after twelve o'clock and took another cup of the tea and a slice of the bread Janet had left on the hearth, ready for Ruby when he should come in, cold and hungry.

The train was late. Mr. Elder read on awhile, but he had walked much and worked hard that day, and could not keep his eyes open before the fire. Ruby, who was coming home for Christmas holidays, had written and begged him not to trouble to meet the night train; he would take an omnibus and be up in five minutes. So Mr. Elder did not go.

He heard distinctly the clock strike one, two, three; but between times he napped. Ten minutes after three he heard the whistle, roused himself, stirred the fire into a blaze, drew up a chair for Ruby, thought how good it would be to see that bright face over there in ten minutes more, thought how unlike Ruby and his sister were and yet how lovely both, and waited for the omnibus.

Ten minutes passed, fifteen, twenty; when the clock struck the half hour he rose. Ruby might have missed the train, but it was not likely. Mr. Elder heard the rain drizzling against the windows, heard the moaning wind, and knew it must be very cold out. He was just going for his coat and hat when a rap which said "Haste!" sounded on the front door. Mr. Elder drew his dressing-gown about him and opened the door. Nan stood there, wrapped round the head and shoulders with the old shawl.

"Mr. Elder," she spoke hurriedly but low, "Ruby came from the train; he—he was hurt on the way; bring some one and come at once! You will find him in Mr. Vane's office. I will go for Dr. Matthews." And she was gone.

Why Nan should come at that hour of the night, why he should find Ruby unconscious on the floor of his father's office, were questions that passed hurriedly through Mr. Elder's mind, but to them he gave little heed. He only thought of getting the boy home and under the doctor's hand.

He and Thomas, Janet's husband, carried him in their arms—it was not far—and Dr. Matthews was at the house almost as soon as they. Nan waited at the door long enough to learn from Janet that Ruby was reviving, and, knowing that there was nothing for her to do, started down the street, she scarce knew whither.

The excitement which had held her up during action was gone now, and she felt weak and sick. But she kept on her way, and when, directly, she saw that Mr. Vane's office door was wide open and the light streaming out, realized that there was something more for her to do, and pressed on.

No one was there. That the light must be put out and the door locked for the safety of the establishment, were the only thoughts in her bewildered brain. To shield Sim or herself never occurred to her at that moment. If any one had asked, she no doubt would have told the whole terrible truth, and lifted a little the burden from herself.

Some one else had seen the light also, and Nan had but just blown it out and was drawing to the heavy door, when another light flashed full in her face, showing the

brutal countenance of the night police. The
strain had been too great; Nan had no courage left. She could but scream and fall in
a half swoon.

Taken aback by this unexpected meeting,
Yanks stood dumb for an instant; then all
the villainy within him broke out into one
long, exulting laugh.

"And so you're caught, my beauty!
Caught in the act! You didn't allow to have
a meetin' with your old frien' to-night, I
reckon; and as it's toler'ble dark, you won't
mind havin' him walk down the street with
you. He! he! But I say now, get out o'
this! No time for playin' off;" and he
stooped and shook her roughly by the wrists.
Then another thought struck him. "I say,
where's that brother of yours? He's about."

Nan had come to herself enough to know
that she must rouse. The question put her
on guard, and for the first time she thought
of shielding her brother.

"He is not here; I do not know where he
is!" she cried wildly.

Yanks shook her wrists again and put his
face down till she felt his foul breath upon
her cheek.

"Tell me where he is! You could not go
in here without the key, and he keeps it!
Am I a fool? Do not lie to me, or I'll -"

But Nan only fell to sobbing. "I do not
know! I do not know!"

"Get up from this and come along!" he
said, at length. "He can't be far, and we'll
track him. I've got one putty prize any-
how! Ha! ha! And as it's cold an' rainin',
you'll enjoy a warm little house in the middle of the street, what's always open to
Yanks' fren's! He! he!"

"Oh, don't take me there!" But Nan
checked as well as she could her sobs. She
knew that resistance or entreaty was useless; besides, the thought that Sim's safety
might lie in her hands gave her strength.
Sim, who without doubt had been doing
evil; Sim, who had, for all she knew, killed
Ruby; Sim, who had fled she knew not
whither; Sim, her brother, she would pro-
tect. Yanks went on with his insults, his
mockery, until, irritated by her silence, he
began to threaten. Still she held her peace.

At the station-house he thrust her into
the women's ward; by the lantern she saw
it was empty, and, glad to be alone, sank
upon the floor.

## CHAPTER XXXIX.

### WHERE ARE THEY?

DR. MATTHEWS, like
Mr. Elder, was too
intent upon reviving
Ruby to give much
thought to the cause
of his injuries. That
he had been violently
handled was evident.
But when the restor-
atives began to take
effect and the first suspense was over, Dr.
Matthews looked up suddenly to Mr. Elder
and demanded:

"What work is this?"

Mr. Elder could only give the facts as he
knew them.

"The girl? How came she to know?"
asked the doctor, a sudden suspicion dark-
ening his brow.

That was part of the mystery.

"I always wondered at Mr. Vane showing such confidence in that— What became
of her?" he cried, and then hurried out to
question the servants.

Janet said the young woman in question
had got there before Dr. Matthews, had
waited until she heard that Ruby was coming to, then left. Janet, like the others, was
too much occupied to think it strange.

Dr. Matthews went upstairs. "You must
attend to this thing, Mr. Elder. I must stay
by him. And send Thomas for Dr. Peters."

He wanted a woman about, too, for, for
the first time in his professional life, he felt
a kind of helplessness. So he called over the
stair, "And bring Mrs. Cole!"

"I—I am surely getting old," he said, rubbing his glasses on a corner of the sheet.
He noticed that his hand trembled as he
held Ruby's wrist.

There was but one thing for Mr. Elder to
do—go to police headquarters and report.
He understood well enough Dr. Matthews'
broken sentence — Sim must be responsible
for the deed.

But Nan? Mabel had told him much of
Nan, and he had watched the girl with interest and often talked with her in the shop
and at her own home. He had watched her
in church, too, and had learned to turn to
her in preaching, for her eye always gave
him ready, often eager, attention. He called
her his listener, and not a few times her
interest roused his own. At first he thought
her thin face very homely, but now saw only

a clear, gray eye, full of intelligence and feeling, and certain lines of endurance about the mouth; the mouth itself having that clean look which we associate with a pure utterance. Into her spiritual life he had never been able to penetrate further than her eyes showed, for, though frank and open in conversation, she never spoke of herself, and the minister felt that under the cover was a mighty reserve force.

As for Sim, the minister knew him only as a straightforward, industrious young man, trusted by Mr. Vane, and possessed of unbounded devotion for Ruby. Yet Mr. Elder could see but one course for him to pursue.

At the station-house he found not the regular night-police, but a substitute whom Yanks had called and warned to keep strict guard while he was away upon an errand of importance. Mr. Elder went alone to the house of Mr. Stoval, chief of police. The man of business soon linked the chain of evidences. "Her brother keeps key; you found office door open; store not entered by violence."

Mr. Elder could not refrain from speaking a word for Nan and Sim also. But an officer of the law must know nothing of previous character, sympathy or indecision; only facts. He would proceed at once to the residence of the accused. Mr. Elder asked leave to accompany him, for he wished if possible to have a word with Nan before the arrest.

A guard was stationed without before Mr. Stoval knocked. It was agreed that Mr. Elder should speak first, and, if Nan appeared, counsel her to accept the situation quietly.

There was no response to the first knock;

at the second a querulous voice called, "Sim! Sim!" At the third a match was struck and a woman, carrying a candle, came into the passage. They could see her through the side lights, though she tried to cover the flame with her hand.

"Who's there?"

THEY CARRIED HIM HOME —SEE PAGE 83.

Mr. Elder responded, giving his name.

"And what do you want? What's the matter?"

"I want to see your daughter, Mrs. Larkins."

"At this time o' night! What's up? I say, Sim, can't you wake up?"

Mr. Elder's heart failed him; the mother

evidently was ignorant of all the dark events of that night and was calling for protection upon the son who was not there.

But he cleared his voice and called again: "I must come in, Mrs. Larkins, and it is better that you open quietly. Trust me; do you not know my voice?"

But the police had no time to waste; he caught the door-knob and turned it impatiently. The door opened.

Mr. Elder kept him back and entered alone, speaking quietly to the disturbed woman. He told her that something had gone wrong at the store and that he must see both Sim and Nan.

Mrs. Larkins went upstairs then quickly, carrying her candle. In a moment Mr. Elder heard a loud call, surprised and alarmed: "Nan! I say, where are you?"

She stepped across the upper entry, opened a door, and all was still a moment. Then: "They're not here! They're not here! Where are they? Where's my girl and boy?" And the terrified woman stumbled down the steep stairs.

The police was standing in the passage with the minister, but she did not notice. "They've gone, both of 'em! What's wrong? Tell me what's wrong!" she cried. There was no acting in it.

But the law must be fulfilled. The place was searched.

Then anger overcame terror in the woman. "Search my house!" She dared them, threatened with what Sim would do on his return, and broke into wrathful reproaches. Because she was poor, her house must be ransacked and her children accused. And nobody had better children than hers. Because something had gone wrong,—what had they to do with it?

Mr. Elder tried once to speak, but she turned on him in a fury.

"You—you, the minister as they call you— to come to my house in the night and makin' me open the door by your sleek tongue!" She forgot she had not opened the door.

Mr. Elder was glad when the search was over, and, in truth, relieved that Nan, at least, could not be found. He had done his duty; he had put the business into the hands of the police and wished to leave it there.

He hastened back to Ruby.

AY broke, and the faint light coming through the window brought a gleam of hope to Nan. She had crept into the farthest corner and crouched there in sickening fear, waiting the return of the police. She heard the steady tramp back and forth by the window, and did not know that it was the substitute, and that Yanks himself had hastened to Mr. Owen with the news. For Mr. Owen had secretly hired the night police to be especially watchful of the Vane establishment. Yanks understood his suspicions, and now his exultation was double: getting extra pay from Mr. Owen and gratifying his own revenge.

And why revenge? Nan knew when her cheek had burnt at thought of him; she knew now when her cheek no longer burnt, for she was cold, yet strangely insensible. It was the only thing she could think about. The number of times Yanks had dropped into the shop and tried to engage her in conversation, the number of times he had attempted to see her home in the evenings, and at length, after she had avoided him often, the evening when, getting off later than usual, she had come upon him suddenly, and he would not be shaken off, even attempting familiarity that made her hot and cold. Sim had to be told then, but he did not know how bad it was, for Nan feared the consequences. Sim had it out with Yanks next day and gave him to understand that he would be reported at headquarters at the least offence in future. Yanks knew well that this was no idle threat, and from that time contented himself with covert malignity, keeping a watchful eye for revenge. The brother and sister knew it very well, but, neither being of the timorous sort, passed unnoticed the leering and lowering countenance.

His time had come now. Poor Nan! Everything failed her, crouching there, in that darkest corner before the dawn—her bodily strength, her courage, her faith. Not a word of prayer came to her lips, not even in her heart was there an uprising; the fountain was sealed. Once she remembered the words she had gone over and over a few hours ago, but those hours seemed many, many, many years; the recollection was more shadowy than a dream—" but deliver us from evil"; she could not recall how she felt when she said it.

" Believest thou that I am able?"

" I do not know," she muttered in a hoarse whisper.

Was Nan's faith weak and worthless, then, because it failed her in the hour of trial? Or was it her faith which failed, or the flesh only?

Nan's examination was much against her. She had two objects in view—to speak the truth, and to shield Sim. In consequence she grew red and stammered, with the knowledge that though speaking the truth, it was not the whole truth. So that not only circumstances, but public sentiment, went against her. She could not have told afterwards what they asked or what she said; she only felt that she had failed and that all evidence pointed to Sim. She made no effort to prove her own innocence, knowing it would be useless and feeling, in a vague way, that holding her was a sort of satisfaction which would make them less eager to catch Sim.

Yet Sim was guilty; he deserved punishment. But he was her brother and she loved him. Besides, fearful visions swam before her—visions of the end that awaited Sim if Ruby should die. And visions not only of that end, but of what might become of Sim's soul.

After the examination Nan was taken to jail, where a stream of the curious and idle flowed in and out. They asked her questions, expressed pity, or merely gazed through the grating as upon an untamed animal. She had scarcely tasted food, and the nervous strain was becoming dangerous. A bright spot burned in either cheek, her eyes glowed like coals of fire; she set her lips together at length and refused a word. The jailer's wife pitied her and entreated her husband to forbid visitors, which he did.

Nan sat perfectly silent the rest of the day, looking through the barred window but seeing nothing.

In the morning the jailer's wife brought her breakfast and she was sitting there still.

" You haven't slept any, have you?" asked the woman kindly, for the girl's face was white and haggard.

" I don't know." And that was all she would say.

But as the day wore on she seemed to gain strength. Visitors in general were prohibited still, and she had the time to herself. About noon her mother came; she wept and wrung her hands and reproached Nan bitterly and went away bemoaning her lot. Nan stood and looked at her without a word.

Toward evening Mr. Elder came. Nan gave him one quick, inquiring glance, then turned from him and looked through the grating. She read " little hope" in his face. The minister stood by her at the window and began to talk. He told her she was not alone; that she could call upon God in the prison cell as well as in His sanctuary. She listened until he was through, then said so quietly that he started:

" I have no hope."

No hope! Was it guilt then? He looked at her drawn face—she kept her eyes turned away—and could not see a line of guilt there.

" Why?"

She was startled by the suddenness of the question, and looked in his face. He saw in those clear eyes only truth and suffering.

" Because," she said slowly, " when I was in the hardest trial, I did not believe that God was able or willing to save me, to deliver me from evil. I forsook God then; now he has forsaken me."

The minister took her hand. " When was that?" he asked gently.

She felt the tears coming into her eyes and dropped her head. " Do not ask me."

His strong hand sent a thrill of strength through her.

" Do you think it is faith that saves you?" he asked.

She raised her eyes with a question.

" If you were falling now and I held you up by the hand, would it be my hand that saved you, or yours?"

She was silent a moment, then for answer asked simply: " But if I drew my hand away?"

" You would fall; and if, too weak to rise, you stretched it to me, what then?"

" You would raise me up."

Nan covered her face with her hands and wept freely, but silently. They were the first tears she had shed. The minister knew he had said enough.

## CHAPTER XLI.

### PITY.

EARLY next morning loud voices in the street attracted Nan to the window. Just outside the jail yard an excited mob was gathering. Directly there were footfalls on the stairs, a heavy door not far away opened and shut.

When the jailer's wife came with Nan's breakfast, she looked pitifully at her. But Nan had slept, and, as she sat down to the little table the kind woman had spread, asked quietly:

"Was that a prisoner brought in just now?"

"Yes."

"Who?"

The woman looked pitifully at her again.

"Was it my brother?"

"Yes."

Nan leaned her head upon her hand in silence.

"He gave himself up," continued the woman; "my man says he don't believe they'd ever have caught him."

"May I see him?"

The jailer's wife said she would find out, and in an hour Sim entered the cell. His face looked as if he had been through a terrible illness, but there was no sign of weakness about his frame.

Nan held out her hand. "Sim!"

He looked at her, around the cell, at her again.

"How came you here?" His voice was hollow and strange.

Then she realized that he knew nothing of her part in the events of that night. Weakness overcame her and she sank into a chair. She told him presently.

"You? Why would they suspect you?"

She told him quietly and in few words the whole story of her following him and of her arrest. His face was full of misery. She saw that his punishment was almost greater than he could bear.

When Sim confessed, telling, without an effort to shield himself, the story of his going to rob the money-drawer, of Ruby Vane's coming in as he was in the act of opening it, of his striking him down and fleeing; telling also that he knew nothing of his sister's presence, that she had no part in the affair except as she tried to save Ruby and secure the safety of the store, sentiment turned mightily in Nan's favor, and she was released on bail.

Yet the cloud was over her. Mrs. King declined to take her again into the shop, which could not afford to lose its reputation by employing a suspicious character. Other attempts to get work were fruitless also, and, sore at heart, Nan saw only want ahead.

Then Mr. Elder did what many considered rash, some presumptuous. He employed the accused accomplice, sister of the criminal, as assistant nurse for Ruby.

For Ruby's life was yet hanging by a thread. Dr. Matthews called in still another physician, and the three came out from a long consultation without a sign of hope. Nan, who was dusting the library, watched eagerly as they came downstairs. She saw the grave faces of two; Dr. Matthews' was covered with his handkerchief, and he went out and up the street weeping, utterly broken down.

The strange doctor remained and talked with Mr. Elder. He said he saw no reason why Ruby should not recover if it were only the external injuries that were to be contended with; but his system had received a severe nervous shock, evidently, which, combined with the violence done him, might prove fatal to the body or to the brain.

Mr. Elder felt the room spinning round and giving way beneath his feet. This child, who had been placed so confidently in his care, how could he return him to the father and mother, even now, perhaps, on their homeward way, a shattered wreck! He groaned aloud, and prayed God that he might present the lifeless body instead.

Mr. Vane had been written to simply that Ruby was sick. They were in the south of France, and traveling from place to place, so the letter might not reach them for weeks.

Nan visited Sim daily. At times she found him quiet, ready to talk, and eager to hear from Ruby; at others his misery was so great, or he was so desperate in his despair, that she could not speak to him. It was on one of those days when he turned his face from her to the darkest corner of the cell, that a visitor was admitted. It was George McPhail. Nan left at once, and the fair, well-dressed young man went over and laid a trembling hand on the prisoner's shoulder.

"Let me alone!" said Sim, but turned and, seeing who it was, sprang up and faced him. "You dog!"

George's knees gave way; he tottered and leaned against the wall. Sim saw his white, terror-stricken face and pushed to him the one chair. The wretched youth sat down and buried his face in his hands. At length he looked up and saw Sim standing by the narrow window, his face haggard and terrible.

"Why—why do you take it so hard, Sim?" he gasped; and then took courage as the prisoner did not turn upon him. "He is living yet, and may get well, and—nothing was touched, no harm was done at the store. If he gets well it won't be hard on you."

"Do you think I care what becomes of my neck?" Sim demanded fiercely. "Let it break; the sooner the better!"

After a pause George crept up and spoke in a whisper, glancing around fearfully. "You didn't give me away, Sim? You didn't make a hint that I—that we—had had a talk that night?"

Sim regarded him in silence.

"You know nothing could be laid to me; I never—I knew you were steady and got good wages; I—"

"Don't lie out of it! I knew what you wanted!"

"Oh, Sim, I won't! It's true! I was so hard pressed I—I was desperate! And you—everything was in your hands—you could have replaced it before—"

Sim's eyes burnt like a madman's; he caught George by the shoulder and the poor creature's teeth chattered.

"Look here! No more words about this thing! I'm a thief and a murderer! You egged me on to it, but the law can't touch you. I wouldn't tell if it could. I have enough to stand without your whimpering. I did it of my own free will, and—I'll suffer for it!"

"But you're not a thief! You didn't take a cent! And—he may get well!"

"It's all the same!" said Sim, with strange quietness.

George rubbed his long, white fingers together as if to warm them; he wiped the cold sweat that was rolling off his forehead. "You haven't let me out, and I'll not forget you, Sim. The Rhodes' place may go; I'll take father's anger and I'll sell it. My creditors are pressing me hard. I'll pay off,

and I'll employ a lawyer to defend you—the best to be had."

Not the former contempt, but genuine pity stole through Sim as he looked down upon this poor, weak creature, miserable because of fear. It was in his voice as he answered: "You may save your money, George; I do not need him."

But George protested with real earnestness.

"There is nothing for a lawyer to say. I will give the plain facts, as I've given them already, and they will act on them. If he lied for me, I'd contradict him!"

Nan wondered at Sim's calmness next day and every day after that; she did not know, neither did he, that pity springing up in his heart had opened it and was sending gentle streams through his whole being.

---

<h2 style="text-align:center">CHAPTER XLII.</h2>

<h3 style="text-align:center">THE VIOLET.</h3>

ARIAN, staid young woman as she was, came rushing downstairs, fairly alarming Mr. Waring, who stood at the foot.

"She's coming! She's coming tomorrow!"

"Who?"

"Who? Mabel."

"That is your cousin, who went abroad for her health?"

"Yes, and I didn't know they had got home. And," Marian's joy was tempered, "Ruby is sick, Aunt Emily wrote. I think he must be very sick, though she does not say so; and I do not understand why she wants Mabel to be away when he is so ill."

"Perhaps she is not so good a nurse as you."

"She is strong and well now," said Marian.

"But you are not strong and well." Mr. Waring spoke gently. "You stay so much up there," he pointed to her father's room, "and so much in the library; you do not walk and ride as you used to do. Why do you not like those things now?"

"Oh, I like them, but—"

"We will walk now," said Mr. Waring; and they went out.

Marian could talk only of Mabel and her coming to-morrow.

"You will like her, Mr. Waring, she is so bright and sweet."

Mr. Waring smiled. "I am sure I shall like her, if she is like Ruby."

"No, she is not like Ruby. Ruby is not like any one, I think." And Marian sighed, for Ruby was ill.

They walked on in silence for a while, then Mr. Waring said:

"Do you know that from the time you came here I have observed you closely?"

She knew that he observed everything closely.

"I could see that you had been surrounded by affection and cheerfulness, and that life here would be a great change for you. You were a child, too, and I wondered when I saw you sitting quiet in your father's room. When you sat there day after day, I knew it was because you wished to serve him. When you decided to remain here, I saw the struggle, or the marks of it, in your face and from that time it was changed. I wondered at your quietness and patience, for I knew it was not your nature to be passive. Do you remember one Sunday when I came in and found you reading?"

She remembered very well.

"You read my thoughts when you caught my eye. Then I set to wondering more and more about you, and what it was that gave you, a mere child, so strong a spirit. You changed after that Sunday, toward me, and I was sorry; you never gave me your confidence again with childish freedom, as before; but you were guarded and seemed to have become, all at once, a woman. Then you were troubled about your faith, and—"

"Oh, Mr. Waring, how do you know everything?"

"And I reproached myself. That made me think about your faith, and I watched you more closely than ever, for I wanted to see if you would come out from under the cloud or if it would overwhelm you. But you came out. Then I wondered more, and from wondering I came to studying the faith that had power like that. It was not a day's work. It would be a long story if I told the whole of it. I only want to tell you that now I believe that 'at the center God is sitting, watching and keeping the worlds right.' And you helped me to the belief; you and Ruby. Those were his words, you remember. These things were so real to him,

he never seemed to think I did not see them."

They had stopped in their walk under the old elm tree. Marian leaned against it. All the world had changed suddenly.

Mr. Waring stooped and pushed aside some green leaves. "Here is something that is like you;" and he handed her the violet he had found. "It is the first to brave the winds, it has worked on quiet, patient and alone, and it helps to sweeten the world."

Marian went up to her own room and placed the violet in a tiny white china bowl; there it floated on the water, and she touched her lips to its fragrance. She was very happy — for Mabel was coming to-morrow.

Mabel came, and they embraced, kissed, cried and laughed, and did other strange things, as young women will. When they got upstairs and had time to look at one another, Marian declared that Mabel was just herself, only a hundred times more beautiful. But Mabel could not understand the change in Marian; she did not like to say much about it, but thought it over when her cousin left her. Marian was taller, but very little, and not so plump; her cheeks were pale, and they used to be so rosy; she did not wear her hair in short curls now, but in a knot. But there was something else; what was it? Marian had always seemed older than herself. To be sure, they were twenty years old; but she, Mabel, was a child still, while Marian was—a woman! What made the difference? Mabel was puzzled. She did not know how many things, besides years, make women.

Marian was delighted when she saw the look of admiration in Mr. Waring's eyes.

"I knew you would like her," she said next day, as she met him in the hall. Of course everybody must love Mabel. She was so lovely, so sweet and so artless.

In the evenings she and Mr. Waring sang together, and Marian sat with her little work-basket and listened. For Mr. Waring staid almost every evening. Marian was happier than she could tell. Even the cloud of Ruby's illness did not hang heavily over these young girls. When alone they spoke of it often and of the strange happenings. There was a mystery about the whole thing which Mabel could not unravel. She told Marian all she knew of Sim's deed, of Nan's arrest. Why Nan should have been suspected she did not know. She believed—she knew—that Nan was innocent. They would not allow her to see Ruby during the few days she spent at home. Her mother looked sadder than she had ever seen her, yet Dr. Matthews did not come so often as he had done in other cases of sickness. She had wanted to stay and help, but her mother had said she must come to Marian.

But it was not long before they heard that Ruby was better, yet Mrs. Vane wished Mabel to stay awhile longer. News came of Sim's trial; he was sentenced for three years, but Nan was free.

The weeks slipped by. May came and Mrs. Vane wrote that Mabel would better come home. Mabel was glad and sorry. Marian felt her heart sink.

"Oh, Marian, if you could go! Can't you, for a little while?"

But Marian answered, "No, not yet."

It was Mabel's last evening, and Marian was sad, yet it seemed to her that nothing could make her sad in the old lonely way since the time when the whole face of the earth had changed suddenly. As she came slowly down the stairs she was thinking of the violet, no longer floating in the tiny white bowl, but pressed between the leaves of her Bible. Mabel was in the parlor, she thought; the door was ajar. Marian pushed it noiselessly, but stopped. The great room was dim. She could see over by the window two figures: one was Mabel, her fair head drooped; then all the light seemed concentrated on Mr. Waring's face, for that was all Marian could see. Or was it that the light was going out from his face, a light she had never seen before. Yet she knew what it was. Marian closed the door more softly than she had opened it.

---

## CHAPTER XLIII.

### NO. 37.

A YOUNG man stopped at the penitentiary gates and showed his permit to enter and see No. 37. He passed through the office and into the open square around which were the cells, the workhouses and other buildings. Near the chapel was a grass plat, and in the center a fountain played, spraying the mass of flowers around its basin.

The penitentiary was not such a dark, dreary place then; he thought no matter how wicked a man might be, he must feel happier and better every time he came by the chapel and saw the flowers and caught their fragrance.

He waited there. Directly No. 37 came. He was tall and strong-looking, and bronzed from labor in the sun. But when he saw who his visitor was, he stopped short and looked on the ground.

"Sim!"

He would not take the outstretched hand. "You would not shake hands with me?" he said.

"Oh, Sim!"

Ruby had seen at first only the tan and the look of health on Sim's face; now he saw something else, deeply cut into every line of it. It was not gloom; gloom is weak and selfish. It was that strong despair which we would hide, but cannot, for it chisels itself upon the face and even moulds the form.

"Let us go where we may be quiet, Sim." And Ruby led the way to the back of the chapel.

There they sat and Ruby talked. For a long time Sim said nothing, but Ruby knew he was listening, and talked on. He told of home things and home people—of Mabel's marriage; of Nan, who was now his mother's housekeeper; of Sim's mother, whom he had seen the day before; of the doings in Greenville; and all so naturally that Sim was taken out of himself and forgot for a time that he was No. 37.

Then Ruby began to talk of other things, not with hesitancy or embarrassment, as you or I would have done probably, but naturally as before, only more gently.

"I wanted to tell you, Sim, how I came to go in there that night. I did not write, because when Mr. Elder and Nan were writing I told them what to say, and I knew I would come. That night as I passed the store I saw a light through the show window. I looked in and saw it came through the glass top in the office door—the inside door. I hardly know why I went round to the office. I thought perhaps the light had been left by mistake, or that you or Mr. Owen were there looking after something. I didn't know it was so late. My watch had stopped early in the night, and I had slept, so I didn't know the train was three hours behind."

Sim groaned.

"I know it is hard for you to hear of these

things, but I think it is always better to talk over hard things—once—and then lay them away. I don't know if we can ever lay a thing away until we have talked it over. Nan has told me a great many things, and before George died he told Mr. Elder—"

Sim started and looked up.

"I knew you would be surprised. Poor George! He wanted Mr. Elder to tell his father and everybody, but Mr. Elder did not. He said it was not as if his confession would make things different for any one else. He only told me and wanted me to tell you."

They were both silent awhile.

"George said if he had to live his life over again he would rather be wicked and fearless, no matter what punishment he received, than to be afraid. He said fear makes you wicked and is itself worse than any torture. And I believe it is true, Sim. Poor George! He was afraid of God; he was afraid to die, and, I think, afraid to live, too. But Mr. Elder knows how to make things plain, and he was peaceful at the last."

When Ruby rose to go he held out his hand again, which Sim took this time, looking also into the grave eyes lifted to his.

"Ruby, you come here and give me your hand as if I had done nothing. It ain't that you don't know the whole of it, is it?"

"Yes, Sim, I know the whole, I think. I have got it from one and another and put it all together. I know your sin was great."— Sim drew a long breath of relief—"and that your punishment is great, also."

"My punishment! If it was twenty-five years, if it was my lifetime, it would not be my deserts, and I would not make complaint."

"I don't mean being in here." Ruby looked around at the great walls shutting them in from the world. "I mean what you have to bear in yourself," laying his hand upon his breast; "that is your punishment."

Sim drew another long sigh.

"But, Sim, I want you to lay aside the past. I want to see another look on your face."

"Lay aside! It ain't like I didn't know better; it ain't like I hadn't — repented once and — been trusted."

Sim's lip was pale and quivering.

"I could tell you of people that knew better, that had repented and were trusted and sinned and found hope again, Sim. The Bible tells us of them, and you have read it. But I'll only remind you of one you have seen, and that may make it more real —

Father Paul. You know how everybody loved him because he was so good and upright, 'The Honest' they called him. And you were at the funeral and heard how he was trusted and betrayed his trust. Yet you don't doubt that he had hope in God, do you?"

The next day was Sunday, and when the blind chaplain of the penitentiary had dismissed the congregation, he felt in the prayer-box. The box with the slit in the top had rested upon the table in front of the reading-desk for years, and every Sabbath day the listeners were reminded that if any wished special prayer in his behalf, he might write his name upon a slip and drop it into the prayer-box. There was a slip in it to-day, and when the blind chaplain reached his cottage and handed it to his little daughter to read for him, she said, "Why, papa, it's a mistake; there's no name on it, only a number."

"What?" asked the chaplain.

"No. 37."

---

## CHAPTER XLIV.

### THERE IS NO FEAR IN LOVE.

MARIAN'S period of daughterly service is ended. One night as she sat in her father's room — she sat there nearly all the time now — he said feebly:

"Daughter, read."

"What shall I read, father?"

"What you read the first time."

Marian wondered. She looked at the row upon the shelf.

"The first time?"

The scientist leaned wearily back in his arm-chair.

"'Like as a father pitieth — a father pitieth —'"

Marian went quickly into her own room and brought the Bible from which she had read that Sabbath morning seven years ago.

The man of science, worn out with searchings in dark places, worn out with the labor that satisfieth not, closed his weary eyes and his daughter read.

She read slowly. "Bless the Lord, O my soul; and all that is within me, bless his holy name. Bless the Lord, O my soul, and

forget not all his benefits; who forgiveth all
thine iniquities, who healeth all thy diseases; who redeemeth thy life from destruc-
tion. Like as a father pitieth his children,
so the Lord pitieth them that fear him; for
he knoweth our frame; he remembereth that
we are dust." And on
to the end.

She asked if she
should read more; he
shook his head. "No,
I will sleep now."

She helped him to
bed.

In the morning when
Marian went to him,
for that was her first
task, he was still.
Those weary eyes
would never open again
to see his little daugh-
ter sitting by his side,
waiting; nor would the
ears hear her gentle
voice. He did not need
her longer. So Uncle
Philip and Aunt Emily
came and took her
home.

Ruby was at the gate
to help them out of the
carriage, brimful of
some mighty secret. He
put one arm about his
mother and one about
Marian and brought
them to the library.
And there was Aunt
Sarah, her real self,
only years younger than
when she went away,
and Uncle Alex, almost
as young.

"We haven't got ner-
vous prostration nor
any other complaint,
we haven't come to rest
up, but just to see you,
and to be happy all to-
gether once more."
That was what Aunt Sarah said.

It was a great summer they had. Marian,
accustomed to service, found herself the
center of everybody's care. It was no
wonder Mabel had told her so much of the
minister. Sometimes Marian thought he was
all strength, sometimes he seemed all gentleness and goodness. When she sat in the old

place at church and heard the hymns sung
and Mr. Elder's sermons, she could not keep
the tears back.

"Is all this for me?" She was like one
who had been cast upon a far-off island and
now after many years was at home again.

HE KEPT HIS EYES FIXED ON THE GROUND.—SEE PAGE 91.

She felt that she had never known how lonely
those years were until she breathed again
the atmosphere of sympathy; yet they were
precious to her.

Ruby took Marian walking with him every
day. It was wonderful how Ruby knew
everybody, not merely their names but
themselves, and what they did and what

they wanted. He always seemed to have the right word ready when he met anyone, and faces young and old lighted up at sight of him.

He took Marian on Sunday afternoons to Father Paul's cottage, where he talked to the factory children. Mrs. Wyman had given up her Sunday-school long ago. Those children had such a low tone, she said; and they were enthusiastic only when there was the prospect of a lawn party or a Christmas tree; indeed, they were just a set of beggars. "And who made them beggars?" Aunt Sarah asked when some one told her about it. The truth was, Mrs. Wyman was tired of fruitless efforts such as she had made for so long. The "church" did not appreciate her labors; Mr. Elder had disappointed her in many ways; "he is not just the man I took him to be." Greenville was getting to be a live place now, so there were many ways of spending herself and her substance which might bring more abundant returns. "Society" appreciates your efforts if the "church" does not; "it" surrounds you with worshipers.

So Ruby had gathered together the scattered lambs. He did not call it Sunday-school, but a "meeting." And at the meeting the children talked and he talked, just as the occasion was, and every one felt that his word had a place. They sang a good deal; some days they sang nearly all through the meeting — that was when the "leader" saw some more restless, or when there were signs of trouble on any little face or marks of anger.

"And you are not going to be a preacher, Ruby?" Marian said one evening as they walked home along the little path by the river.

"No, I never thought God called me to that; and besides —"

He stopped short, with his hand upon a fallen tree, and looked at the river dashing over the rocks. Grave as Ruby always had been, even as a child, Marian could hardly remember that she had ever seen him sad. It was a kind of sweet gravity that broke into merriment at any moment. But as he spoke and looked at the river, a deep sadness settled upon his face, making it paler and his eyes darker in the fading light.

Marian's first impulse was to ask, "Besides — what?" but she did not, and directly was sure she understood. Ruby had never been strong enough since that last illness to resume his studies; he was frail and his face

no longer ruddy. Ruby had never been one to talk of the great things he expected to do, and was not considered ambitious, as the word goes, so that no one knew how many hopes were buried in secret when the verdict came — he must live an out-door life and have little to do with books. Uncle Alex guessed the truth when he saw his frailty and remembered the night when he had stood up and said, "But I want to live now, Uncle Alex. I want to be a man." And Marian understood partly when that sadness changed his face so suddenly; she understood, too, why he did not wish to speak of it.

One rainy day Ruby had a sore throat, and Marian took her work-basket and went up to his room to sit awhile. "I can't talk, Marian, and as it would tire you to do it all, I'll give you these to read. I love to have you sit with me;" and he got down from the shelf an oak box. "I have never showed them to anybody, but I knew you'd be interested; you have heard me speak often of Thomas and Carter. Carter was my room-mate."

Marian read Thomas' letters first; there were several of them, tied in a little bundle. The first told how he missed Ruby at college, then of various happenings; at the last:

"I made up my mind to do it. Ruby — you know what we talked about that night. I could have gone in with you after Carter left, and I could have taken your room and been all to myself when you didn't come back. I wanted to do it bad enough, but made up my mind I would be out-and-out or nothing. So I stayed with my room-mate and let them say their say. There wasn't much of it, though. I believe the meanest fellow in the world respects you more if you stand by your colors, with no parade about it. One of them wanted to know if 'Elijah' had left me his mantle, and I said I wished I could think so. But I must confess it got next to me when one night Rowe, my room-mate, said, 'Rejoice, brethren, over the backslider reclaimed,' and then they all struck up, 'Welcome, wanderer, welcome; Welcome back to home.' I was nettled a second, then I said, 'Let's sing it all,' and got my book. They joined with me, and Ruby, when it came to 'Eyes of love are on thee, my son! my son!' and our 'meeting' broke, I never saw a quieter set."

The last letter was of recent date and

short; it told of Thomas' entering the ministry.

"I have enjoyed reading them, Ruby," Marian said, as she tied the bundle. "Mr. Thomas must be a fine young man."

But it was Carter's letter that brought the tears to her eyes.

It began by reminding Ruby of their last night together, of Carter's disgrace, and went over some of what he had told of his family affairs.. Then:

"I did catch it, Ruby, as I told you I would, and they caught it from me, too, for over a year. For I laid myself out to be sullen, though that never did work well with me, and I took on airs and lost no chance to hint about how the wheel turned round—and I felt mighty mean. Well, I'll just leave you to imagine what a nice mess we had there, and at last my uncle came to see me and he said my father was too hard on me and that he mustn't keep me moped up there doing no good. My father wouldn't hear to anything at first, but my uncle is one of those men who hammer on till they get their way, and the end of it was I was allowed to go traveling. It wasn't just a pleasure trip; I had work to do to pay my expenses, and that gave me a good, independent feeling. I had been gone about four months when my father died; then my uncle wrote that I must be at home in two months to settle up matters, for I would then be twenty-one. I could see well enough what he wanted; he never liked my stepmother. My father left nothing but debts, and the family was at my mercy. I was mean enough to be proud of it. I didn't get home till the eve of my birthday, and I greeted them all like some lord. I went all about the place, criticising, as consequential as only a fool knows how to be, and my uncle was there to back me up. Some fellows came to take me to a frolic that night, but I refused. It was something new for me to want to be alone, but as soon as supper was over I went to my own room. My uncle followed me and began to talk. I was moody and wouldn't speak if I could help it, so he went out, pretty angry. I've thought of you many a time, Ruby. I've thought of what a brave little chap you were, and 'long-headed,' as Thomas used to say. But that night I couldn't get you out of my head. I could see you sitting there with your solemn eyes just reading me through. I thought of the morning I left you in bed, so sorry for a wretched

sinner like me that the tears were in your eyes, and saying, 'Carter, I wish you had a happy home like mine.' 'If I had a home like his, I would not be what I am,' I said, 'And whose fault is it?' I can't tell you the whole story of that night, only I didn't go to bed. I didn't close my eyes, for a battle was going on inside, and one side had to be whipped before it was done. When day broke I got down on my knees, so you may know which side won then. I went down to the breakfast room early, and when my stepmother and little sisters came in, kissed them and handed mother to her place. Everybody understood. My uncle was red with rage and would eat no breakfast; but I couldn't help it. I was happier than I had ever been in my life. Now, there isn't anybody I'd tell this to but you, Ruby, but I want you to know, for it's a big part owing to you that I have a happy home and a kind mother and the dearest little sisters in the world."

"Dear old Carter!" said Ruby, when Marian had finished and looked over at him. "I'm so glad he's happy. He was such a kind-hearted fellow and always wanted somebody to love."

Ruby asked his father, mother, Aunt Sarah and Marian to meet him in the library at a certain hour, and there he laid before them a plan which, he said, he had thought over a long time. Mr. Vane drew his lips together and shook his head. Mrs. Vane looked surprised, then grave. Marian wondered, but Aunt Sarah spoke:

"It is the very thing. Farm life will be the making of Ruby. Do you intend to imprison him in that musty store? Nobody with any sense can live idle. And Sim Larkins has had three years of the best training."

Mr. Vane looked at his sister in wonder. "The farm life is the best for Ruby, I know; but as to Sim, it is not alone training that he needs. I bear him no ill-will, poor fellow, for with his bringing up and temptations some of us might have done worse, and I intend to give him employment as soon as he is free, for I believe he is a changed man. But I am afraid this plan is not wise."

After a pause Aunt Sarah said, "For Ruby's sake, let us try it," and her eyes had something more than the old shine in them.

Her brother leaned his head upon his hand in troubled thought; it was hard to deny Ruby anything. Mrs. Vane sat near her husband, pale and silent. Ruby went and stood between them; he put one arm about his mother and one hand on his father's shoulder.

"Let us not be afraid," he said.

The plan over which Ruby had thought so long was perfected at length. He was to take Glenwood, with its beautiful farming lands, which Sim was to manage. Mabel and Mr. Waring, with their little Philip Vane Waring, were to live with them, and Nan — her mother was dead — was to be their housekeeper.

It was the last evening of the "reunion," as Ruby called it. To-morrow was breaking-up day. They were all gathered in the library.

By the wall sat a young man, tall and strong-looking, with a bronzed face and close-shaved head. He did not join in the conversation, but listened, and when Ruby talked kept his eyes fixed upon his face; and that was nearly all the time, for Ruby was doing most of the talking. Marian was by the fire. Mr. Elder next her, for they had just come in from a walk in the cold.

"When we get settled down," Ruby was saying, "you will all come to see us, and you'll find out what fine farmers Sim and I are, and what a great housekeeper Nan is. Father will retire after a while, then he and mother will come and live with us and help to subdue this young tyrant," caressing his nephew. "And Marian, of course she'll come, only — we can't leave Mr. Elder by himself —"

He stopped short, for Marian drooped her head so low upon her hand that he feared she was not feeling well, until he saw how rosy her cheeks were. Mr. Elder looked as if he did not know exactly what to say, which was something unusual. Everybody was silent, and Mabel was smiling behind her handkerchief.

Aunt Sarah hastened to the rescue. "Ruby, when you were a little boy I thought you would be our preacher; but, next to that, I'm glad you've taken to farming, like your grandfather, whose name you have. Still, I'm sorry we can't have a preacher in the family."

Deeper waters. A silence that might be heard.

Aunt Sarah was angry with herself and wanted to throw the blame on Ruby. She darted him a glance, and a faint light broke upon Ruby's understanding.

Mr. Vane thought he must say or do something, so he caught Ruby's throat playfully. "Preach with these vocals!"

Then a truly solemn silence fell in the room, for every one saw the quick spasm of pain that passed over Sim's face. Everybody, unless it was Ruby — I cannot answer for him, for he was not disconcerted in the least, but said:

"Well, if I can't preach, I can sing. Come, Philip, your uncle will sing for you." And he cleared his throat and sang in a voice inexpressibly sweet, though not strong:

"I think when I read that sweet story of old.
 When Jesus was here among men.
How he took little children as lambs to his fold,
 I wish I had been with them then.
I wish that his hands had been placed on my head,
 That his arm had been thrown around me—".

The door opened; it was Nan to say supper was ready.

"There, we will have the rest after supper;" and Ruby gave his hand to Aunt Sarah.

And is that all about Ruby? Oh, no; but our time is out, and I'll have to put it all into this: He still loves, and is not afraid.

THE END

www.ingramcontent.com/pod-product-compliance
Lightning Source LLC
Chambersburg PA
CBHW020028030726
47499CB00007B/2318